SAYONARA BITCH

RICHARD TONG

Published by
O GROUP LTD

FIRST EDITION November 2015
Printed in Hong Kong by Asia One

ISBN 978-988-12563-1-7

SAYONARA BITCH
©2015 BY O GROUP LTD

Written and directed by Richard Tong.
Graphic characterization and illustrations by James Ng.
Cover, layout, design and typography by Iain Richardson.

Comments, enquiries and information?
ogroup.com.hk

Also by Richard Tong

THE DURIAN EFFECT

ME & MY POTATO

BITCH ON HEAT

There are six million stories in the neon city. This is one of them.

SAYONARA BITCH

RICHARD TONG

SAYONARA BITCH

1. BEYOND THE VELVET CURTAIN

Wan Chai

Wān Zǎi

灣仔

Doesn't matter
what you call it,
how you spell it
or the way you say it.

Wan Chai means trouble.

Dominated by Central's towering confidence.
Subjugated by Causeway Bay's mass of humanity.
Wedged between the two. It slipped through the
cracks in Hong Kong's relentless energy and ambition.

If your family
had three kids...

Wan Chai
would be the
fucked-up one
in the middle.

Spurned, burned.
The bastard by-product
of a Saturday night
knee-trembler.

Wan Chai sweats in the shadows of wealth, desire and exploitation.

It's been called a red-light district. That, however, is an affront to places like Sham Shui Po. In that regard Wan Chai is not even Mong Kok. It's red-light lite. A theme park of vice for beginners and old hands. A furlough for the US Navy. It's Suzie Wong. Joe Bananas. Popeye's, Club Hawaii, The Cycle & Carriage, Neptune and Makati. Pole-dancing, faux English pubs and basement discos. Full-service saunas. Discount plumbing and luxury cars. Ricky Tattoo.

Come sundown, Wan Chai is the empty page.

People reinvent themselves here. Some are reborn. Spirits are raised, if only for the night. Identities are erased. Souls are crushed. Lives are destroyed. Some for the evening, some forever. A good person will be reborn, how much more so the evil person. A close friend of the Buddha Amitabha said that, after a weekend bender. This is where the beginning meets the end. For better or worse, everyone gets a chance to be whomever they want and do whatever they like.

Except for today.

I'm here with my daughter. And she wants to be anywhere else. Mei is three going on thirteen. I'm taking her to dance class. She does ballet twice a week. She's not crazy about it, but it's something her mother wanted for her.

I can't wait 'til Mei is old enough to go to ballet, she said. A little pink leotard. Hair in a bun. And a pair of wings on her back at Christmas.

Dance class is one of the ways I try to live up to the promises I made to Ling on our wedding day. It's a way for me to honour her, since that mini-bus ploughed into a crowd on Nathan Road and made her a memory. I've been trying hard for two years now. I like to think I'm improving. Mei is better at it than me. She has an advantage, of course. She is her mother. The living embodiment of her.

I don't her out of my orbit for extended periods. Another of the vows I made in the wake of Ling's passing. I'm also big on taking responsibility for what's yours. Sometimes my mother-in-law has to proxy for me, or I get Angel to do me a favour. If I'm caught in a meeting, battling a deadline or entrenched in an edit. Some days are a struggle, in every sense.

Like today.

Mei has to be at class earlier than usual. Her teacher wants a word about something. Wouldn't tell me what. Neither would Mei. Women and their secrets. They'll be the death of me. They nearly have been, a couple of times.

It's early evening but the day is just beginning on this stretch of sidewalk. The smell of rotting vegetables, bad eggs and decomposing flesh retreats into the walls, wrested by a redolence of incense and smouldering paper.

An aging mama-san stoops over a red bucket. Burning tributes to the gods of harlotry at Club San Francisco. She's opened her golden gates early, hoping to get a jump on the competition and lure twilight punters beyond the velvet curtain.

Nothin' But A Good Time blares from within. Poison.

A lycra-clad nymph, sporting the latest in aerobic fashion, stands in the doorway. Every bar has a theme, from Beach Party to Japanese Schoolgirl. San Francisco is leveraging the recent Olympics in Seoul. This floozy could be a South Korean rhythmic gymnast. A willowy devalgate siren, she attempts to draw seamen from the streets. Marooning the hapless on a fetid reef of bar stools. Ripe for plunder, pillaging wretched cargo. Her eyes widen, a Pavlovian reaction. She smiles. Her make-up cracks.

The mama-san senses a trawler. Potential shipwreck. She straightens her back.

Mr Jack! We not see you at happy hour for longest time!

Busy, Mama.

Too busy for Mama? How sad. Got beautiful new girls, see?

Got a girl of my own now, I remind her, lifting Mei's hand in mine.

And what a beauty she is! You're a good man, Jack So. A girl should spend time with her father. You're a good man.

Trying, Mama. I'm trying.

You try too hard! Take a break, come see us! I buy you drink!

She throws another wad of demon-cash at the flames. The smile on her teenage sentinel slackens. The opportunity to show me the charms of the Bay Area and climb Coit Tower has passed.

It's not the first time I've drawn salutations and invitations along here. I'm a known quantity. Or rather, I was. The unknown known. It's not a part of my life I return to often.

Mei wants to know why everyone is so friendly to me.

I used to work here, Sweetheart.

You worked there?

Not *there*. Around here. Sometimes. Long ago.

What kind of work?

Helping people.

How did you help them?

I tried to make sure they didn't get into trouble.

Like when Uncle Benny gets into trouble?

Something like that, Sugar-pop. Yes. Something like that.

Oh, she says, and ponders the deeper meaning of my admission.

We turn off Lockhart into Fleming. Enter the Tung Kai Building. Climb a flight of tired stairs. Walk the length of a weary, grey corridor. A beacon of polished brightness lures us like moths to flame.

Irina Wang School Of Dance.

Walls have been knocked through to create a studio about half the size of a basketball court. Oak floorboards. Fluorescent tubes in aluminium shells hang from the raw ceiling. Shatterproof smoked-glass windows bisect the opposite wall, diffusing whatever light the surrounding buildings allow. Floor-to-ceiling mirrors, on the right and left, double the space. A small office hides in the back corner. Classical music floats in sub-arctic air.

Chopin, or Schubert?

Irina Wang stands at the office door. An inscrutable oriental aunt. Big perm. Her clothes would've gone out of style a long time ago if she'd let them. She acknowledges our arrival with a crease of her lips. A big effort for her.

The focus of her attention stands at the other end of the studio.

Sam Wang.

Lithe limbs *à la quatrième*, reflected in the mirror. A demonstration for a pint-sized protégé, *noblimente*. Her tight frame combines with the flesh-coloured leotard to present a study in naked athletic elegance. Schubert's Quintet In C Major pays a sublime compliment to the complexity of her biological fresco. Confidence is evident in her posture and gait. A soft crop of black hair is parted on the left and tucked behind her ears. It gives her an elfin quality. At this distance you could mistake her for a teenager.

I know her too well for that.

Sam and I grew up together. Half-brother and half–sister, for want of a better term. Asami, to invoke her full name, is half Japanese. In the same way that I'm half Chinese. You can't really tell. She looks as local as I do foreign.

We were both misconceptions, the corollary of occupational hazards.

A Japanese businessman left more than a stain upon her mother's mattress.

My miracle of birth wasn't quite so glamorous. An American matelot wouldn't take no for an answer.

Our matriarchs met when they were seconded to the Cultural Work Troupe of the Central Garrison, circa 1955. They performed for Mao and select guests. A few years later they moved to Hong Kong. They both got knocked up, just as the Great Leap Forward gave birth to the Cultural Revolution. They both went on to corral hostess girls at Club Big Spender.

Irina was one of the few who genuinely cared for my mother in the months before she died. As cancer devoured her, one organ at a time.

My childhood was intertwined with Sam's in other ways too. We traded virginities at twelve. It was an experiment that grew out of boredom and curiosity more than affection. I can't even say it was a loss of innocence. That had been taken many years before by the circumstances of our existence. If you really want to hear about it, the first thing you'll probably want to know is where I was born and what my lousy childhood was like, how my mom was occupied before she had me and all that Holden Caufield kind of crap. But, like Salinger, I don't really feel like going into it. Still, as Sam walks toward me now, *legato*, eyes warm and welcoming, pushing a broad smile before her, I'm reminded of the way those dark pools searched my soul eighteen years ago, while I tentatively poked at her loins. She bit the corner of her lip. I hoped that meant I was doing it right. I wanted to impress her.

She's not the type of person you want to disappoint.

Our formative years shared common ground in a Tsim Sha Tsui sauna. On different ends of the customer experience. I would see them before, dispensing towels and robes. Sam would see to them. She quickly worked out, however, that giving handjobs to strangers wasn't for her.

All she wanted to do was dance. With those legs who wouldn't?

Her mother pumped everything she had, and more, into helping Sam open this school. To get herself out of the *mizu-shōbai*, as they call it in Japan, the water trade, and make sure her daughter was never immersed in it.

The past, however, is only ever a step *en arrière*. It pursues us all relentlessly.

Our lives are conjoined platonically now. Strictly business. Very strict, as far as Irina is concerned. Family business, from Sam's point of view. I give her a hand with the school's marketing and collaterals. She gives Mei dance lessons. My first thought when she requested a precursory chat was she might want to add a cash component to our barter arrangement.

Hong Kong had been hard hit by last year's crash.

The Year Of The Rabbit may have been shot, and The Dragon was on the rise, but many of the princesses populating her classes would still have pocket-money problems.

Sam greets Mei with a sisterly embrace, *dolcissimo*. Go and warm up, Mei-mei.

Bye-bye Ba-ba, she says and skips across the polished oak.

We watch her for a moment, like proud estranged parents.

You wanted to talk about something? I ask, a lifetime of familiarity dispensing with the need for small-talk. Her smooth, almost featureless face doesn't turn to me. Her eyes remain locked on Mei.

I probe a little further into the silence. How's business?

We're fine, for now. It's a week-to-week proposition.

Anything I can help with?

We had an incident last week.

I dread the direction this is heading. Incidents and I have a long-standing relationship. An incident, I repeat. With whom?

With Mei. She got into an argument with one of the girls.

Sam's gulliver swivels to me, followed by her shoulders and then her hips, in one fluid motion, *largo*.

They seem to be getting on now, I observe, glossing over the unseemliness of this divulgation.

It wasn't this girl, Jack.

Uh-huh. And?

Mei has a strong, determined personality.

She gets that from her mother, I reply. Sam doesn't see the humour in this comment, or my attempt to sidestep the issue. Kids will be kids, I offer in apology.

She head-butted a classmate.

Ouch. She okay? The other girl, I mean. Mei didn't mention it.

She'll be okay.

I really don't know what to say. Sorry? There's probably a bunch of stuff that could be said about acting-out and Mei needing a consistent feminine influence or role model. How much she misses her mother.

We all do.

Thing is, Mei has plenty of x-chromosomes in her life. Good ones. She spends a lot of time with her grandmother. Angel, my PA, is like a big sister. Sam is a favoured aunt and not afraid to impart her strong sense of values. The real issue is more likely to be the y-chromosomes that shade her years.

Many would venture she spends too much time with her father.

How do I explain that the reason Mei went the nut might be because she saw me resolve an issue that way in the Marco Polo Suite of The Peninsula? Do I mention she witnessed a pistol-whipping in her living room, and saw me drag a corpse through the creative department too?

I don't. I can't. If Sam found out she'd kill me.

I know I have to moderate my approach to parenting. My responsibility, however, is to prepare her for life. Not shield her from it. I'm making advances in the tempering of my temper, yet it remains a long-term work-in-progress.

While I'm contemplating a short-term response to today's boggle, one that will satisfy Sam, I become aware of a dark presence behind me.

Sam is distracted by it too. She scowls and steps away, *allegro*.

A thick arm reaches toward her. Instinct compels me to block it.

I turn and brace for conflict.

He's a broad man-child. Heavy set. Nudging six-foot. Raw muscle coated in a protective layer of puppy fat. His cherubic mien and medium-length perm lend him a comical appearance. Like a mythical beast, in a bright Versace print. If it wasn't for those glazzies you'd write him off as a puerile joke. The windows to his soul are mean. Angry. Unforgiving. They've seen things. They're looking for things.

Irina Wang materializes beside her daughter. She plants herself in harm's way, between Sam and The Qilin. She speaks in Cantonese. Her tone is low, calm and fearless, fortified by years of dealing with grim realities.

What do you want, Lion Tamer?

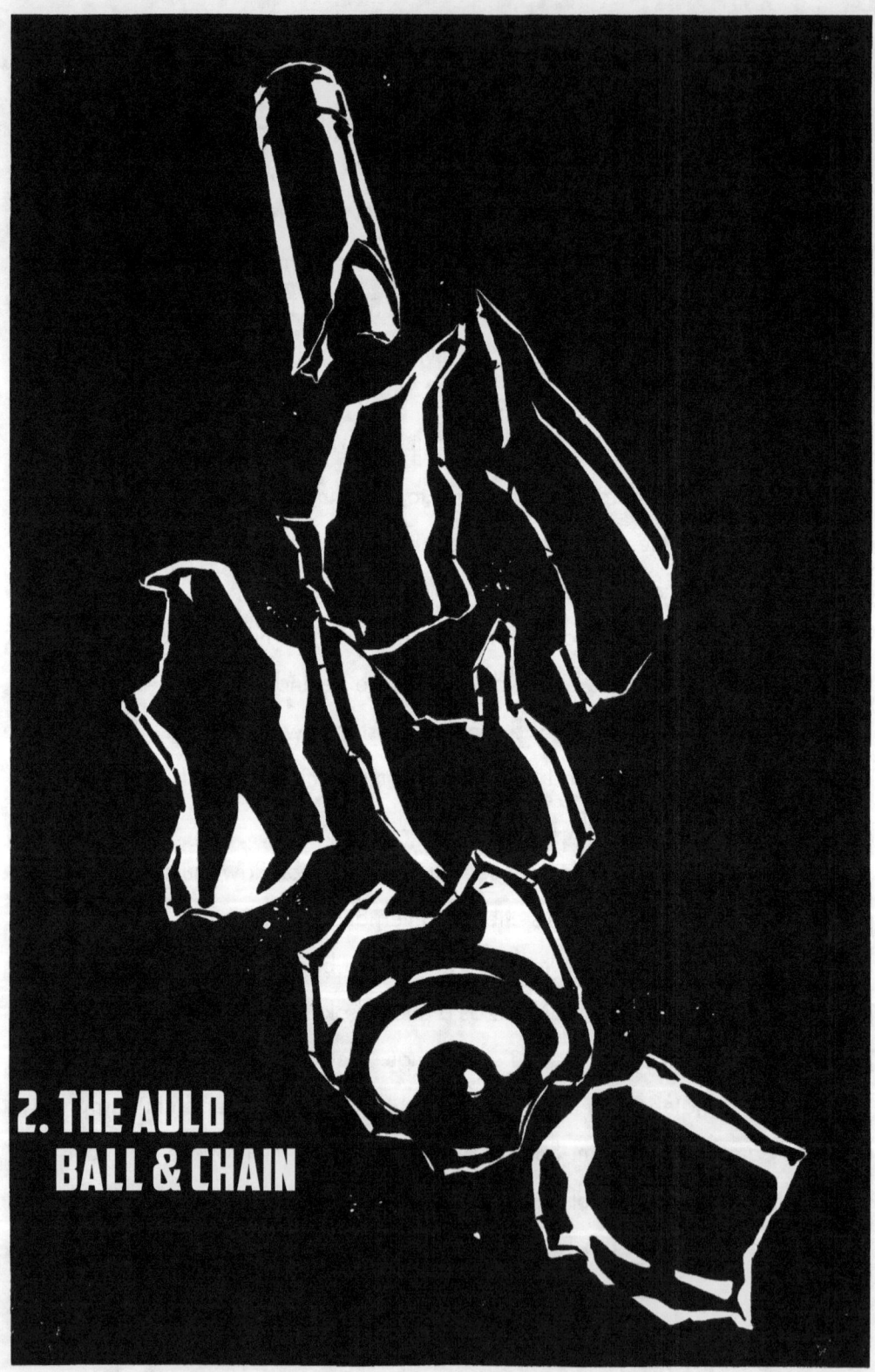

2. THE AULD BALL & CHAIN

Bronson *Lion Tamer* Chung. I should've recognized him. His mugshot was plastered across newspapers for weeks. I thought he was still locked up. Maybe he got time off for good behaviour. Although it's hard to imagine anyone with a childhood penchant for torturing cats keeping his hands clean for an extended period, or that he might've thrown himself upon the mercy of the court.

Oscar Wilde knew the Hong Kong Correctional Services Department as well as anyone.

Vile deeds like poison weeds bloom well in prison air,

It is only what is good in man that wastes and withers there.

Chung strikes me as the recalcitrant type. A man of few regrets, operating with impunity. Essential characteristics in his vocation as a Red Pole. An enforcer among triad communities. He has the enviable distinction of being both feared and respected. He was the only one to get stitched up for the Securicor heist. A brazen, ballistic robbery that involved half a dozen bandits. He didn't rat anybody out. It's probably a mitigating factor behind his early release. A reward for good behaviour of a different genus. He's connected to the kind of money that sort of thing requires too. Of course he could've just smashed through the back wall of Stanley Prison and most people would be too scared to say anything. I'm seriously thinking of apologizing for the impudent nature of my recent actions.

I decide to see how Irina Wang handles him.

Personal experience has taught me you interrupt tribal elders at your own peril. Irina's driving this stagecoach now. It's best for everyone if I just stand ready, betwixt this rock of a man and her resolute face.

I'm looking for Kitty, he says and shifts his gaze to Sam. I'm sorry, Little Sister. I thought you were Ki-

Irina slaps him.

This is a bold move. All of us would agree on that. You'd have to be crazy, a woman, or a crazy woman to contemplate that.

The sharp shot of palm-on-cheek draws attention. Just what we need on top of the head-butt conversation. Sam will file this among the other negative influences that are polluting Mei's development. She instructs the children to continue their exercises and leaps across the room to join them, *pretissimo*. I've half a mind to execute a *pas de chat* of my own.

Do not sully my daughter or this school with that name, commands Irina.

I'm sorry. I thought Ki-

Madam Wang slaps him again. I'm probably not alone in thinking she may be pushing the limits of Chung's tolerance. Do not think, she orders him. She is no longer here. Nobody knows where she went. We have not seen her since she betrayed us. So you will leave us in peace.

This statement is not entirely correct. All of us grown-ups know where Kitty went. She just hasn't been sighted for quite some time.

Chung furrows his brow and internalizes his options. I wonder if this is as awkward for him as it is for us to watch. Although, in fairness, I can see where some of his confusion comes from.

Kitty is the same age as Sam, and they do share a resemblance. Look at them in the cold light of day, however, and it's bad apples to oranges.

Taller, with a fuller figure, Kitty had more ambrosial camber. Her mouth was wider, lips leaner and nose broader. Hair longer. At Big Spender they called her an exotic. Her almond eyes, alabaster skin and general appearance were nonspecific in terms of ethnicity. She could pass for whatever a man was willing to pay for. When cunning linguists questioned her command of Asian dialects she told them she'd been orphaned and raised in a convent. She held conversational Cantonese, Mandarin and English, with the ability to tease in half a dozen vernaculars. People didn't come to her for conversation anyway. She was more than able to satiate that minor kink in their appetites. I'd been told she was part Japanese part Filipino-Chinese. A jalapeño, in more ways than pun. The type of broad MacArthur had his eye on in 1942 when he said he'd return. Men have made fools of themselves, laid waste to civilizations and forsaken futures for less.

What did Chandler say?

If you're not thinking about cooze all the time, you're just not concentrating hard enough.

Establishments like Big Spender were almost a thing of the past. They were being consolidated into superclubs like Volvo. Don't let the name fool you. There's nothing safe about this Volvo. The dangerous curves of a hundred hostesses, from every corner of Asia, braced the floor. There was a miniature Rolls Royce to transport you across the whoreditorium. When raided by the Anti-triad Squad, management were forewarned of the incursion by sympathizers in blue. Only a token handful of unlicensed females were nabbed. A patron was caught driving the mini-Rolls, also without a license, while under the influence.

Irina had liberated Kitty from penile servitude and brought her to the dance school. The kid was grateful at first. Then she decided carnal *contagion, pas de ciseaux, effacé* and *entrechat* were her forte. She returned to the more lucrative side of the performing arts. Her Lear, so to speak, was the toast of the town. A darling of the critics, she worked off-Broadway. Wan Chai's bars and hotel lounges. She hooked up with a *gweilo.* A white ghost. The foreign devil.

No one dared speak of Kitty at Irina Wang School Of Dance. Especially in front of Irina Wang, who'd leveraged more than goodwill to secure the young woman's freedom.

Kitty was a four-letter word.

Parents and Filipino maids have begun arriving at the studio. Delivering children to the class. The sight of Madam Wang confronting a known gangster is not projecting the desired convivial image, particularly in a post head-butt world. As a contributor to this reality I figure I'm in a good position to arrogate additional unpleasantness. And, just maybe, endear myself to Irina.

Brother Chung, I say. I want to apologize for my rudeness. I can be too protective when it comes to my little sister, Asami. Perhaps we can leave Madam Wang and her young friends to their dancing?

The children entering the school are attempting to navigate around the three of us. Irina smiles and welcomes them. She apologizes for the two uncles standing in their way, and adeptly ushers us to one side. It probably looks like the whole thing is being telepathically orchestrated and executed with precision. Between my days in security, and Irina's in hospitality, we have a lot of experience in diffusing volatile situations.

Chung goes with the flow, tentatively, like he's still confused by the dynamics of the encounter. Perhaps the sting on his cheek is interfering with his ability to process information and commanding the bulk of his cognitive ability.

I can help you find her, Brother Chung.

This seems to inflame. His voluminous frame is immediately engorged. His expression hardens. Tension fills the space between us. His feet sink into the floor. He squares himself, primed to explode in one-point-three seconds.

You know Kitty?

I have not *known* her. I know of her. Through this school. She was here, once, long ago. I know a better place to look for her.

Why? What interest have you in her?

It's in my interest for you to find her. That will please everyone. She is obviously important to you, and if I'm in a position to help others I do. Come.

I'm lucky this doesn't sound as pontifical in Cantonese as it does in translation. I'd be writing it posthumously, like William Holden in Sunset Boulevard.

The poor dope. He always wanted a pool. Well, in the end, he got himself a pool, only the price turned out to be a little high.

Doubt lingers in the sulcus of Chung's forehead, yet he concedes to my request. He's as uneasy as the rest of us in this environment and would, no doubt, welcome the opportunity to continue the exchange someplace more familiar. The street springs to mind. This will also allow me time to formulate a nonviolent strategy. The alternative would not end well for me. I say that without fear of contradiction. In the right frame of mind Chung could twist off my gulliver quicker than most could rip the scab off a beer.

On Jaffe Road I point him in the direction of Lockhart, taking a leaf out of Lao Tzu's book.

To lead the people, walk behind them.

Where are we going, Jack So?

To get a beer. And find out what happened to Kitty.

He stops and weighs my response. As if getting beer and finding Kitty are mutually exclusive choices. You said you knew where she was.

I know where she went. Maybe the guys there can help with what happened to her after that.

Why don't you just tell me where?

These men might be more inclined to help me rather than you.

Why?

Gweilo.

Gweilo, Chung repeats, confirming my unspoken antipathetic assessment of Westerners. The type that only know two kinds of people. Us and them. My ambiguous pedigree meant I was often mistaken for one of them.

We wheel onto Lockhart and cross to the sunny side of the street. The red pill is nearing the end of its arc. Burnt light filters through the buildings.

What's Kitty to you, Brother Chung?

Kitty was my girl.

I hear she was quite a lady.

She was like all girls. Until she danced. Then she would take you places.

I can see them together now. Hand in hand. The Lion Tamer and his Lolita. Humbert Humbert and his Kitty Ho.

Lolita, light of my life, fire of my loins. My sin, my soul. Lo-lee-ta. The tip of the tongue taking a trip of three steps down the palate to tap, at three, on the teeth. Lo. Lee. Ta.

Sounds like you had a groovy kind of love, I remark, figuring Phil Collins might be more his speed. I resist the urge to make a quip about Kitty being a Red Pole dancer.

Why did you leave her? A man turns his back on a dame like that for too long, well, she ain't going to dance by herself.

I didn't leave her. He took her away from me.

I'm not sure who he means by He. The judge? The cop who arrested him? A business associate? The Brit she bedded? The Nazarene?

I haven't seen her in a long time, he adds, peering into the past.

I bet, I reply, not sure if I should be making droll comments about his incarceration but, well, fuck him if he can't take a joke. I'm pretty confident I could outrun him if he can't. Besides, the *gweilo* comment had lowered the intensity of things. There was a fraternity developing between us. The kind that comes when two people share a common sense of purpose or experience. Madam Wang was truthful with you, I tell him, hoping to avoid any backtracking should we meet with a dead end at The Auld Ball & Chain.

I didn't get a chance to say goodbye, he says, ignoring my thinly veiled plea for clemency.

Fair enough, I think. People need endings, or a chance to start over.

We arrive at the pub. Kitty used to spend a lot of time here, I inform him, assuming he knows what that implies. He had to be aware of her duties at Big Spender. He would know old habits die hard. You can take the girl out of the game but not the game out of the girl. The game doesn't worry men like Chung. They just need to know they're the number-one ticket holder.

I push the door, figuring I'll order a couple of beers and re-introduce myself to the owner. I'll tell Nifty my friend is looking for his girlfriend. And see what happens. See how the ambiguity of that statement pans out.

We enter the dimly lit boîte.

I let my eyes adjust to the light and direct Chung to the bar at the back. He meanders through the wobbly tables. The walls are festooned with World War Two memorabilia. Old photos of Hong Kong during the Japanese occupation. British military and naval flags, punctuated with traditional pub art. Toucans. *Lovely day for a Guinness.* Neon signs advertising Carlsberg, Blue Girl Beer, San Miguel and Löwenbräu. My feet stick to the carpet. INXS are halfway through Devil Inside. The bass-line triggers low-end fuzz in the cheap speakers.

Four expatriates are playing darts. They probably have been for the last ten years. Their stuffed frames, augmented by large bellies, stretch the limits of old rugby jumpers. Thick necks. Sozzled noses. I recognize a couple of them. They give Chung the once-over. I can almost hear them sneering.

I sit on a stool in the corner. Back to the wall. Bar on my left. Expatriates to my right. A view of the whole joint. Front door to rear exit, toilets and the storeroom. Chung stands beside me. I kick a stool, the international language for sit down. He looks around, lingers on the dartboard for a moment, then slides the seat beneath him. Having his back to the room doesn't seem to concern him.

The barmaid throws a couple of coasters on the counter. I order two pints of Carlsberg. She returns with the beer. A thin head of foam slops over the lip and runs down the glass. I raise my pint in salute to Chung. Then, just for fun, I send a round of drinks to the other patrons. This is met by puzzled expressions. She explains the source of the complimentary beverages. The men look to me, seeking further explanation.

Boys, I say, toasting their success. Triple-twenty, one hundred and eighty!

Only one of the punters lifts his pint in appreciation. Of course the others didn't send theirs back either. Fine. Be like that.

Chung drains his glass. He stares at a point behind the bar. And burns a hole in it.

Guns N Roses launch into Sweet Child Of Mine.

I've got almost an hour to kill before Mei finishes her class. The agitated way my companion is bouncing his leg on the footrest suggests the sooner we get this show on the road the better. Kitty is out there, somewhere. It's rude to keep a lady waiting. I ask the barmaid if she has seen our quarry around lately.

Kitty.

The name cuts through the ambient clutter like the crack of a whip. Like a one-eyed man looking at his wife I realize what a big mistake I've made, instanter, coming here.

These are not the droids you're looking for.

The barmaid's eyes dart across to the gang of four. I follow her gaze. One of them is moving toward me with purpose. The grunt of the litter. He was probably a decent Prop Forward in the halcyon days of his weekend rugby career. Raised on a diet of lager, lager and scotch. By the look of his face they hit him with the bottles as he finished them. It was unlikely he had a life outside these walls. I can feel the floorboards suffering under the strain.

Chung seems unaware of this massive disturbance in The Force.

You looking for Kitty? Prop Forward asks. Friend of hers, are ya?

Kind of. Sort of. Not really.

What is it? Kind of, sort of, or not really?

I'm looking for her, interjects Chung, standing. She's a friend of mine.

Is that a fact? Well maybe we can help you out. Mabel, tell Nifty someone here is looking for Kitty. He's a friend of hers.

This wasn't going to end well. You don't have to be a Rhode Scholar to recognize that. A basic, public school education would tell you what was coming.

Two of the big man's friends, Scrum-half and Fullback, join the inquisition. The well mannered Stand-off remains at the dartboard, politely nursing his beer.

Mabel walks on egg-shells to the back of the pub. She disappears into the storeroom. Nifty has an office there.

Neil *Nifty* Teplice. He'd been part of Hong Kong's pub scene since launching himself into it in the seventies. He had a reputation as a bit of a lad. I thought he was a bit of a loud mouth. A chancer. A one-time Swire Boy and ex-banker, he came out to Hong Kong and went a too far up Wan Chai's river, metaphorically speaking. Like Kurtz in Heart Of Darkness. He owned this bar and a couple of others. I have nothing against him but, like all men, he has weaknesses. One of these is women like Kitty. She took up with him after abandoning Irina Wang and her School Of Dance. Judging by the reaction to her name, we're either on the right track or the wrong side of it. How Chung deals with the next five minutes will tell us.

You looking for Kitty, the dancer? asks Prop Forward.

She could dance, says Chung. She could sing too.

Yeah. And she could play the flute. Kitty's not here, China. Maybe you shouldn't be either. She's long gone. Danced on Nifty's nuts and hoofed it with his dough. You looking for that bitch, Jackie Chan, you're in the wrong fucking place.

In my younger and more vulnerable years, one of the first books I stole was The Great Gatsby. It begins with Carraway recalling some fatherly advice. Whenever you feel like criticizing anyone, he said, just remember that all the people in this world haven't had the advantages you've had. I was living in a 300 square foot apartment at the time, with four clapped-out karaoke hostesses, watching my mother die. Even if I had a sense of irony there was nowhere to keep it. I had a hard time appreciating all the advantages I was supposed to have over others. Turning this advice over in my mind, at The Auld Ball & Chain, it was clear that if Prop Forward had read Gatsby it had failed to make an impression. And, if I'd learned anything else about Bronson Chung in the last half hour, which I hadn't, it's that he was old school. He would not respond well to criticism. Constructive, literary or otherwise. Someone smug would soon be revisiting the classics, and acquiring a very hard but valuable life lesson.

If silence is a source of great strength, Bronson Chung was drawing deep from the well.

Chung would've made a handy Front Row himself.

It had taken him less than thirty seconds to dismantle the room.

I'd encountered this type of thing as a doorman, and when I handled security for visiting indignitaries. The Rules Of Engagement are simple. It's about when, where, against whom, how and how much force is used to meet predetermined ends.

You first duty is protect the interests of whoever is paying you. Then comes a responsibility to innocent bystanders. And, finally, you have to look out for yourself. Although not necessarily in that order. Get in first, get in fast and get out. The default option is simply wait for the melee to subside, then find a workable point of entry or exit. Look away, walk away.

If you are patient in one moment of anger,
You will escape one hundred days of sorrow.

I've honoured the primary principles of that code. I'm weighing up exit strategies when I see Nifty at the back of the pub. He's watching in disbelief. Mabel is behind him. Her look leans more toward abject horror.

Chung recognizes Nifty and storms to meet him.

Nifty heads for the tradesman's entrance.

The men disappear behind saloon doors. There is shouting. Wood furniture is turned into pulp. Fear turns to anger and anger turns to hate. A gunshot. Something is thwacked. Repeatedly.

Sweet Child Of Mine gives way to cheerful whistling. Don't Worry Be Happy, suggests Bobby McFerrin.

Mabel looks to me for instruction, or advice. Something. Anything.

Chung appears. Blood smudged across his Versace swirls. A pistol in hand. He tosses it on the floor and limps toward the street.

Thanks for the drink, he says. Kitty's gone.

The scrum on the floor is moving, kind of. Just. Chung picks up a bar stool and tosses it upon them. They decide to lay-low for a while longer. Stand-off stands on the bench seat of a booth, trying to disappear into the panelling. He's still nursing his complimentary beer. I admire his priorities at this juncture.

The Lion Tamer exits The Auld Ball & Chain.

I embark on a recce of the storeroom.

There's so much blood splashed about I wonder if Nifty has any left in him. His gulliver has been bludgeoned beyond recognition. Dispatched to the boundary, you could say, by the sturdy Gunn & Moore willow beside him. He must have kept it back there for emergencies, when circumstances at The Auld Ball & Chain called for a little Peter Grant diplomacy. A show of Harold Shand on long Good Fridays. A bit of the Dunkirk spirit.

Apart from his arsehole being fifty yards from his brains, and the choirboys playing hunt-the-thimble with the rest of him, he ain't too happy.

I pick up the phone beside the cash register, hand the receiver to Mabel and punch in the number of a cop I know. I tell her to ask for Detective Oldham. Let him know what happened and that Jack So will come by the station to give him a statement in an hour. I drop my business card on the counter and walk to the door.

Lockhart Road lies oblivious to the horrors behind me. Chung has vanished.

What has he left me in the middle of? What have I got myself into?

Nifty Teplice, and maybe a couple of others, dead. Stuck to the carpet of The Auld Ball & Chain.

Nothing unusual, he says! Eric's been blown to smithereens. Colin's been carved up. I've got a bomb in me casino. And you say nothing unusual?

The neon above Crazy Horse flickers into life. It's six in the evening and Wan Chai is waking up. Stretching and yawning. Putting its feet on the floor.

Somewhere, Michael Jackson sings Man In The Mirror.

San Francisco's Olympic athletes, gymnasts and pole-vaulters have retreated behind the velvet curtain.

A siren wails.

I walk back to the Tung Kai Building and hope Mei managed to get through her lesson without assaulting anyone.

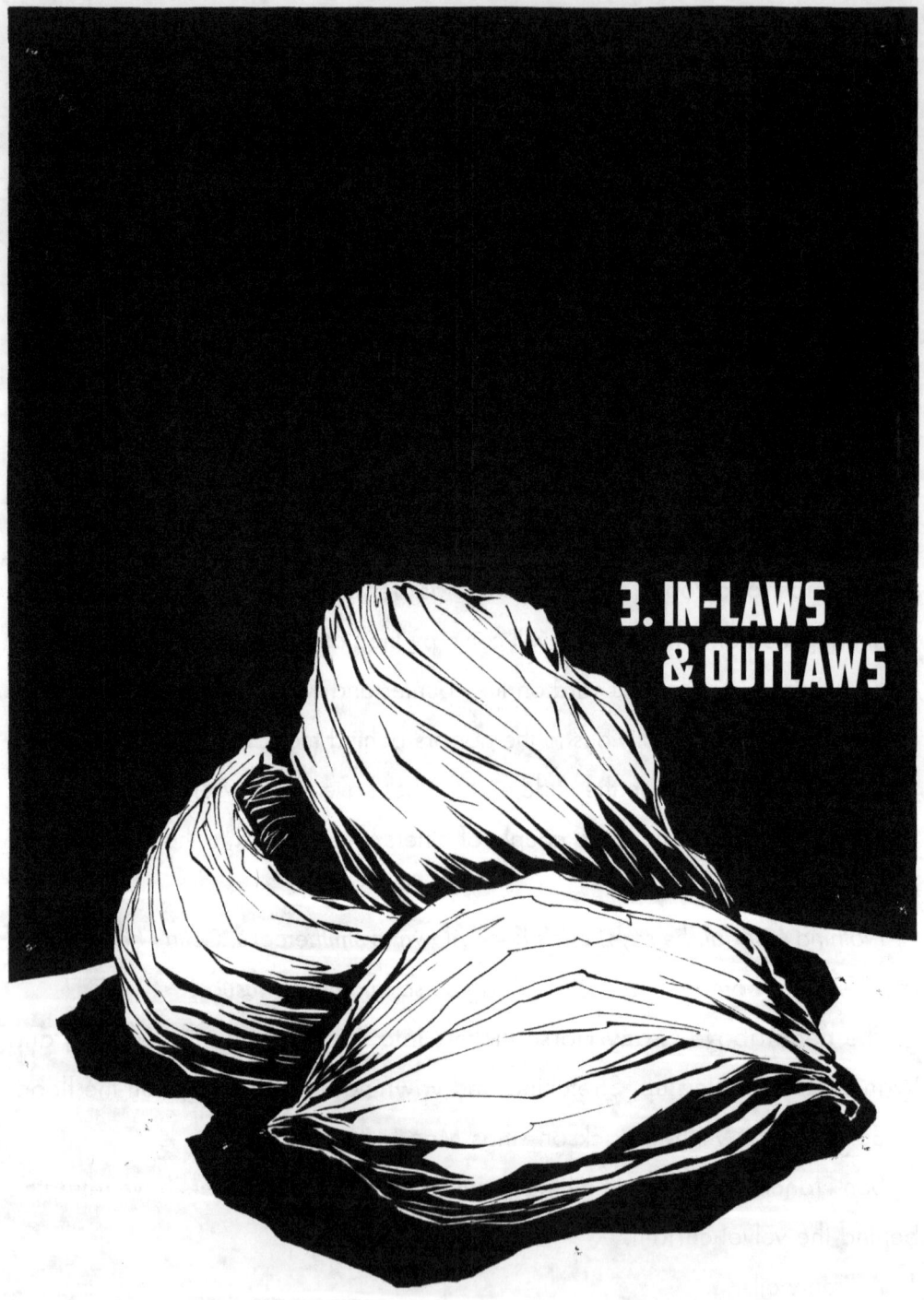

3. IN-LAWS & OUTLAWS

Sam studies the blood on my shirt, *agitati*. Her mother watches from beneath a dark cloud, on the other side of the studio. Their eyes demand answers. Chopin carries on regardless.

You okay? asks the lissom étoile.

Compared to what's lying on Lockhart, I'm in great shape. Sensational. And I'm getting better.

Will Chung be back?

I doubt it.

Did he find her?

Not exactly.

What happened? Did he find out where she is?

He found out where she isn't.

Where isn't she?

The Auld Ball & Chain.

Why take him there?

To get him out of here.

But that was years ago.

I thought she might've left a forwarding address.

So what do we do?

You do nothing. Unless the police drop by.

What are the chances of that?

Quite high.

What do I tell them?

Tell them what happened.

I don't know what happened.

Tell them that.

Mei runs over. Hey Ba-ba! Look at me! She executes a near-perfect pirouette.

Wow! That's fantastic, Cream-puff. Did Sammi teach you that?

Yes!

Can you teach me?

Boys can't dance like that, Ba-ba. It's a girl dance.

I sling Mei's backpack over my shoulder and tell Sam not to worry.

Her glare is still burning into me when we arrive on the footpath outside. In light of recent events I figure it's best to avoid Lockhart. We walk to the car via the road less travelled. I hear more sirens. Oldham must've dispatched a unit or two. He'll be waiting for my explanation.

I steer towards Old Bailey Street.

I tell the sentry at Police HQ I've got an appointment. He lets me park in the compound. A privilege not afforded to all, but I have a curious and somewhat spurious relationship with The Law. I wouldn't say I'm welcome here. I am, however, known to a lot of people. Known to have walked both sides of the thin blue line. There are some who'd like to see me admitted formally, only to be allowed out on parole.

Oldham isn't one of those, although I have pushed the boundaries of our relationship more than once. He's sitting uncomfortably in his fishbowl office, behind a standard-issue desk.

I usher Mei into the room.

We got her Chief, I say. She put up a fight but we got her. Ma Barker has pulled her last job. Mei giggles. I pick her up by her shoulders and look her in the eye. You think it's funny? There won't be laughter where you're going. They'll throw the book at you.

What book Ba-ba? The Sneetches? Green Eggs And Ham? Horton?

I ask Oldham if he's got a copy of Horton Hears A Who. He calls a female officer to take care of Mei while we talk. I tell the young constable to put Mei in handcuffs and throw away the key, then sit to face my accuser.

What can I do you for, Officer?

You called me, remember? Thanks, Jack. Just what I need. Another homicide file with your name at the top.

That's what friends are for.

I don't have friends. I've no use for them.

Just trying to do the right thing.

The right thing for you to do is stay home with your kid. Forever. Just stay home. Tell me she didn't see your friend redecorating The Ball & Chain, please.

She didn't.

That yours? he asks, inspecting the sauce on my chest.

No.

Whose?

I'm not sure to whom it belongs.

Fantastic. We'll need it.

I'll send it over.

I should take it now.

Only if you've got something else my size.

Don't leave it soaking overnight.

I won't even iron it.

What were you doing there? I thought you'd purged that part of your portfolio.

I was helping a friend.

Great help you turned out to be. Hell of a crowd you run with.

I don't really know them. I mean, I know who they are. Chung just turned up at Mei's dance class.

Looking for lessons?

Looking for someone who used to teach there.

Nifty wasn't much of a song and dance man either. Who?

Whom.

What?

Whom. *Who* is used in the subjective. *Whom* is used in the objective position and more appropriate, in this case.

In this case, Professor Higgins, grammar is the least of your worries. Whom was Chung looking for when he split Nifty's infinitive and conjugated his verb?

A past participle. Kitty Ho.

You'll have to fill in the blanks.

I know the owner of the studio, and her daughter. Mei takes classes there. Chung turned up and looked like he was going to make a bit of scene. I told him Nifty might be able to help him find his Kitty-cat.

Why'd you go with him?

To make sure he left the building, and discourage him from coming back. To see what happened. Those classes are an hour long. I had some time to kill.

So did Chung. Why did he punch Nifty's ticket?

He was looking for his girl. Nifty dated her. Split her infinitive, to borrow a metaphor. Conjugated her verb. They might've even got married. Maybe that was enough for him to compound his subject. He would've ended up there whether I took him or not. He'd traced her from Big Spender. If I hadn't told him where Kitty had gone someone else would've. She wasn't one of those people who disappear into the background.

So what happened to her?

She disappeared. Into the background.

Jack-

I took a guy to the pub. I bought him a beer. That's not a crime.

When that guy is Bronson Chung, and he commits half a dozen crimes in less than a minute, that makes you an accessory to at least one.

After the fact.

Still a fact. We'll need a full statement.

I just gave you one.

Do I look like I'm taking notes?

I thought the Lion Tamer was with the circus, at Stanley Prison.

Released a couple of days ago.

He doesn't waste any time.

He made short work of Nifty. Why did he take the place apart?

I think that's just how he expresses himself, when he's frustrated. It's why I took him out of the studio. He was tightly wound.

We're joined by another plain-clothes Peeler, with an eye-patch. I wonder if he still blames me for that.

Detective Chau, haven't seen you around in a while. How's things?

He acknowledges me with a grunt and monocular scorn. We have a love-hate relationship. I love to wind him up. He hates me. Losing that eye in a tussle with a client of mine hasn't helped. The fact it was a broad that stuck him only rubbed more salt into the wound. It added insult to his injury. He tried a glass eye for a while but it had a mind of its own and would wander off during conversation. That could be a distraction, if you were a cop trying to get people to take you seriously.

Cyclops Chau is one of the reasons I steer clear of dark alleys. In case he's waiting down one of them.

Where's your boyfriend? I ask, enquiring after his partner in anti-crime. He's also named Chau. It can be confusing, until you see them. The other is Bud Abbott to this one's Lou Costello. Crockett and Tubby, I said once. And got a punch in the guts for it.

Chau works south side, replies Oldham on his subordinate's behalf.

Too bad. I love a reunion, even if they do always end in tears. Do you miss him? I do and it's only been a couple of minutes.

Leave it, Jack. What were you thinking?

I was thinking I prefer the blind justice of Chau's patch here, over the bung-eye of the law that used to wander about. I was thinking I had to get Chung away from a class full of women and children. I was thinking I could help him out.

So help us out. The pieces of this puzzle are missing or dead.

Except me.

We'll never be rid of you, mutters Chau.

IT'S NOT 20 GUYS WITH MEAT CLEAVERS BUTCHERING SOMEONE IN A CROWDED RESTAURANT, AND NO WITNESSES.

YOU'VE GOT A *WHITE GHOST*. YOU CAN BURY LOCALS, BUT WHEN MEMBERS OF THE RULING CLASS GET DUSTED IT DOESN'T REFLECT WELL ON THE COLONY.

PARTICULARLY IF IT'S SEEN AS A HARBINGER FOR LIFE AFTER THE HANDOVER. THIS'LL BE FRONT PAGE OF THE PAPER.

MAYBE THE GOVERNOR
WILL GET INVOLVED.

HAVE TO GET HIS NOSE
SURGICALLY REMOVED FROM
BEIJING'S ARSE FIRST.

I'm impressed with Chau's uncharacteristic display of wit, although not surprised by the sentiment. Governor Wilson hasn't endeared himself to the people of Hong Kong with his kowtowing to the rulers-in-waiting.

Maybe this will help, offers Chau. He throws a folder on the table.

Oldham opens it. Scans the contents. Puts it down. I reach for it. He drops his palm upon it, denying my curiosity. Police business. Come on, I plead. What's in there that won't be in tomorrow's paper?

A lot. And I want to keep it that way. Who else has seen this, Chau?

Today? Probably no one. I pulled it myself.

I bet you did, I interject. Lonely at the top is it?

Chau tenses. Oldham diffuses him with a wave of his authoritarian hand and asks what I know about Kitty Ho.

Wang bought her out and across to the dance school, from Big Spender. She didn't stick around. Went to work in Wan Chai. Hooked up with Nifty. She had a relationship with Bronson Chung at some point.

What point?

The point of ejaculation. That's all I know. How about you?

What I know stays in this room.

Where else would it go?

Neil Teplice put in a call not long after the Securicor job. It seems Nifty fingered Chung, so to speak. You'd have to wonder how he would get that kind of information, wouldn't you?

And why he'd be stupid enough to act on it. Maybe Kitty had her claws into both of them. She might've let it slip that Chung was part of the heist and Nifty phoned in the tip. He eliminates his nemesis and earns a few Plod-points at the same time. Kitty trades up and out of her nefarious circle. She mixes with a different class of rogue. Maybe Chung was looking for more than a dame and a cuckold's requital. Maybe he was looking for payback on time served.

Maybe, agrees Oldham.

Look for the girl. Chung is. Maybe you'll meet them both on the road to Oz. Shouldn't be that hard.

Thanks for the tip. We'd never have thought of that. They're not exactly standing up to be counted. And you can't see the trees for the wood. The only thing harder to nail than a mobster in Mong Kok is a whore in Wan Chai.

You're probably not doing it right.

Easier to catch crabs on a hill, snipes Chau, invoking a cryptic Cantonese idiom.

If it's crabs you're after, my friend, you'll find all sorts and sizes down there. Easy to catch and more fun trying. Give you an excuse to go undercover too.

I don't need an excuse, says Oldham.

Send Chau then. He can keep an eye out for her.

Two sets of eyes are better than one, he replies, then realises the insensitivity of his comment. Sorry. That's not what I meant.

Chau stares blankly. Either it went right by him, or he's past caring what either of us say. Or the chain of command renders him mute in these situations.

Oldham reminds me how well I know that part of town.

Used to know, I correct him. The past is a different country. They do things differently there.

It's changing, but not that much.

What's in it for me?

We're in it for you, Jack. You've taken a lot of withdrawals from the favour bank. It's time for a deposit. Last year's donation to the Benevolent Fund, much as it was appreciated, can only hold a man in good stead for so long.

He's talking about the shituation I'd gotten us into last year. The one that cost Chau his binocular vision. The one others had paid for with their lives and left one of my business partners confined to a wheelchair. The mess I'd cleaned up with some cash and diamonds that had come into my possession in the denouement of that scamellum. I still have a gonad full of stones stashed away. You can't drop them all onto the market at once. It does more than lower their value. It draws unwanted attention. Struggling advertising agencies aren't supposed to have such resources at their disposal. We adopt the same approach as the Dutch and the South Africans. Release a few at strategic times, like Chinese New Year, or when our cash flow is stagnating. No one knows about them, apart from Angel Luk, my other associate at the agency. Oldham and Chau had turned blind eyes to many of the inconsistencies in the story. More for the sake of clean paperwork than financial gain. The money I donated went to Chau's medical expenses and widowed police officers. It was recompense. Reparations. Not a lifelong Get Out Of Jail Free card. We were all crystal clear on that and bonded by the insoluble truth of it.

I'll have a word with a few people.

Oldham leads me to a desk outside. He instructs Chau to take my formal statement regarding the showdown at The Auld Ball & Chain. Cyclops begrudgingly releases me into Mei's recognizance half an hour later. I ask if he'll validate my parking and have the car brought around to the front. He doesn't see the humour in this.

I remind Mei that's not entirely his fault.

It's dark by the time we pull into 88 Sing Woo Road. I bypass the agency on the first floor and head straight for home, fourteen storeys above. My mother-in-law's scorn preferable to Angel's inquisition.

That can wait until tomorrow.

There's an unfamiliar clatter of chatter coming from within the apartment. Por-por is noisy but, even when delivering a sermon to our God-fearing domestic helper, she rarely sounds like an over-heated Legco debate.

Mei reaches for the door handle and questions me with her eyebrows. I bring my hand to my mouth in mock horror. She laughs and enters the apartment.

Eight sets of glazzies turn to greet us.

Por-por's demeanour is not as disapproving as it usually is when I bring Mei home this much past dinner-time. The congregation before her has taken care of that. It's one of the few things we have in common. A dislike of crowds. Particularly at home. Especially after the last time we played host to uninvited guests and the bloody mess they left in the lobby. She's so embarrassed about it she still can't look our neighbours in the eye.

Bing pokes her Filipino gulliver out of the kitchen and looks at me. She's worried and wondering if I'm aware how dire the current situation is. Her eyes drift to the crimson splash on my t-shirt.

She'd rather deal with that than what lies in the adjacent room.

Mei is coaxed out from behind my legs and introduced to her distant relatives. They're all women, apparently. The sisters and daughters of their wily leader. An elder stateswoman of the Zhang Dynasty.

Gu-por.

I've heard of her and the family's legendry predisposition to hunting in packs. Her arrival was said to be a sign of The Apocalypse. This prophecy appears to be grounded in truth. Por-por informs me Gu-por and her clan intend to stay with us.

For dinner?

For longer.

For our holidays, chirps one of The Aunties, like this is a good thing.

Oh. That's great.

It seems they've taken it upon themselves to start The Handover early, prematurely granting each other the right of abode. It's pointless asking how long they plan to occupy our territory. They probably don't even know. To be uncertain is to be uncomfortable, as the saying goes, but to be certain is to be ridiculous. It could be anything from a few days to a few weeks. Or whenever the food runs out. Like locust and viruses, they move from one host to another at irregular intervals. As the reunification of China and Hong Kong draws closer I guess we can expect impromptu visits on a regular basis. It was part of the deal Thatcher brokered with Deng. For the immediate future I'm more concerned with how we're going to accommodate them at bed-time. No doubt it's been worked out. Apart from a couple of large, industrial grade garbage bags, luggage is relatively thin on the ground. Rooms must've been allocated and commandeered. That'll teach me to go out carousing until the early hours of the evening.

Por-por or Bing would usually give Mei a shower at this time of night. Under the circumstances, however, any port will do in such an uncertain storm.

Is it safe to go into the bathroom? I ask, in case there are more of them camped in the shower recess.

We take refuge for as long as can be considered polite. Mei wants information about Gu-por. I don't really have much. She's a wealthy widower. She'd have to be to support a posse like hers. None of the siblings made their marriages work. They all live with her and live off her. I don't know how her husband died, or how she came into so much money. I suspect it's all related. Maybe he's not even dead. Maybe he married out of the family. Or is hiding.

I could identify with that.

Their ménage is headquartered in Guilin. A beautiful part of China's south-west. They have two homes on the same block. A newer, second realm Gu-por built to accommodate her burgeoning responsibilities on the domestic front. The original kingdom was abandoned and left empty for a while, earmarked for demolition. Until it became a sanctuary for swallows. Word spread amongst these prized members of avian community. Thousands of them relocated from nearby cliffs. Gu-por now houses one of the great swallow sanctuaries in Guanxi. She reaps the benefits too, harvesting the nests. She sent us inordinate supplies of them during Ling's pregnancy. This odd commodity is one of the reasons Mei has such lovely skin. That's probably what's in the garbage bags out there. Two hundred thousand dollars worth of bird spit.

None of this, of course, would make any sense to Mei. So I simply tell her that Gu-por is the queen of a magical land.

What about the others?

They are her loyal subjects. They follow wherever she goes.

Like Thidwick? she probes, referencing Dr Seuss' big-hearted moose.

Just like Thidwick, I reply, and wonder what Gu-por's antlers would look like on the Harvard Club wall.

There's already a mattress on the floor in Mei's room. And no bags. This is where I am to be sequestered for the duration of The Occupation. I fall asleep in here most nights anyway, during or after storytime.

Mei puts on her pyjamas. The ones with the Yodas.

I inspect Por-por's room. Two large suitcases dominate the *mise-en-scène*.

In my official abode there's three carry-on bags. It could be a bit tight in the double bed, depending on the combination of refugees. At least they'll have something to read. This was also my literary fortress of solitude. Xanadu with Dewey Decimals, from 101 ARI to 426 DIC and 828 YEA. The walls are plastered with lettered loot purloined from Hong Kong libraries in the folly of my formative years.

It was the best of times, it was the worst of times.

It was the worst of times, to be honest. The age of foolishness and the epoch of incredulity. The season of darkness and the winter of despair. Nothing before us, no heaven above us. We were all going direct the other way. It was a tale of one country, two systems. And there was little else worth salvaging from the annals of that bleak period. The books, along with bootleg films, are where I learned English. They precipitated and facilitated my assault on advertising too. When I was stuck for words I could always steal from others. Like Aristotle said, habits fostered at youth make all the difference. On the other hand, nothing so needs reforming as other people's habits. Like the habit of turning up unannounced. And with two more irrelatives to be housed somewhere we're encroaching upon yet another Dickensian epoch. The sofas in the living room may not live to tell.

It is a far, far better rest that I go to than I have ever known.

In the arrivals lounge every surface is paved with Styrofoam lunchboxes. The outlaws are reaving a buffet of entrails and appendages.

You can't have any pudding if you don't eat your feet.

Mei devours the extra attention being poured upon her. And doesn't look like head-butting anyone for encroaching upon her space. It's a shame Sam isn't here to see how we've answered any concerns she may have regarding female influences in my daughter's life. She could OD on feminine mystique this week. And the next.

I decide to control the dotage and put her to bed.

Tonight's story is, unsurprisingly, Thidwick The Big-hearted Moose. Mei's asleep before the bear holes-up in the titular twig-eater's antlers. I should be so lucky. The events of the day have taken roost in my gulliver. I can't shake them off. They mill about like free-loading relatives on a couch.

I pick my way through the throng in the living room, informing the fray of my plans to take care of a few things in the office. Don't wait up, I suggest. Or rather, request. They barely acknowledge my departure. I can still hear them discussing meals past, present and future as I descend in the lift.

Approaching the glass doors of So Fuk Yu I decide that whatever is waiting for me there can wait until tomorrow. I turn into the first floor stairwell and walk to the carpark. Since buying the Range Rover I've taken to late night driving in much the same way, for the same reasons, as others go jogging. To put their troubles behind them.

Without thinking too much about it I find myself on Lockhart Road.

Business is brisk. A higher police presence than usual. It probably has something to do with this afternoon's slaughter. The US navy also appears to be in town, en route to some policing exercise of their own. Girls take pot-shots at the servicemen, playfully assaulting crew-cuts and dragging them from the street. They meet with little resistance.

Who's sexploiting whom?

The Auld Ball & Chain is cordoned with tape. Punters gather at the front, wondering what to do, like this is the only bar in town. Now what? Where do we go from here? It's a good question. They consider their options. A convivial, congenital working girl beckons them into Waikiki. The answer, it seems to me, is obvious.

You follow the girl.

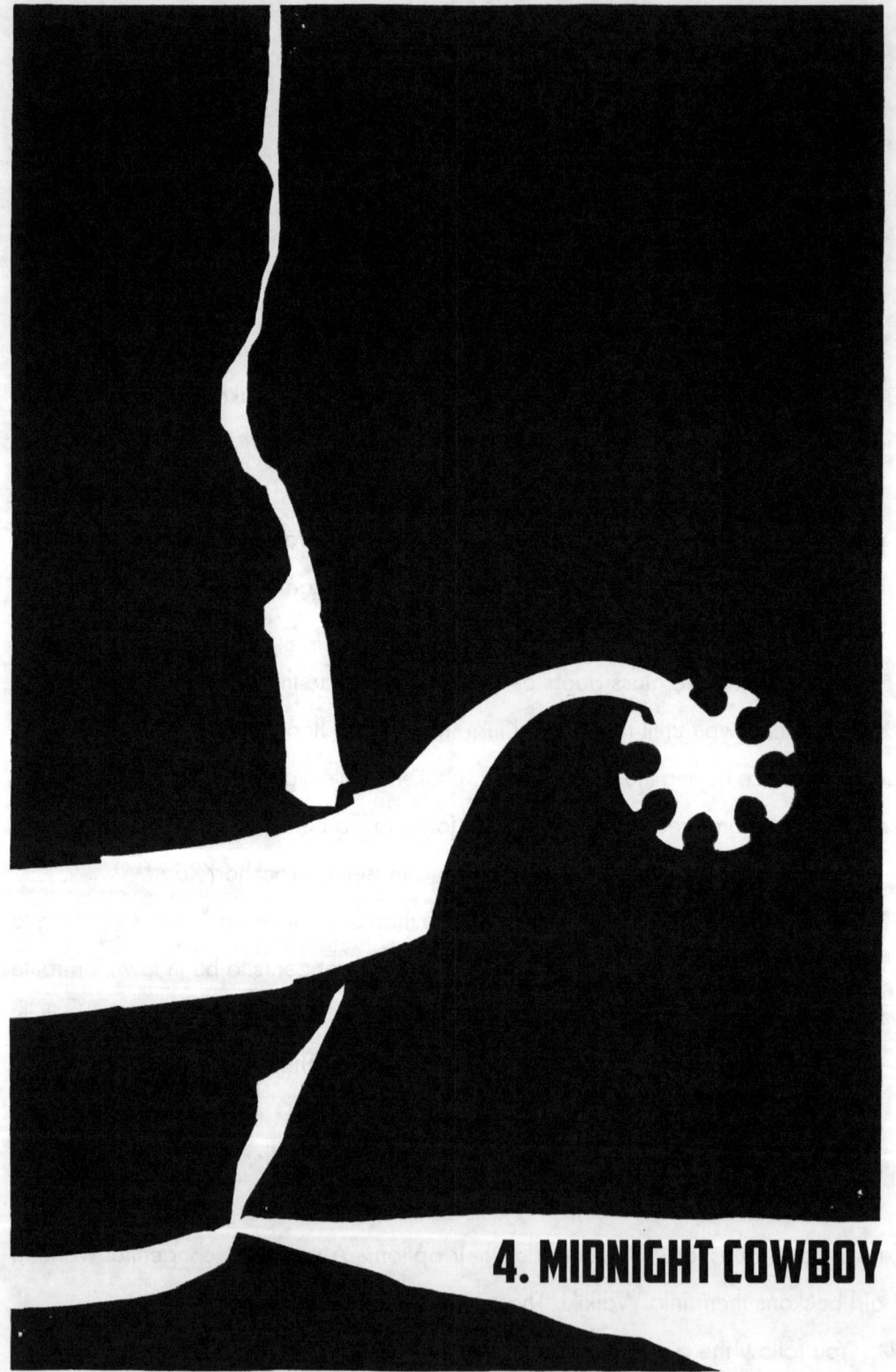

4. MIDNIGHT COWBOY

I swing into a parking spot outside The Horse & Groom. It's a reflex action. They're rare. See a space, take it. This bar is as good as any to ask questions. Kitty was fond of post-coital kibble, according to her homicidal lover. She would've come here. Many make it their first or last stop of the night. The faux English pub does a hearty faux English breakfast.

The manager is Kenny *Cowboy* Lau. He has a preference for country music and western attire. He rides midnight to dawn and wrangles a harrase of *filles de joie*. Most of which he's proudly broken-in himself. The man knows the macellarious market and his product intimately. No one understands the comings and blowings of Lockhart Road better.

The bar is thick with smoke. Most of the tables are occupied. It's a study in Darwinian Theory. A collection of different species at various stages on the evolutionary trail of the evening. A few sailors, fresh from the dock, are getting their bearings. Working on a plan and slipping a little ammo into their clip before embarking on an overdue sexual sortie. Locals, midway through a moderate session of Liar Dice, bang plastic shakers onto the table. They call bluffs and howl when the truth is revealed. Tourists and expatriates are getting their first real glimpse of the Filipinos they bought-out from the girlie bars. Some tread softly toward the business end of the evening, others brazenly steam toward it. Office workers and traders catch up after a brutal day. The bar counter is lined with lone wolves lamenting bad bets and poor decisions, planning a moonlight flit, or putting off the return home because there's six people trying to find a space of their own in a shoebox.

The jukebox plays The Escape Club. Wild Wild West.

Kenny sits at the far end of the bar in a cloud of carcinogens. He gets through a couple of packs of Marlboro a night. Right now he has one eye on me while he talks to a barmaid. It's Mabel, formally of The Auld Ball & Chain. She's still wearing the same Guinness promotional polo shirt.

People move on quickly.

A man collapsed on the train as it arrived in Admiralty. Heart attack. A group of passengers picked him up. They lifted him onto the platform, put his briefcase beside him and returned to the carriage. The doors closed. The train pulled out.

This city can be a bitch. It waits for no man and mourns even less.

I pull up a stool south of Kenny and give him a nod of acknowledgement. Not a lot of men can get away with wearing rusty cavalry boots and stonewash jeans. Kenny isn't one of them. His leg bounces to the music.

I order a bourbon on the rocks from Mabel. She gives no indication we've met before. The eclectic horseman tells her to pour me an extra shot of the good stuff. Three fingers of Olde Regret hit the deck.

I raise my glass to him. Yipee ki-yay.

Yippee ki-yay motherfucker, he replies, like he's been practicing it in front of the bathroom mirror. John McClane meets Travis Bickle.

You talking to me? Well I'm the only one here. Who the fuck do you think you're talking to? Oh yeah? OK.

Mind if I ask you a few questions, Kenny?

Is that one of them?

It's about The Ball & Chain.

What about it?

What do you know?

Nothing.

Mabel didn't tell you about her boss ordering his last round of drinks?

No.

You heard about it?

About what?

Someone put Teplice out of business.

That's too bad.

You know who?

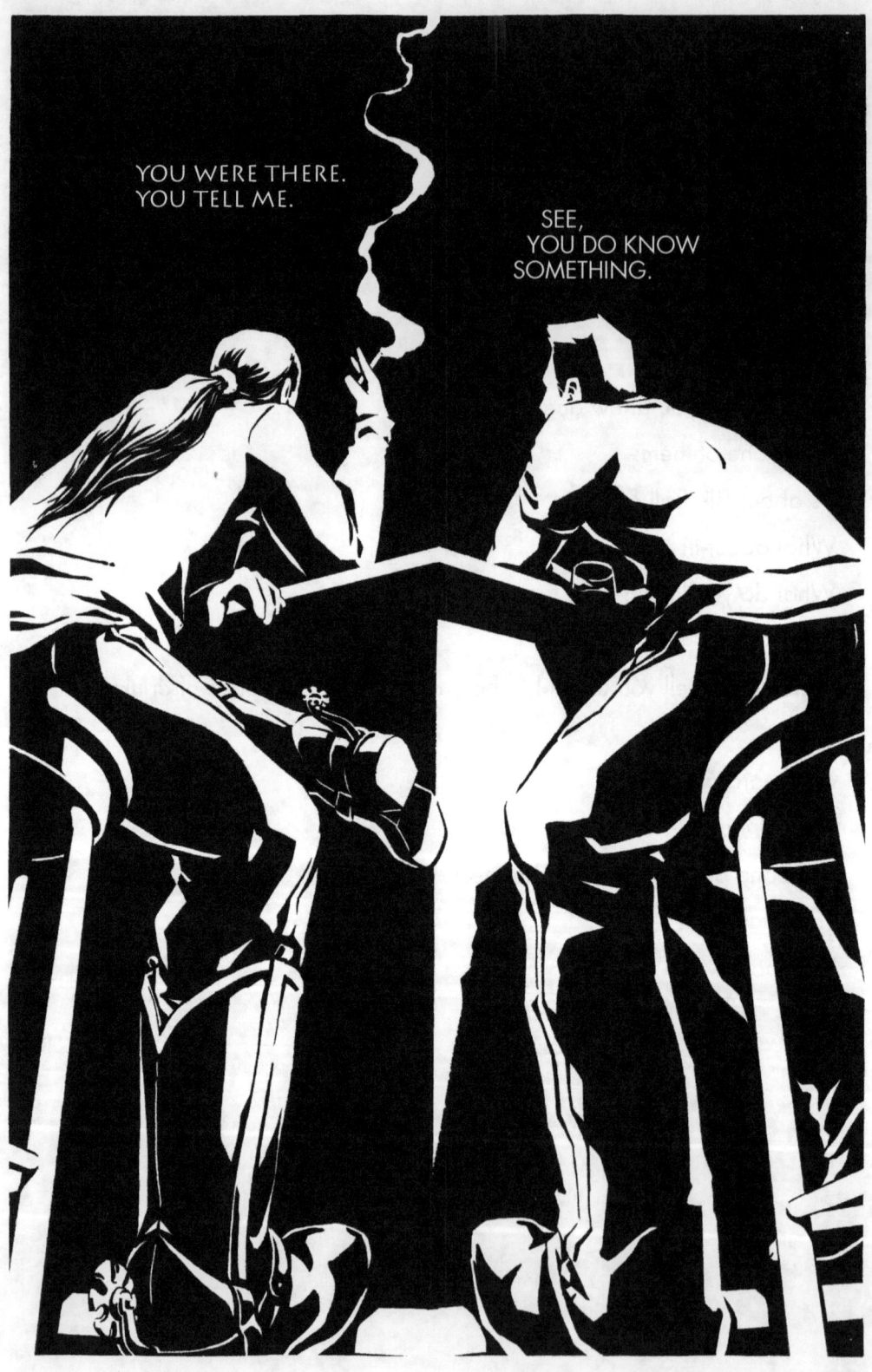

YOU KNOW WHY
THEY PUNCHED
HIS CARD?

Why you looking for her?

I want to offer my condolences.

Good luck. You find her you tell her to call me. She was good for business. Hasn't been seen for a long time. Since the divorce.

They were married?

Maybe. They split. She got more than half the money. Messy business, divorce.

Didn't end well today. Know where I might find her?

No.

Mabel worked there. Maybe she knows.

Maybe you have to ask Mabel.

Mind if I do?

Not if Mabel doesn't. She's on a break. Make it quick.

Mabel is drifting across the room to an empty table in the corner. I drop a hundred on the bar and tell Kenny to get himself something special.

I don't drink.

Buy yourself another packet of Marlboro. You can thank me later. Yippee ki-yay motherfucker.

Yippee ki-yay.

Poison get started on Every Rose Has It's Thorn. I take a seat opposite Mabel. She lights a menthol and looks over my shoulder.

You okay, jeh-jeh?

Okay.

You speak to police?

Of course.

What did you tell them?

What happened.

Anything else.

I don't know anything else.

Didn't take you long to find work.

I'm good at my job.

How long were you at your last one?

Long time.

How well did you know Nifty?

Better than he know himself.

Mind if I pinch a smoke?

They're menthol. Make you sterile.

I fired my last bullet a long time ago.

You and Teplice. Kitty tease him about it. When she drink. She say he was only half a man, in front of his friends. She not give him any face. Said she'd go back to her old boyfriend if he wasn't locked up, he knows how to treat a lady. Teplice beat her. Didn't care if anyone watching. Beat her bad one night. Knocked her down. She get up and go.

Go where?

Nowhere. Just gone. Easy to do. People do it every day.

Stole his money?

Took his keys one night. I never seen him so angry.

You think he more angry about the money, or her?

Both. Maybe money more. He had a lot of girls.

But he married her.

Maybe.

Maybe?

They had party. She wore a big ring. Maybe they register for marriage. They fight like married couple. She keep working though. He say he didn't mind. She was good for business. Her business is my business. What's hers is mine, he say. I think maybe he mind more than he say. Sometimes. Maybe.

You know where they lived?

He had a place on Bowen Road. Jackie used to make delivery there. Or take the money there at the end of the night, if Teplice leave early.

Jackie?

Bar manager. There was another place too. Corner of Jaffe and Fenwick. No one lived there. No woman, anyway. He throw parties. Private parties. Him and his girls and his *gweilo* friends.

How do you know that no woman lived there?

No woman could. He sleep there sometimes. Keep a change of clothes. But if you looking for Kitty you won't find her there.

Where would I find her?

You wouldn't. Teplice look everywhere. She's gone, like the tide.

Great, I think. Another infuriating metaphor. Cantonese love their idioms. And speak in riddles half the time. This one has me thinking of Longfellow.

The tide rises, the tide falls,

The twilight darkens, the curlew calls;

The day returns, but nevermore

Returns the traveller to the shore,

And the tide rises, the tide falls.

Where was the place on Bowen Road, Mabel?

I don't know. Jackie make delivery.

How do I find Jackie?

I don't know. He's gone. Like the-

Like the tide. I get it.

Question time is over. It's not that she doesn't have Jackie's number. She just can't give it to me. That would be against The Rules. I thank her for the cigarette and take a step toward the door.

He wasn't a good man, adds Mabel, expelling a lungful. But he wasn't a bad boss. He pay good. And he pay on time. Not a lot of people do that. Do you do that?

Me and Nifty. We're a dying breed.

Go around the back. Maybe the door unlocked. Look above his desk. Maybe you find a list of numbers. Maybe Jackie's number there.

Maybe.

Teplice was a good boss, she says.

Maybe, I reply, agreeing to disagree and leaving her to fondly reminisce.

Some say you can't judge a man or his life by the way he lived, only by the way he died. There are no evil men. Just evil deeds surrounding the goodness of a man, like a lotus flower. Or some bullshit like that. Maybe Nifty was a lotus flower and his life had folded in upon him. Whatever his shortcomings may have been as a man he'd garnered Mabel's respect as an employer. I wonder if that small floral tribute is the only one I'll find laid at Neil Teplice's feet.

I exit, cross the road and duck into the service alley behind Lockhart.

Deep in the shadows, Bon Jovi are prescribing a dose of Bad Medicine.

I make a sharp right at the back of The Auld Ball & Chain. I give the door a gentle kick. It swings open.

The night lights have been left on. Even without the spectre of death in the air it would be an eerie scene. Stale booze and cigarettes ooze from the floor, cling to the walls and hang from the ceiling.

Nifty's blood has coagulated on the desk. I gag, more at the memory of his final moments than the smell.

A cork board above the desk is flecked with syrup. Likewise the list of employee phone numbers. I pull a pencil from among a dozen pens cradled in an empty beer glass. I scrawl names and numbers on a coaster. There's a stack of envelopes by an out-tray. I lift one. The name at the top is familiar enough. Neil Teplice. It's the address that gets my attention.

5C Bowen Road.

It's been crossed out. Re-addressed to The Auld Ball & Chain.

Bowen Road.

He may no longer be in residence, and been declared *persona non grata*, but whoever's there knows where to find him. Maybe they know other things too.

I'll drop by in the morning and pay my respects.

Returning to the car I notice someone behind the wheel of a white sedan, three spaces back. His eye patch is unmistakable.

I approach his blind side. Hammer my palms on the bonnet. Startle the bejezus out of him. He throws the door open, intent on confrontation, then recognizes me and settles back into his seat. I offer two thumbs-up, a wink and tell him not to stay up too late. It's a school night. He stares at me and begins plotting my downfall in half a dozen novel ways.

I drive home pondering the murky muskeg of Nifty's life, knowing I'll soon be wading through the flotsam and jetsam of another existence.

Mine.

5. THE MERRY WIDOW

The outlaws are holed-up for the night. There's one on the couch, bathed in the familiar glow of late-night television. Another is nesting on the adjacent vinyl island, dribbling saliva like a septuagenarian swallow on the cliffs of insanity. I tiptoe through the refuge to the bathroom and brush my teeth. Twice.

In Mei's room I pull the Ewok blanket over her shoulders, kiss her forehead, then tuck and roll into the mattress on the floor.

I hate days like today. Homicides can really take it out of you.

I'm being chased through the New Territories by bar girls. They're all wearing the same almond-coloured leotard with thick, pastel blue stripes. They're all the same girl, just with different hair. Giant perms. Vidal Sassoon bobs. Joan Jett crops. Long and straight. I get to the top of Castle Peak Road and Sonny Bono points to Lion Rock Tunnel. The Filipino hunting party is hot on my heels. A giant silhouette stands at the end of the tunnel. A Cheshire Cat grin spread wide across his round face. A bald woman is by his side. She has no eyes.

What's the matter, Jack? Don't you recognize me?

I try to sit up. Mei is perched on my chest. Ba-ba? What's that noise Ba-ba?

I try to focus. What noise, Sugar-pop?

That noise, she says, looking toward the furore beyond the door.

I don't know. Maybe Gu-por and everyone else?

When are they going?

Good question. Let's find out what's got their knickers in a twist.

At the epicentre of enlightenment a full compliment of family members have gathered. They are gravely concerned about the lavatory. Our lone ablution is out of commission. I'm not surprised. Of course it's broken. If I had to broaden the appeal of this situation comedy I'd inject some toilet humour too. The sudden increase in traffic would test the load-bearing capacity of any comfort station. A relic from a simpler time, it was only ever one bum away from retirement.

I tell the incontinent masses not to worry. I'll get someone to fix it. Until then they are hereby granted the right of commode in the first floor washroom, at the office. One at a time, I caution, handing the key to Gu-por.

Mei and I have errands to run and a lead to chase down. We'll get breakfast at the *dai pai dong*. After we drop by the office. It's only fair I warn Angel of the irregular visitors she'll be receiving during the course of the day. Throughout the week. Indefinitely. Until further apprised. Like everyone in Hong Kong she knows the day is coming when there will be hordes of Mainlanders squatting in our Special Administrative Region. She just wouldn't be expecting that day to be today.

I leave a note on her desk, asking her not to call Immigration.

Mei wants to know why we're driving, not walking, to breakfast. The *dai pai dong* is around the corner.

We're going somewhere after, Doodle-bug.

Where?

Lake Winna-bango.

Woo-hoo, Waldo Woo! Let's roll! she shouts from her booster chair in the rear, and puts on her seatbelt. Click-clack, front and back! Safety is everyone's business!

We pull up at the shopfront on Yik Yam Street. The proprietor is a plump shouty dwarf, another of Mei's adopted aunties. I wind the window down, bark a salutation and order. Fried-egg sandwiches, a warm soy milk and a strong coffee. To go.

Mei unbuckles, opens her door and runs inside. She returns a couple of minutes later, laden with the morning lode.

Leave the lid on your soy milk, Bingle-bear. Until we get to Bowen Road.

Are we going to the swings? she asks, unwrapping her sandwich. It's finished before we get onto Queen's Road East. I tell her she can have mine. She hesitates for a moment, then devours it.

I turn off Magazine Gap into Bowen.

It's a comparatively undeveloped belt that cuts across the low-slung hips of Victoria Peak. Starting here, in the Mid-levels, snaking around behind Admiralty and Wan Chai to a point on Stubbs Road, above Happy Valley. Much of its journey is closed to traffic. This makes it a popular haunt for those running themselves into an early grave. A couple of expats jog by as I throw the car on the curb at 5C. A few aging dawn-walkers dawdle along. They're probably on their way to a Tai Chi session at the park, if they don't die before they get there. Mei's quite fond of the playground down that way too. A young, optimistic couple walk hand-in-hand. I'd wager they've been to worship at Lover's Rock, a small monolith in Bowen's nether regions that's been known to ensure happy marriages, when it's in the mood and doesn't have a headache. Further down, at the opposite end of the street, a teenage girl sits alone on the curb, staring vacantly at a recently opened home for unwed mothers and their unwanted progeny. Crisis pregnancies. Adoption. Foster care. Second chances and last resorts. One too many trips to Lover's Rock.

That aside, signs of life are few and far between. Even at the busiest times. A handful of well-tailored professionals will exit this row of walk-up apartments in an hour, and trickle down the hill to Gotham.

For now it's just me, Mei and the silent minority.

I take the plastic cover off the foam cup of coffee and cauterize my senses with its contents. It's not coffee in the traditional sense. The secret, they tell me, is the eggs shells that infuse the brew. The litre of condensed milk it's cut with plays an important part too. Opiates make it habit-forming.

Mei is valiantly attempting to take the lid off her milk without spilling it. I tell her to be careful. It might be hot. I twist awkwardly in my chair to assist.

It would be better if I was allowed to sit in the front, she reminds me for the one-hundredth time.

No it wouldn't. Yours is the safest seat in the car.

It's also the most boring. All I can see is the back of your head.

Better that than the front of a mini-bus or a taxi.

What are we doing here, Ba-ba? The playground is miles away.

I have to see a client. Won't take long.

It's already taking forever.

I'll be back in a minute. Drink your milk. I'll be quick. You can listen to your Sesame Street tape. Here we go.

I punch the cassette player. C Is For Cookie kicks into gear.

Half-way to the apartments I stop, remember something important, and return to the car.

That's was quick, says Mei as I open the door. Can we go to the slide now?

Sorry, Beetle-bomb. Forgot something.

I wind the window down a bit, to let some air in. This is the right thing to do when leaving pets or kids in the car.

That okay, Grumble-guts?

Fine.

I take The Sneetches And Other Stories from the backpack and give it to her.

How much longer are you going to be, Ba-ba?

Not long, I promise. And close the door on that discussion.

The exterior walls of the building would've been creamy white in their glory days. They're off-yellow now, like a chain-smoker's teeth, and sweat-stained with tropical grime. The block clings to the green skirt of the slope. Stairs lead down to 5A and 5B. Up to 5D. The path ahead ends at 5C.

I ring the bell.

It occurs to me I'm on the verge of speaking with someone who may or may not know their ex-whatever was clubbed to death with a cricket bat.

What was I thinking?

The heavy door looks like it's taken a pounding over the years. Beaten within an inch of its life, it hangs drearily on to the hinges of actuality.

Likewise the middle-aged frump who answers it.

She's not the thirty year-old scorcher I was expecting. It's hard to imagine this one inflaming passions or igniting anything other than the cigarettes she's clutching in her chubby hand. You could strike a match on the skin beneath the faded towelling bathrobe. She's five-foot-eight and hauling thirty-five kilos of excess freight. A mess of bottle-blonde hair is struggling to maintain itself, long overdue for some attention. Two inches of black roots are having their moment in the sun. Narrow, grey eyes drag heavy bags beneath them.

It looks like she's been drinking all night.

In a way I kind of hope she has. For a woman to look and smell this way after eight hours of sleep would be nature's cruellest joke.

Sorry to wake you.

I look like I've been sleeping?

Oh. Okay. Thanks, I reply, lost for words.

I'm Lynne Sprudel. I didn't take his name. I took everything else. All his bullshit. But I didn't take his name. Lucky, huh? At least now I don't have to change it back.

The voice has English tones. Wannabe-posh. Like she wishes her name was double-barrelled and had gone to a better school. Even in this dilapidated state she's trying hard to maintain appearances.

The ginger tomcat rubs against her thick ankles. She pushes it into the apartment with a bare foot. The cherry-red polish on her fat toes is faded, cracked and chipped.

I figure I don't have to tread too carefully here. As far as the Teplice-Sprudel relationship goes there doesn't seem to have been a lot of love to lose. I'd say she blasted through her mourning period about three-fifths ago.

Who are you? she demands, squinting into the harsh morning light.

I was acquainted with your husband.

Wasn't everyone?

I'm here in a more professional capacity.

Really? What profession is that?

Solicitors, I ad lib, recalling the firm of my unofficial legal counsel. Callett, Crambazzle, Dratchell & Feaque, ma'am. One of our clients is looking for an associate of his.

He didn't have associates. Swifty had debtors, creditors and whores.

I resist the urge to ask which of those classifications she fell under. Our client is seeking a known companion, Ms Sprudel. A female.

Good luck. Man had more slatterns than a Mong Kok madam, she says, looking over my shoulder. That mongrel in the car is not his, is it? Mother's Choice is a few doors down.

No, ma'am. That mongrel in the car is mine.

She looks at me like I've just given away the ending of Vertigo.

Alright Lynnie? a gin-soaked voice calls from within.

Man here's looking for one of Nifty's tarts, Haze.

A man? the curious woman replies, drifting out from the shadows.

Haze is just as frumpy. Fifteen kilos larger. She gave up bleaching her hair a while ago. Probably around the time of The Boer War. If Haze is not Lynne Sprudel's sister she's a close relative. She gives me the once-over.

Well don't keep him all to yourself. Bring him in so we can all get a look.

She punctuates this request with a porcine snort. And I can tell this bad idea of mine is rapidly turning into a waste of time.

You better come in then, Lynne concedes.

Mei is watching intently. I raise my hands and signal ten-minutes. She sticks out her tongue. I give her the thumbs up. She puts her gulliver back in a book.

I enter the apartment and immediately regret the decision. The stale smell of smoke is augmented by the unmistakable aroma of cat's piss. It's plain to see why.

There must be half a dozen moggies roaming the living room.

Sprudel shoos a large Persian from a worn armchair and drops into it. A bottle of gin and a tumbler stand on a side-table. Both are almost empty. Or a quarter full, depending on how you look at these things.

You going to make the introductions? asks Haze, nursing a drink and spreading like Jabba The Hutt over the adjacent sofa.

Sprudel looks at me and realizes she doesn't have the information to answer that question. She lights a cigarette instead.

Jack So, I offer politely.

So far so good, guffaws Haze. I give a flat smile, acknowledging her pun. So, So, you're looking for one of Nifty's disposables?

I was led to believe Ms Ho was slightly more than that, Ms...?

Hazel, Mr So. No need for formalities in here, is there Lynne? Makes us feel older than we are. Call me Hazel. And you can call Ms Ho exactly what she is too. A home-wrecking, money-grabbing, whore-on-heels.

Clearly Hazel hasn't read Gatsby either. She thinks this comment is hilarious and throws her gulliver back as she cackles. I'd laugh but it's the second time I've heard it.

Lynne stares into her tumbler. She's as past-it as the nicotine stained walls.

For a house in keening the air isn't exactly heavy with sorrow. Although it does have a lot to compete with. The stench almost has me dry-heaving. How long must she have lived among this to be immune to it? Maybe the thought of Nifty's estate has contributed to her buoyancy. I ask when she last saw the deceased. Her husband.

I told the police last night, I haven't seen him in years.

Since?

Since he started fucking the natives, interrupts Hazel.

I ignore the peanut gallery and add a firmer tone to my voice. Lynne, we really could wrap this up quicker if there were less interfations.

Ooh, get you, responds Hazel, and lights a cigarette. So tetchy. Don't mind me, Mr Interfations. I'm just a neighbour, lending support to a friend in her hour of need. I might need a lawyer myself if my old man doesn't pull through. He was with Nifty last night. Got more stitches in his head than a football. Lost a lot of blood. Still in intensive care.

I hear it was quite an ugly scene.

Been living with me for twenty years, he's used to ugly.

Snort.

I'm beginning to understand why Prop Forward would rather spend more time at the pub than at home with his Scrum Half. Have you spoken to him? I ask.

He doesn't remember much of anything. Although he's been like that for ages. The damage might not be too bad.

Snort.

That's lucky.

Yeah. Lucky me.

Snort.

I return my attention to the merry widow. You last saw Neil a few years ago?

I kicked him out. He'd stopped being discreet about his indiscretions.

And you haven't seen him since?

Not if I could help it.

You've spoken with him?

Not really. Not in the last six months.

Hazel cackles, snorts and almost coughs up a diseased lung.

Where was he living?

At the pub.

Anywhere else?

He had a fuckpad.

Did you know any of his indiscretions?

Oh yes, we were all great friends. Karaoke on Friday. Mahjong on Saturday. Gosh we didn't half have some nights, didn't we Haze?

Did you know Kitty Ho? I heard she was quite special.

They were all special. They were all Kitty Ho. They were all the same. You don't look Chinese.

Pardon?

You don't look Chinese, for a name like So.

You don't appear to be grieving. Doesn't mean you're not hurting.

Sprudel quietly appreciates the sentiment, and pours three-fingers of gin. Neil's death doesn't surprise me, she admits. Someone was always going to hit him back. I never had the guts. When he left, when I threw him out, I was glad to have him gone. We were separated. He could do whatever to whoever, whenever.

Separated? Not divorced?

Our papers were before the court, as you legal types are fond of saying.

He didn't get remarried?

I wasn't invited. Doesn't mean he didn't. He was a lot of things. You could add bigamist to the list and no one would raise an eyebrow. It's the Chinese way isn't it? Another wife stashed away somewhere.

He wasn't Chinese.

Neither are you. Doesn't mean you can't act that way when it suits you.

So you never met Ms Ho?

If I met her I would've warned her. If she walked in now I'd buy her a drink. I'd like to meet the one that said enough is enough. I'd congratulate her for getting out and getting even. I hear she robbed him blind. Good for her. Apart from that, what's so special about Kitty Ho?

I'm just following up on behalf of the estate.

The estate? That's a good one, isn't it Haze? The estate! Does this look like an estate to you? This is all he left me and no one is taking it away.

I don't think anyone would try. What about The Ball & Chain?

She turns to her neighbour and raises her glass in a congratulatory fashion. Didn't think of that, did we, Haze? A place to call our own.

There may be some dispute if he'd re-married. The people my firm represents have a substantial interest in the building, as a whole.

That would make him a two-timing, wife-beating, cheating bastard. What would your lawyers have to say about that?

If we can find Ms Ho we can determine if she has any entitlement. If not we can deal directly with you. Make you an offer.

Sprudel sits straighter in her chair. She puts down her drink. A lot of people are interested in that pub. And your Kitty Ho, she adds. A big lump of man turned up last night, right before the police. I figured Neil owed him money or had put one through his girl. Or both. I didn't know what had happened. Gives me the chills thinking about it. He was right here. Now I think about it, he was a tad off balance when I opened the door too. Like he was expecting someone else. Same as you. I guess I've always been a disappointment for men.

No you haven't, offers Hazel. You're just too good for them, that's all.

You have no idea where she might be? I ask.

Could be any one of a thousand brothels. You find her you tell her I'd like to buy her that drink. At my pub.

Snort.

Our pub, suggests her partner in grime.

One thing was certain. If Kitty Ho ever turned up, there was no shortage of people who wanted to buy her a drink.

Sprudel stands, uneasily, and wobbles toward the back of the unit. Wait there, she says. I've got something that might help you find her.

Rather than be left alone with Hazel, and the discomfort that comes with breathing the same air, I step outside to check on Mei.

She averts her eyes as I approach, trying not to look guilty. I ask her what she's hiding in her lap.

Nothing.

I lift the book. She attempts to stop me but has neither the speed nor strength. A cassette sits in the folds of her skirt. The brown magnetic tape lies in an unruly pile.

I tried to change it, she offers sheepishly. I didn't do it on purpose.

I know, Sweetheart. Don't worry. I'll get you a new one.

Now?

Soon.

How much longer?

A couple of minutes. It'll only take a second. I promise.

I'm going to count. One.. two... three...

I walk back to the apartment. Sprudel is standing in the door.

Thought you'd gone without saying goodbye, or waiting for your goodie bag, she says, and presents me with an envelope. Maybe Kitty Ho's in there.

Photographs. Glossy four-by-threes. Polaroids. Girls. Nifty with girls. Girls with other girls. Girls with Nifty and some of the rugby team. Celebrating. Christmas. New Year. Chinese New Year. Anything and everything. Some wear nothing more than a bikini. Some not even that. Nifty is amongst them, alabandical and oblivious to his bloody destiny. They hang off him. Drape across him. He's soaking it up. Lapping it up. Living it up. So many women, so many times. One stands out. A post-modern Portrait Of Carlotta.

Kitty Ho.

Even if I hadn't seen her before I'd know it was her. Like the first time Yossarian saw the chaplain in Catch-22. It all made sense. The eyes. The lips. The smile. The body. The way she used them all, effortlessly. At the same time. To extraordinary effect. Sure, her nose was a little wide and there were a couple of small blemishes on her rich, almond skin. The extra pound of baby fat added dimension to her estiferous curves. And if she asked for anything you'd surrender it to her. Even if there was only a slim, seductive hope of getting something in return. A man would kill just for a piece of her.

You didn't show these to the police, Lynne?

Didn't seem important. You're the only one who asked about the girls.

Is Kitty Ho one of these?

You tell me, she replies. And I wonder who is testing whom.

Do you mind if I ask why you keep photos like this, of your husband?

Ex-husband. I thought I might need them, at the divorce. Ammunition. Irreconcilable differences? My arse. He was so stupid. Bastard stashed those with his skin magazines. It was the last straw. Keeping them under this roof. He had the cheek to ask if he could have them back. I told him he could take plenty more. I'd send him one every now and then. Birthdays. Anniversaries. Christmas. I'd cut the girls out of them. Leave him there, on his own, with that idiot grin. I guess it was a bit cruel but nothing compared to what he did to me. I'd kind of forgotten about them. The photos. Until now.

Before we walk so far down memory lane that we can't find our way back, I thank her for her time and apologize for her loss. I tell her I'll be in touch if I have any news and ask if I can keep a couple of photos.. I'll return them later.

About as close to her as you'd want to get, I reckon. No good ever comes of women like that.

I walk back to the car.

Hazel shouts a last-minute invitation. I'm downstairs if you want to ask me anything, Jack So. Anything!

The snort that follows almost chokes her. It sounds like the last breath of a man on the executioner's vine. A death rattle that will haunt me for all my days.

Angel sports ambitious heels and a ruthless sheath of black lycra. The latter begins where most underwear would end. It stretches over every shameless curve, across trabeal shoulders and down sinewy arms to delicate wrists. Long, straight hair flows in a ponytail from atop her gulliver. She's straight out of a Robert Palmer video. Simply Irresistible. Desirable is her natural state. Each pocilliform ear is studded with a single two-carat diamond. I could say something about gilding the lily but that would be like telling Van Gogh the sunflowers are too orange.

Her glazzies pour scorn upon me. They demand an explanation, as if the elephant in the room just farted. I feign ignorance and try to distract her with a compliment.

Is there something different about you today? Hair? Perfume?

Yes. I'm using a new strawberry douche. And when I ran in here to answer the phone I accidentally whipped up a daiquiri. Fancy a cocktail? Hors d'oeuvre?

Vulgarity is Angel's other language. It's a provocative, crude counterpoint to her physical refinement, strict Methodist education and partiality for classic literature. Strange bedfellows indeed. Part rebellion and part defence mechanism, a cultural revolution rages between her bookends.

A little early for Happy Hour, I reply. Still, maybe you should put little umbrellas behind your ears. Presentation is everything.

I had my ankles pinned up there for a while this morning, but it reduced my mobility. Got your note. How many are up there, Jack? I got to six, although I may have counted one or two of them twice.

She opens the top draw of her desk, pulls out a translucent shell of sparrow spit and waves it about.

We're cornering the market in bird nest too. I appreciate the gift but it's not mandatory, like a toll, every time one of them wants to split the whisker.

I'll pass it on. We'll have to bear with it for a while.

Can't be worse than my family at New Year, or during Golden Week. They come out of the woodwork and fucking trash the place. Speaking of riots, was it you or Mei-mei causing all that trouble in Wan Chai yesterday?

I don't know what came over her. One minute she's sitting there, nursing a pint, and the next she's ripping the place apart.

Angel gives a curt smile and exits. The conversation is over, for now. She'll tell me when she wants to hear the whole truth and nothing but the truth. We should probably wait for Benny anyway, or I'll have to repeat the story when he gets here.

I reboot the Apple Macintosh and attend to a pile of artwork.

Honda Legend. *A regal expression of luxury.* Philips Prestige Portable phone. *Only $17,500!* Repulse Bay Hotel. *Barbecue by the Bay.*

Business hasn't been too bad. Looking at this stuff, it should be worse. Unfortunately, our overhead has increased. Benny isn't as productive since he became a paraplegic. He rolled out of his coma with a new lease on life. I'm beginning to understand what Chuang Tzu meant when he said everyone knows the use of usefulness, but nobody understands the usefulness of the useless. This is especially true of art directors.

Benny's approach to his craft has become somewhat Confucian.

Besides the noble art of getting things done, there is a nobler art of leaving things undone. The wisdom of life consists in the elimination of nonessentials.

I have neither the wisdom nor the will to act on this. He copped a beating and a bullet on my behalf. I've carried the guilt and the gimp ever since. We brought in a creative team to pick up his slack. Our part-time team is now full-time.

Harris Tweed and Paris Garters, Mei Calls them, based on a favourite Seuss poem.

Wing *Harris Tweed* To is a hard-working art director. 25. He rarely speaks, and doesn't look at you when he does. Advertising seems to attract people that aren't good at communicating. He has a fondness for oversized baseball caps. New York Yankees. Chicago Cubs. Cleveland Indians. These stop his gulliver from exploding with built-up rage, and keep that mop of hair off his face.

Flora *Paris Garters* Kwok is a bilingual copywriter. English and Chinese. She has a pageboy haircut, round coke-bottle glasses and looks like she's twelve.

It's the quiet ones you have to watch out for, says Angel.

Benny wheels in at ten-thirty, on the back of another heady night in Tsim Sha Tsui. The chair might impede his ability to chase girls but not his desire. He thinks they all want a spin in the driver's seat and a peek under the hood, to see if the engine still purrs. He takes the wheel-chair in his stride. Works it to his advantage. A sympathy fuck is as good as any other, he'll tell you. And you don't have to work so hard. Just lie back and enjoy the ride.

Angel used to be repulsed by him, now she nurses him. Tough-love. She bought him a vacuum erection-pump for Christmas.

You're more talk than torque, Ironsides. Got a dick like stinky tofu. This invention will solve half your problem.

She approaches like a spouse that's found lipstick on a collar, and a receipt from Cartier for gifts that have failed to find their way home. Narrow eyes, hand on hip.

Some think we're married. We kind of are, professionally. Angel is a ratified member of So Fuk Yu & Partners, but a love of books is all we've shared. We've flirted with taking our relationship to a more biblical level. When push came to shove, however, neither of us had the courage to thicken the plot. And when I say neither of us I mean me. All mouth and no trousers, as the saying goes. I'd declined a number of open-ended invitations and wild-card entries. Withdrawing at the last minute, we never made it to the folk dancing finale. All mouth and no trousers. It's a bit of a running joke now. A euphemism for all-talk-and-no-action. Not an invitation to oral sex, as Benny often assumes.

Oldham is on the phone, Angel informs me.

I wonder what he wants. It's not about the library books, is it?

Yes, Jack. He's joined the Special Branch of the Library Police.

She holds my gaze for a moment before striding to reception. Her way of letting me know she's not finished with me. Not by a long shot. She returns immediately. Arms folded across her accusatory chest. Challenging me with her stance. Legs apart. She demands a full recount of what happened.

I was a bright cold day in April, I begin. The clocks were striking thirteen...

Knock it off Jack. It's not 1984. We're balls-deep in '88.

Two fat ladies.

Clickety-click, she replies, impressing me with her knowledge of Orwell and bingo calls at the same time.

The Party has started, Angel. It will be in full swing by '97. Control the past, control the future. Control the present, control the past. War is peace, freedom is slavery and ignorance is strength.

To underline my last point, Benny trundles into the discourse. By the time I get to the bit about Big Brother Bronson braining Nifty at The Ministry Of Love, Flora and Wing have downed their tools and walked over too.

When I recap this morning's visit with the widow Teplice, Benny wants to know what I'd rate her, on a scale of one to ten.

With one being Jessica Rabbit and ten being Beetlejuice? An eight. A solid eight. A pair of steatopygic eights, actually. Two fat ladies, as it were.

Clickety-click, repeats Angel.

A couple of Hooray Henriettas, contends Benny.

The only thing they're light on is Hooray. There's some secret government lard experiment going on over there.

Steady on, reproves Angel.

Bigger ruins than the Ming Tombs. More cracks than a Terracotta Warrior.

It's our scars that make us know our past was real, Jack.

Come on, Jane Austen, for what do we live but to make sport for our neighbours, and laugh at them in our turn?

The lady is in mourning.

Not this morning.

Nifty wasn't discreet in his extracurricular activities.

No man is, even when they think they are.

I never got caught, proclaims Benny.

And there the prosecution rests, Your Honour.

She didn't know about a marriage between the two love buzzards, I submit. She didn't seem to care. She only got animated when I mentioned another party could claim ownership of the pub, or someone wanting to buy it.

How did you know that?

I didn't. I was fishing.

Catch anything?

Crabs, just from looking at the ones that got away. She showed me some pictures of Nifty's women. Told me Chung called by the night before too.

The pictures of the women, inquires Benny. Can I?

No you can't. I'll have to turn them over to the police. And I think they'd prefer they weren't stuck together.

Just asking. Not even a peek? Go on. You know you want to.

I give him one of the Polaroids and tell him I want it back. Unsoiled.

Ooh-ah! he says, like a monkey that got the last mandarin. He pops a wheelie and pirouettes. I bet she'd like a bit of Benny's *buri-buri*. I'd give her a spin around the block and back again.

You'd run out of juice before you got halfway home.

Pulling a cow up a tree would be easier for you, suggests Angel.

Not if you pull it for me.

We're talking cash cows, donkey breath. Not your burrito. Do you think Chung was more interested in getting his girl, Jack, or stitching up the man that grassed him?

I thought it was all for ardour. Now I don't know.

If one is strong one loves more strongly.

She's gazumping me with Henry James now. I shouldn't be surprised. Her passion for reading hung around her like the cloudy envelope of a goddess in an epic. A somewhat strawberry flavoured envelope today, apparently.

If you've been hated you've also been adored, I counter.

The phone rings before she can exercise her right of reply. Hold that thought, she says, lifting the receiver.

I'd rather you held it for me, confesses Benny.

You just keep pulling on that cow of yours, I remind him.

Angel delivers standard greetings and deferments into the handset. Then covers the mouthpiece. You might want to take this, she whispers. It's Liu Pang.

Pull the other one. Who's on line two, Governor Wilson?

No really. Liu Pang.

Well, well. We are attracting a higher class of scoundrel.

6. OPPORTUNITY KNOCKS

Liu Pang and I move in different circles. That's an understatement of planetary proportions. If Hong Kong is the sun, Liu Pang is Venus. I'm one of Jupiter's moons. Most of what I know about him I've gleaned from the tabloids. His face is regularly splashed across Society pages. Captions preface his name with phrases like *philanthropist and raconteur*, or *businessman and patron of the arts*. He's friends with everyone, sits on the board of half a dozen companies and has a hand in mounds of property. He recently opened a chain of high-end boutiques and restaurants. Han Dynasty specializes in proving money can't buy taste. He's on his sixth or seventh wife. This probably means he's some kind of perverted sociopath or gay. Or both. People like Liu don't call people like me unless they want something. Even then they have an Oompah Loompah arrange a meeting. If he wants to speak, personally, it has to be urgent, embarrassing and/or illegal.

Either way it reeks of money.

I assume you know who I am, he says with a plum of some sort or someone in his mouth. Lynne Sprudel would die for an accent like that. I wonder if you'd be so kind as to join me at my home this evening.

That may be a little late in the day for me and my associates.

Perhaps we could manage without them.

Manage what?

I was told you might be able to help me with something. A job, of sorts.

What sort of job and who said I'd be interested in helping you with it?

Eric Tsoi. He said you sometimes-

Eric sometimes says too much.

Eric Tsoi is my unofficial lawyer. Senior Partner at Callett, Crambazzle, Dratchell & Feaque. We've helped each other out of some unauthorised situations. If Eric put Liu Pang onto me then it's a safe bet they've discussed the full scope of services in So Fuk Yu's portfolio. The grapevine would've given him a decent précis too. A recent affair and ensuing brouhaha generated considerable public interest. We'd had a slew of calls requesting assistance with delicate matters in its wake.

You can still see the blood stains in the lobby, if you know where to look.

It's not the type of work I actively pursue. It just has a way of finding me. I'm quick to turn it down, most times. With Liu Pang, however, there's the possibility of a healthy profit margin and the prospect of larger, legitimate rewards to follow. Once I get in his good books. Besides, I'm curious. And Angel will never forgive me if I turn down the opportunity to stick my nose in such high profile business.

I owe it to her to hear what he has to say.

Eric does go on a bit sometimes, doesn't he, Mr So? Still, splendid chap. Jolly good lawyer. Utmost respect for you. That's why he thought, you know, you'd-

Six o'clock you say?

Yes. That would be fine. Thank you, can I just say how-

Say it at six. You still at Belleview, Repulse Bay?

Yes, of course. You know where I live?

Everyone knows where you live. See you at six for cocktails and canapés.

I've barely cradled the receiver when Angel tells me to pick it up again. Detective Oldham will not be denied.

I was just thinking of you, Detective.

That's why I called, Jack. My ears were burning.

I went to see the widow Nifty.

I know. Her neighbour told us. She said another person of interest had been there too, asking questions. Local guy. Snappy dresser. Had someone with him as well. Might've been Chung.

What made her think that?

His picture in the paper. Not the sort who's easily mistaken.

We all look the same to them. Chung was there yesterday. Just before or after he advanced down the pitch and smashed Nifty's head over mid-wicket

He's got balls. Why would he go back?

Maybe he's fucking her.

What did you find out?

No one's seen ass nor tit of Kitty Ho for years. And you'd remember if you saw her. She's no pork chop. I've got the pictures to prove it.

Say again?

Sprudel gave me some happy snaps of Ho. Uncensored.

That's nothing in your book?

Nothing I haven't seen before. They'll amount to nowt too. Unless you arrest me for possession of unlicensed pornography. She's a ghost, Oldham. Blown or flown, busted or dusted. Found any broads decomposing in acid baths lately?

Only about fifteen. You going to share your pictures with the rest of the class?

I've got a small business to run into the ground first. You guys don't start work until after lunch anyway. What did Hazel have to say?

You know the neighbour?

I'm fucking her.

Stop fucking with me. What did you find out?

Nothing. She was there, consoling the recently bereaved. Getting a jump on the massive crowd expected at Nifty's wake. Hazel's old man was collateral damage at the pub. But you know that. What happened?

We sent a car. All quiet. No answer from Sprudel. Left a team out front.

Why are you telling me this?

I thought I'd do you a favour. In case you're thinking of laying a wreath, and paying another visit. Anyone turns up and it'll go into a report. I'd rather not to see your name in it.

Very Christian of you, but I won't be going back. I couldn't handle either of them again. The air's toxic there. You should wait until the EPA give it the all-clear too. I'll send the snaps over this afternoon. Right now I've got headlines to write and deadlines to meet.

You and me both.

Headlines?

Deadlines.

7. BELLEVIEW DRIVE

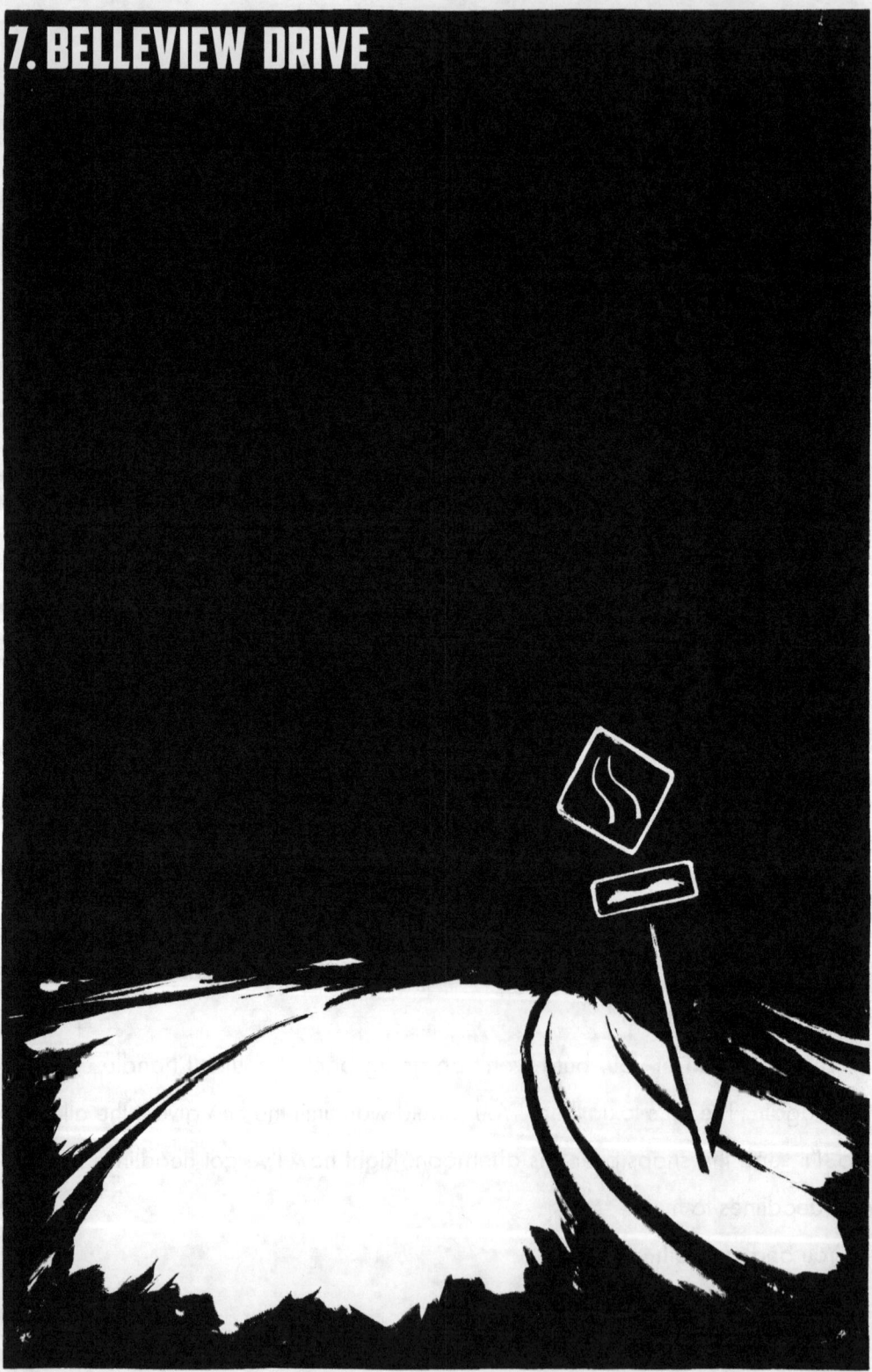

I have a relatively distraction-free afternoon. This is not the same as an afternoon free of distracting relatives. Like ill winds they come in threes, visiting the ablutions in triplicate. While one spends their penny the others mill about the creative department, smiling broadly when eye-contact is made but never speaking. They compliment Harris Tweed and Paris Garters nicely.

Angel wants to know when the toilet upstairs will be fixed. I tell her I'm not sure because I haven't had time to call a tradesman. She gets onto it, as I knew she would.

Sometimes the best man for the job is a woman, I remind her.

Depends on the job, she replies.

Those Bangkok lady-boys aren't bad either, admits Benny and immediately wishes the aretaloger in him had kept that behind closed doors.

Gu-por brings Mei down at 5pm. Naps have been taken, yet neither appears to have taken much from the experience. Unhappy is Gu-por's natural state. Mei's misery is rooted in the pink dress she's wearing. The lace trim and big red bow at the back aren't thrilling me either. This outfit would not have been her first choice.

Hello Sweetheart. Look at you! So pretty!

Poor thing. She must be going stir-crazy up there. I ask if she'd like to come for a drive to Repulse Bay. She jumps at the opportunity and I spend five minutes explaining to Gu-por this is not an outing for the whole family.

I promise to take everyone for *yum cha* on the weekend.

Skies are clear on the south side of the island. The sun hangs low and, having no alternative, lazily bathes the water in gold.

We plunge down and around the mountain.

British troops fled through here, on their way to Stanley, in 1941. They kept the invading Japanese at bay for two weeks before surrendering. A century before that it was a home for pirates.

Repulse Bay is an upper-class retreat these days, sheltering raiders of the corporate variety. You could almost forget you were in Hong Kong. There was no sign of the city's huddled masses on Belleview. Just large, landed mansions on swathes of verdant slope. The illusion is only betrayed upon closer inspection. Filipino domestic helpers, in starched uniforms, wait by entry gates for deliveries of children and groceries. Some walk dogs. Some are walked by dogs, dragged down the street by canines so large saddles would have been more appropriate.

It's like a castle! exclaims Mei as we approach Liu's house.

She's right. It's big and ornate. Tudoresque. I park the car twenty metres from the front door and grab Mei's backpack from the rear seat. We walk across loose, grey stones to the entrance.

I caution Mei to be wary of Reformists, Norfolk Rebels and dragons.

The door is large and swings wide as we approach. Our arrival has been anxiously anticipated and observed.

Liu Pang emerges from the shadows. He looks flustered, in a Brideshead Revisited kind of way.

Where can we hide in fair weather, we orphans of the storm?

The navy blue blazer and Rodney Dangerfield slacks need pressing. He sweeps a mop of hair out of his eyes. A Don Wan facial hair experiment tickles his lip. He's taller than he looks in the social pages, probably because he's not stooping to put his face next to another. The man is in good shape too. Anything between 45 and 60, if you count wives in dog years.

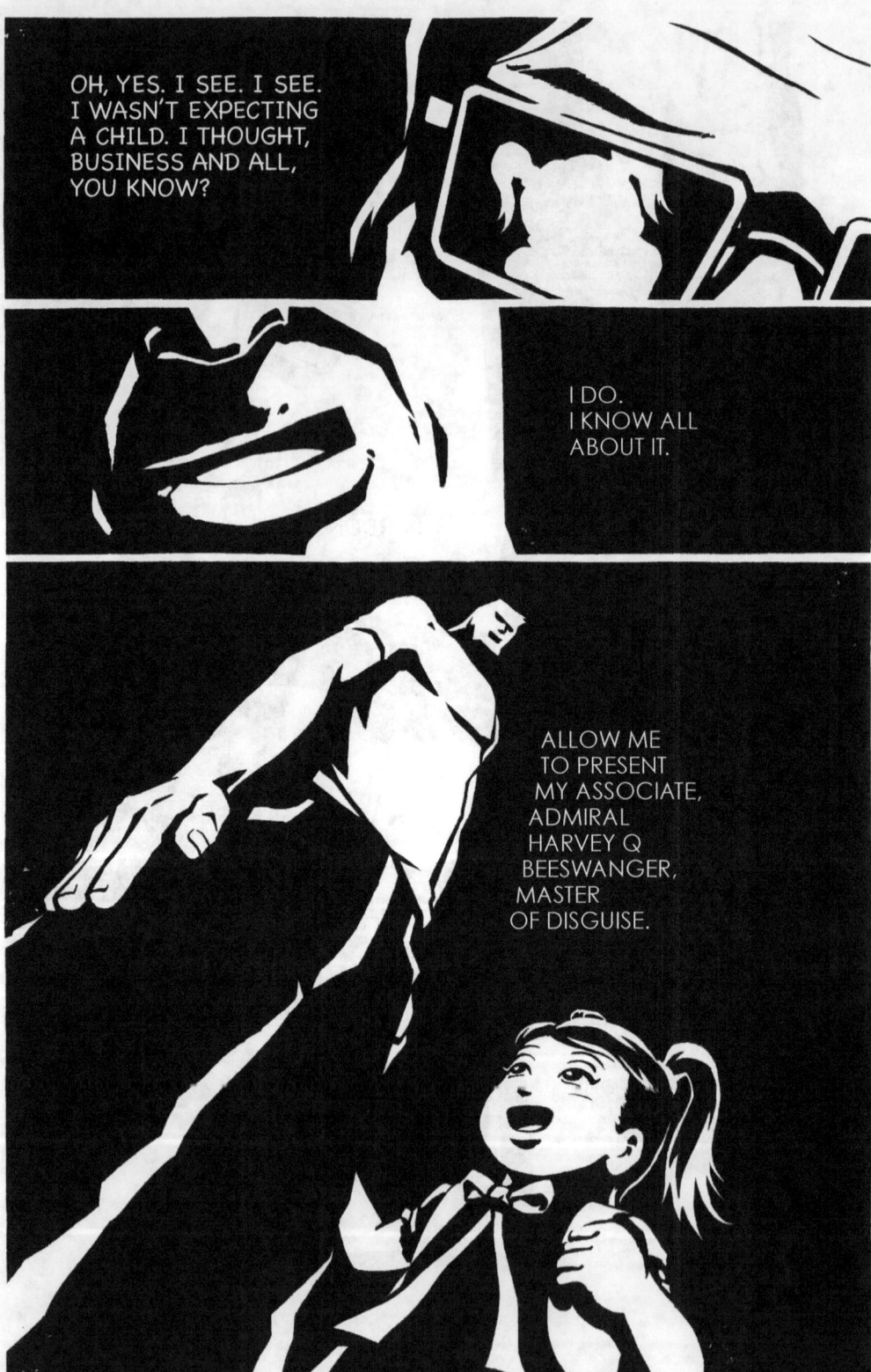

Liu brings us through the dark, quiet interior, past stacks of cardboard boxes. He walks like a man with a dame on his mind and the rock of Sisyphus on his shoulders. I can hear the mills of fate grinding slow and small.

We're ushered into a plush room.

First Editions line one wall. A triptych of Hockney, Johns and Pollock look out of place on another. But what do I know? A Japanese department store just spent 82 million on a Monet for their frozen meat section. You could call it a drawing room. If you drew. Or an observatory. The south side of the island can be observed through the large bay window. Imported sand on the distant shore is like a burnished band of precious metal in the fading light. Still, it's cold in here. There should be a widow and a casket in the corner.

Sometimes, I feel the past and the future pressing so hard on either side that there's no room for the present at all.

Drink? No canapés tonight, Mr So. The maids are with the wife, in Europe. She left me with the other one. The one we employ other maids to clean up after. Ha.

Can hardly look after herself. Been with the family for so long we can't get rid of her either. Good help is hard to find, eh?

I want Ribena, demands Mei.

I want Ribena please, I remind her.

I want Ribena *please*.

I'll see what I can do, says Liu. Excuse me for a minute, won't you?

Excuse me please, Mei instructs.

Yes, right. Ha. Excuse me *please*, says Liu. He exits the room. His footsteps echo down the hall.

Mei stands in the window counting boats. I pull paper and crayons from her backpack and ask her to draw them.

Why?

This is a drawing room. You have to draw in here.

What are you going to draw?

I draw a deep breath and tell her I'm going to sit and talk with Mr Liu.

Liu returns carrying a tray. He places a glass of water, a big plastic cup of Ribena and a tumbler of whiskey on the coffee table. Towering above them all is a portable phone. The Boss Phone.

Someone moving in or out?

Pardon?

The boxes in the hall. Someone moving in or moving out?

Oh. Neither really. They're for the boutique. Bits and pieces. Prototypes. We're developing a line of prestige *feng shui* chattels.

Ah, *feng shui*. The ancient art of furniture arranging.

Luxury goods, for the wealthy.

The morally and spiritually bankrupt. Those who need a change in fortune the most.

Ha! Yes. Big market. Especially since the crash last year. Everyone's looking to improve their lot, eh? Alter their destiny. Change their fate.

Almost as many as are looking to exploit it.

It's important to diversify your portfolio. Particularly in times like this. Waiting for the market to bounce back. I'm looking at a number of property ventures as well.

I like the sound of all this. Waffling aside, he'd be a good client. Cash-flow. So Fuk Yu could survive on the brochures and catalogues he'd need alone.

Anything I can do to help? I offer, hoping he takes the hint and gets to the point before Mei turns this into The Bored Room.

Yes, of course. That's why we're here, eh? Down to business. It's a discreet matter. And, well, you know, he says, looking in Mei's direction.

Don't worry, she's very discreet.

Ha. It's just I wasn't really expecting her. It complicates things.

Not really. Children are easy. Adults complicate things. Kids just want to know how much fun they're going to have, and will there be enough to eat.

It's just we might be joined by some, er, associates.

See, you're complicating things already.

Some matters of business are best left to adults.

Consider her my associate then. That should even things out. A person's a person, after all.

A person's a person, no matter how small! chimes Mei.

Why don't you tell me what we're doing here, Liu? I was under the impression there was a brief?

Yes, there was. There is. A couple of things, actually. I thought you might be interested in both. And we could, well, kill two birds with one stone.

You could start by telling me about one of them.

He takes a swill from his tumbler, as if it would be impolite to get to the point quickly. Yes, he says. I have, I think, mentioned a property venture. A large one. I'd like to create an air of expectation and excitement. Give it a real international feel. It's not far from here. Redhill? I could show it to you.

Not in front of the children.

Pardon?

You wanted to show me something.

Redhill Peninsula.

I've seen it before.

Of course you have. Ha. I've acquired a substantial parcel of land there. With other investors, naturally. But it will be my project.

Sounds exciting.

Oh it is.

And the other matter?

Other matter?

The one you've been dancing around since we got here. The discreet one. The one you don't want anyone to know about. Not even me.

I guess it must seem that way. Ha. Sorry. More of an indiscretion, if you know what I mean.

No, I don't know what you mean. Why don't you tell me?

I need your assistance with a transaction, this evening.

A transaction? If it's a witness you need, Mr Liu, I know a good lawyer.

Yes, so do I. That's why I called. Eric gave me your number. He felt, we both felt, after reviewing things, you might be better suited to the job.

Go on.

The transaction pertains to an indiscretion. And we need to be quite discreet about it. The transaction, that is. And the indiscretion. Do you see?

It's becoming clearer, yes. The old cat has burnt his whiskers.

Yes. Ha. Well, you have the gist of it.

Why don't you give me the guts of it?

Pardon?

The details. Give me the details.

Yes, the details. It's quite a large sum of money.

Cash.

Yes.

A bribe?

Certainly not!

Blackmail?

Not exactly.

Not exactly?

The word, it upsets me.

How about *insurance* then, is that a better word?

Ha. Yes, that's great. Insurance. Ha.

Against fire? Flood? Acts of God? Critical illness?

I can't really say.

Can't, won't or don't want to say?

A bit of both really. All three.

Can we talk about what you want me to do? You didn't call me here to help you with those boxes and ship the tangerine trees. What is my role in this top-secret transaction you're so keen not-to discuss? And what's in it for me. I can send you a rate card for marketing services when it comes to your property venture. These other things, however, operate on an *ad hoc* basis and are priced accordingly.

Yes. I'm sure they are. What might be the going rate, do you suppose?

Lin Yutang said there were three great vices. Efficiency, punctuality and the desire for success. But there was something else fuelling Liu's anxiety and unhappiness. Something beyond the *have much and be confused* adage. Whatever it is I've had enough of it.

Come on, Mei. We're going.

Mr So, whispers Liu. Please sit down. Try to understand how difficult this is.

Try to understand how annoying *this* is.

Are we going Ba-ba? I'm not finished yet.

It's okay, Cream-puff. Keep drawing. We'll be going soon.

Twenty thousand? offers Liu.

Tell me more.

An acquaintance of mine borrowed something. A string of pearls. Black pearls, attached to a large sapphire, set in diamonds.

Quite a trinket.

Yes. Ha. A trinket. If only, eh? It's been, well, misappropriated.

And you need to get it back, before your wife finds out it's missing.

He blushes. Embarrassment, tinged with relief. Yes. That's pretty much it.

I doubt it. I'm sure there's much more to it. This acquaintance of yours, Liu, she won't give it back without payment?

She can't. She was, we were, leaving a nightclub. We left together. And were set upon.

Where?

Which nightclub?

Where were you bailed up?

Oh, yes. I see. Here.

In this room?

Not exactly. Out there. Where your car is. Thereabouts. It was dark.

How much do they want?

Half a million.

Is the necklace worth that much?

The embarrassment it would cause to me, and my…

Wife? Acquaintance?

My wife and acquaintance. It would ruin us all.

Which is why you don't want the police involved.

You understand my situation.

They have you both ways. And by the short hairs.

Yes. Ha. Both ways. Burnt whiskers, eh?

And your wife, she won't miss half a million dollars half as much?

It's much easier to account for, and attribute to other expenses. Half a million here. A million there. Three hundred thousand into that. It's easy for her, for us, to lose track of money.

Yes, my associate and I have the same problem. With that kind of money you can lose track of all sorts of things. The hand-off is this evening? When and where?

They said they'd call. Soon. Any minute now.

You're leaving this a little late aren't you?

I'm not in a position to negotiate.

To get me involved, I mean. What if I wasn't available, or said no?

Oh. I hadn't thought of that. Ha. I guess I'd be on my own, eh?

You might still be.

What?

You might still be on your own. I haven't agreed to anything, yet.

You mean you won't?

I mean, as you say, you haven't thought this through.

I haven't had the time, or your experience, Mr So. I don't know what to think.

Well, let me help you. These associates of yours will stick to their end of the deal, or they won't. If they do you won't need me. You'll be home free, so to speak. If, however, they move the goal posts...

The goal posts?

They could change their mind about any number of things. The price. Returning the sapphire. Your personal health. Half a million is more than enough to ensure there are no witnesses. And if your acquaintance is so compromised by the situation, well, she's not going to come forward. Not if you disappear.

Good lord. They wouldn't, would they? I'm sure it will go as they said. They were very precise and, er, professional. Ha. I got the feeling they've done this sort of thing before. I've heard, you know, stories. I think I just, well, I just felt it would be better if someone else was there, eh?

When you think everything is going according to plan, that's usually when you've just walked into an ambush.

Ha. Yes. Never trust a recruit with a weapon.

Or an officer with a map. Look, if they're so organized, and have such rigid instructions, my presence could upset them. They might alter their plans.

Do you think?

I think this little indiscretion of yours is anything but venialia. And it's going to cost you a little more. Forty-thousand, for me and my associate.

That's blackmail.

I thought you didn't like that word.

I dislike it even more now. Why, you're no better than-

Than whom? The alternative? I don't think so. I wouldn't be here otherwise. So we'll do this my way, all the way. Cash up-front.

This is-

Highly irregular? How much do you know about these things? What do you know about these people? File a complaint with the Small Claims Tribunal if you're unhappy with the service provided.

What makes you think I have that kind of money? That sort of cash?

You're about to do a deal for half a million. You'll have some change lying about. Eric would have told you my services don't come for free, and the way payments are structured. I'm not even charging you ten percent. Standard industry commission is seventeen-point-five. You're getting a preferred rate.

He leaves the room, Boss Phone in hand. I consider my options.

Leave now, miss opportunities. Current and future. Stay, and hope we don't earn our money the hard way.

The distant trill of portable telecommunications routs these thoughts.

Liu returns shortly after, worries compounded by the Louis Vuitton keep-all he's carrying, the call he received and the weight of the moment.

Good news? I quaeritate. He gives a puzzled look. Like I just said quaeritate and asked him to spell it. The phone call. Was it good news?

That rather depends on your point of view, eh? I'm not sure there's good to be found in any of this.

He hands me four bundles of notes. These look pretty good, I tell him, and put the money in Mei's backpack. It'll be safe in there. Who'd steal from a child?

We should get going, Mr So.

To where?

Redhill. Pak Pat Shan Road. You know it?

Of course I knew it. I'd attended lavish parties there once upon a time, in a previous life. Lately it had made headlines for different reasons. Construction workers dug up a number of unexploded bombs from the war. One of them detonated and took two hardhats with it. That aside, it's a nice spot overlooking Tai Tam Bay. One way in, one way out. No way out, if things went south.

His associates had chosen well.

We can take a look at the property you mentioned earlier, I venture, maintaining a sense of optimism. While we're there. Kill two birds with one stone, as you say.

Ha. Yes. I suppose we can. If there's time, eh?

In a hurry are they?

I think we all want this resolved quickly.

Yes, you're right. It's not as if I'm getting paid by the hour. A quick game's a good game, hey what?

What game? Mei asks.

I-spy, Bar-ba-loot. We're going for a drive.

Where are we going? Will it be fun?

Lots, for everyone.

I'm hungry.

We won't be long, I assure her, then look to Liu standing by the door. The defence rests, m'lord. Simple. Uncomplicated. How much fun, and will there be enough to eat.

Do you think, you know, she should accompany us?

I should leave her with your maid? The one that can't look after herself?

Ha. Well, no.

We have time to swing by my place?

I don't think so. It's just-

It's just the way it has to be. Be more up-front about the business at hand, next time. Don't worry, she'll help keep everyone in line. She's stopped me from doing many things that could be considered anti-social and counter-productive. We'll take your car. They'll be expecting that. You've already deviated from the plan. Don't want to disappoint them too much. Mine's low on gas. And you'll get upset if I ask you to chip in for petrol money.

He leads us down the hall, like it's knee-deep in molasses. We pass through a spacious kitchen. His leftover maid smiles feebly as we walk out the rear door.

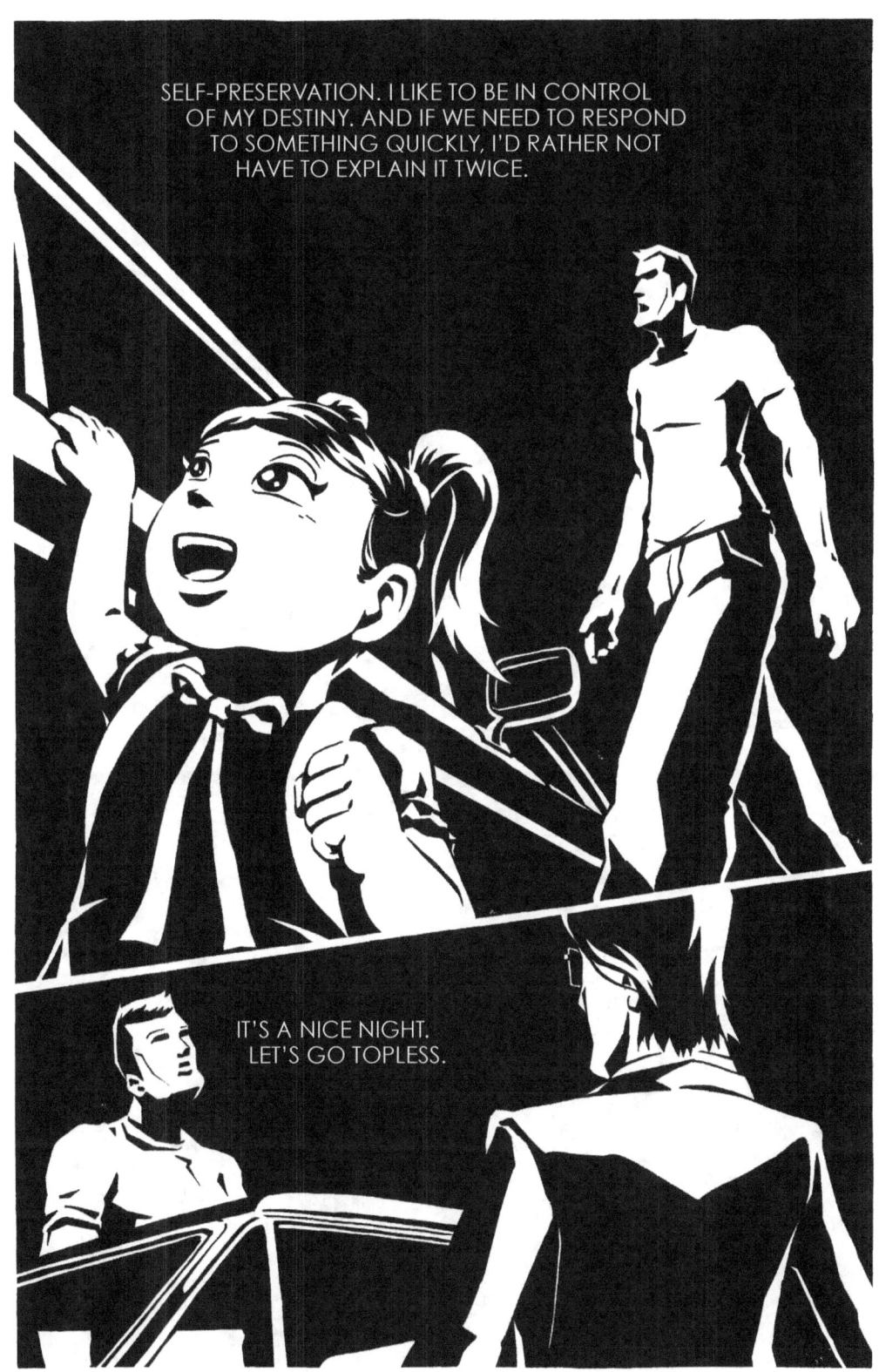

SELF-PRESERVATION. I LIKE TO BE IN CONTROL OF MY DESTINY. AND IF WE NEED TO RESPOND TO SOMETHING QUICKLY, I'D RATHER NOT HAVE TO EXPLAIN IT TWICE.

IT'S A NICE NIGHT. LET'S GO TOPLESS.

8. SITE SEEING

We cruise around the coast in silence, past the Repulse Bay Hotel. It's just been renovated. There's a seven-storey hole in the middle. The dragon that lives in the mountain behind needs an unobstructed view of the bay and direct access to the beach. Architects and developers making such considerations for the environment seems just as implausible. The *feng shui* consultant who sold that idea must be laughing all the way to the bank. I ask Liu if he had a finger in this pie. He's preoccupied with the portable phone cradled in his hands. Staring at it, like he's waiting for it to ring. Or hoping it doesn't.

Apartment blocks are few and far between on Redhill. Hidden homes and low-rise estates reign. Duplexes, under-construction. Part building site. Part bomb site. No streetlights. I turn into Pak Pat Shan. Dead-end ahead. Out of the blue, into the black.

Which one is yours, Liu?

Which what?

Your development. Where is it?

Further round. We can drive by after, eh? Best not to be late and all that.

It's your funeral.

Pardon?

You're the general. What number?

Sorry?

The house. What number is it?

Oh. Sorry. The pump house.

Pump house?

The, er, water station thinggy. Just here, on the right.

A boom-gate blocks a narrow access road.

Are you sure they're expecting us?

Oh, yes. Ha. Maybe we're early.

They might be waiting down there. We should take a look.

We should wait here.

You wait here. I'll go down for a look.

Look for what, Ba-ba?

The Once-ler.

Ooh. Can I come?

I think about this for a moment, caught between unknowns, unsure which is the lesser of two imperilments. I've made a lot of bad choices lately. This will be another.

I need to go to the toilet, she adds.

I lean over and take some tissues from Mei's backpack. Come on then.

Maybe I should come with you, suggests Liu.

I think the young lady would appreciate some privacy, don't you? What if they turn up while we're down there? You could lose the cash, the car and any hope you have of salvaging your dignity.

Yes. I guess so but, well, you know. Be careful, eh?

I'll try not to step on any unexploded missiles. If you get lonely you can always reach out and touch someone.

Pardon?

Phone a friend, I say, eying the weapon of mass communication in his hands.

Oh. Ha. Doesn't work too well out here. Hard to get a signal.

I reach into the car and turn on the stereo. Leave the engine running, I instruct him as The Pet Shop Boys get started on a tune.

I come here looking for money…

I lead Mei around the boom-gate. The Bentley's headlights illuminate the way, until the arc of the road takes us down a gentle incline. The night swallows our footsteps. My eyes adjust to the dark. Mei's grip tightens on my hand. I tell her not to worry.

I'm not afraid, Ba-ba.

Neither am I, because I'm here with you. See the moon?

The lunar bulb is in full bloom above us.

You can go here, Moon-face.

Okay, Balloon-face.

She squats and hums a tune while she pees.

Two and two are four. Four and four are eight.

I pass her the tissues. She takes a moment to organize her drawers.

Hey look!

What, Ba-ba?

The Lorax!

Where? she asks, searching the sky.

Too late. He's gone.

She breaks free from my grip and slaps my thigh. Ba-ba! Don't trick me!

I thought I saw him, behind that Truffula tree. Maybe it was a Bar-ba-loot.

Ba-ba!

Ba-ba ba-loot!

Ba-ba ba-loot! she repeats.

Up gully! Through gulch!

And down slippery sluice!

The road comes to an end. A wire fence guards the pump-house. The muffled mechanics of a generator rumbles within. And that's all. Not a Bar-ba-loot nor a Swomee Swann in sight. Not a Humming Fish to be heard.

What's that noise, Ba-ba?

The Once-ler. This must be his Thneed factory.

Not that noise. *That* one.

The lights of the Bentley have been augmented. Another vehicle has arrived.

Come on, I whisper, leading her up the garden path.

A voice cries out in protest. An almighty clap destroys the night. Wheels spin in the soft shoulder.

Silence. Almost.

A high-pitched tone rings ominously in my ears. I look at Mei. Fear swims across her face. I gather her in my arms and move into the shadows of the road.

Rubber screeches on bitumen. Glass breaks and metal collapses. More lights. The Bentley is bathed in a pale yellow sickness. Doors open. Heavy feet move from one car to the other.

He's dead, reports someone in apathetic Cantonese.

The money?

Here.

Come.

What about-

We came for money. We got money. You want to explain this to the police?

Doors close. The vehicle backs up and splits the scene. Mei and I stay huddled in our dark latibule, among the Brickel Bushes. Breathing heavily, inching closer to the car. The stereo plays on. Dusty Springfield duets with The Pet Shop Boys.

Since you went away, I've been hanging around,

I've been wondering why I'm feeling down.

I put Mei beside the boom-gate and ask her to wait. She shields her eyes from the glare of the headlights and tells me she has Brickels in her britches.

We'll get them out in a minute, Possum-chops.

Where's Mr Liu?

I don't know. Maybe he's gone for a walk.

I know exactly where I'll find him. Although I'm still hoping it was just a warning shot, to scare him. Maybe he's cowering somewhere, counting his blessings. Or maybe the interlopers have taken him with them.

I inch closer to the vehicle.

What have I, what have I, what have I done to deserve this?

It was a warning shot alright. A warning for me. And it scared the living daylights out of my client in his Continental.

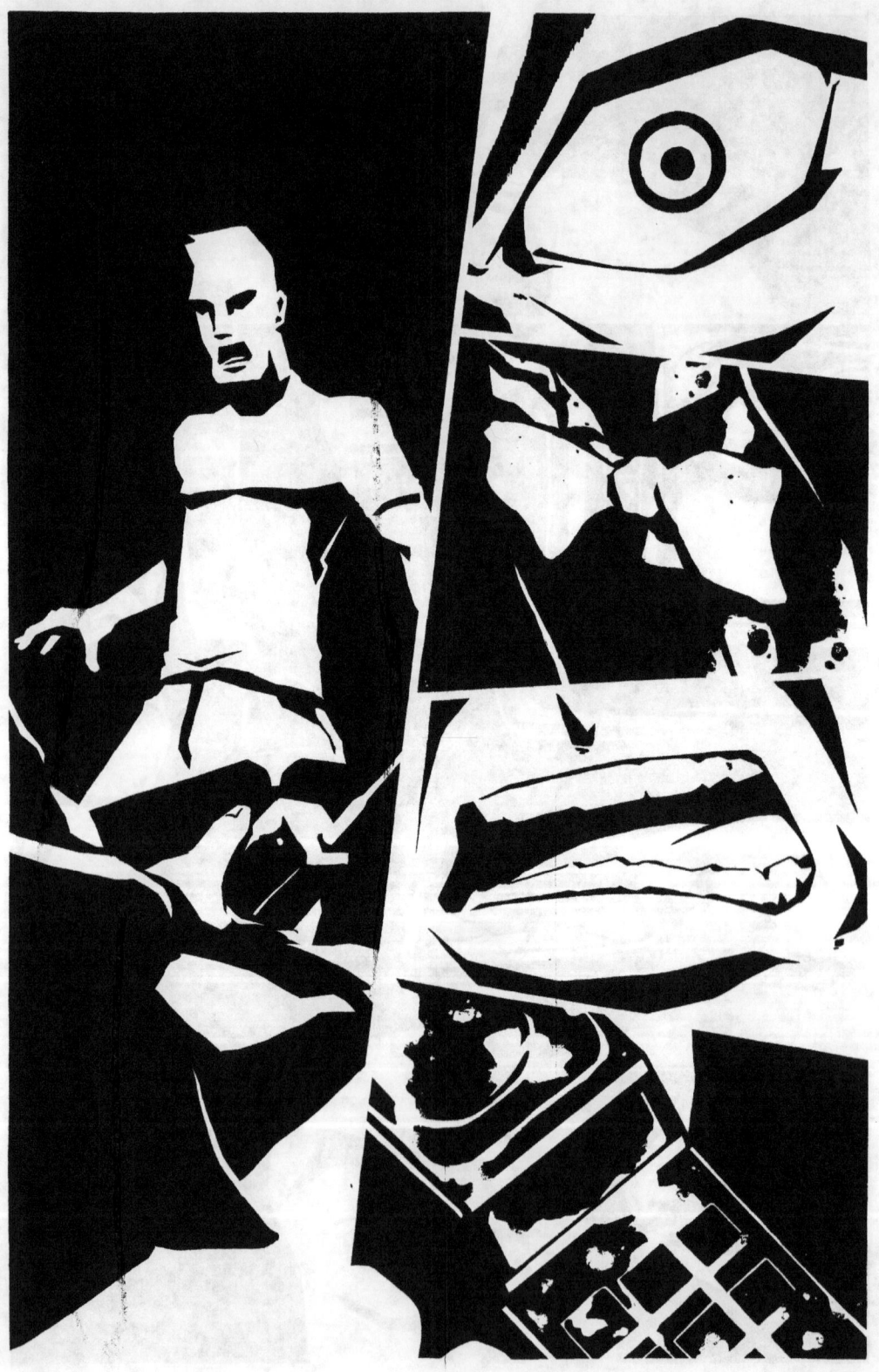

The old cat had got more than his whiskers burned. The blast had taken his head clean off. Bits of his skull were sprayed across the leather, the door and the roadside bushes. The Pet Shop Boys would still be crooning in his ears, somewhere. He'd barely had time to open his door and greet his executioners. The Boss Phone was still in his lap.

I kill the motor. Turn off the lights and contemplate the bloody stump where Liu's head had been revisited. It was a post-modern rendering of Waugh.

He wasn't a complete human being at all. He was a tiny bit of one, unnaturally developed. I thought he was a sort of primitive savage, but he was something absolutely modern and up-to-date that only this ghastly age could produce. A tiny bit of a man pretending to be whole.

Ba-ba?

Hey Doodle-bug. Wait there.

I take her backpack from the rear seat.

Where's Mr Liu, Ba-ba?

He's gone Bar-ba-loot. Let's find a taxi.

Why we don't take the car? I like driving with the wind in my hair! Don't you like driving with the wind in your hair?

I do, Daisy-mei. I do. That's why we're going to leave the car right here.

I'm thinking I should just get her home, then go to the police. I'm thinking that would be fine provided no one else came across the car with the headless passenger, and my prints weren't all over the wheel. And the last time Liu's maid saw her employer alive he wasn't leaving the house with me.

One way in, one way out.

The neon noir of the city glows behind Mount Parker, vibrating with energy. Rising and falling, expanding and contracting. Throbbing, like a luminous apparition.

The shrill of the portable phone attempts to wake the dead.

Someone probably wants to know how the exchange went. I've half a mind to answer it. Then decide I don't want to be the bearer of bad news. What if they're the type to shoot the messenger?

The phone dies in the murk of the night.

Ahead, torches congregate in a driveway. Rays of light dance across us. We're caught in a tractor-beam. A Rebel Blockade Runner drawn to the Imperial Cruiser. Moths to the flame.

One way in, no way out.

9. NIGHT PATROL

Three of the shadows wear raspberry berets. Not the kind you find in a second hand store. The rigid frames and measured gaits beneath them suggest something better equipped and more professional than standard, portly guards awakened from golden slumbers. These troops are combat-ready. Gurkhas.

Bravest of the brave, most generous of the generous,

Never had a country more faithful friends.

The crest of this legendary Nepalese regiment tells you all you need to know. Two lethal, curved blades laid across each other in an X formation. Gurkhas could go into the jungle for a month, with nothing but bark and their own urine for sustenance, and emerge stronger. Their feats on the big stage were legion. Just this week a grenade was lobbed through a window at their barracks in the New Territories. A British Major and a Gurkha Lieutenant were inside.

Only the Gurkha survived.

It's an injustice of colonial rule that this unit, which has served The Crown so well, will be stateless come 1997. This elite force has been reduced to the ignominious role of security guards, protecting the property of Hong Kong's wealthy for minimum wage. It would be a grand comedy if it wasn't such a tragedy, and you had the courage to laugh in the face of a Gurkha.

The voice emanating from within the squad parading before me is sternly female. And English. What are you doing out here? she demands to know.

Just walking by.

With a three year-old girl, at this hour?

I'm almost four! objects Mei.

Just a man and his almost-four daughter, on a moonlight stroll, right Mei-mei?

We were looking for the Once-ler!

The Once-ler? replies our female inquisitor, warming to the occasion. Well, the Once-ler hasn't been seen around here in the longest time.

Where'd he go?

I don't know. Maybe to teach the Sneetches on the beaches.

You can't teach a Sneetch!

We need a ride home, I interrupt. Could we call a taxi?

Your friends abandon you did they?

In a way.

Which way?

That-a-way, I reply, pointing up the road. You heard them?

Hard not to. They come here to spin their wheels on our unofficial racing circuit. And hold impromptu parties in the vacant lots and building sites.

Her lanky silhouette steps out from behind the guards. At a glance you'd say she's old enough to know what she's doing, young enough to drop a mixed-tape of her favourite songs in your mailbox in the morning. Medium-length hair is piled atop her gulliver like a pineapple, the fringe partially obscures large eyes. A dark cotton skivvy hugs her torso. Slender arms are folded across a flat chest.

Black cycling shorts, popular with the young and impressionable, accentuate a thin waist, gird narrow hips and highlight svelte pins. Chunky sneakers anchor her to the ground.

This mistress of the night, to borrow from Eliot, has the kind of beauty which seems to be thrown into relief by casual dress.

Sometimes it's mainland squatters lifting materials, our neo-minimalist Miss Brooke of Middlemarch continues. Or they break in through neighbouring construction sites to steal jewellery and cash.

You always come down from your ivory tower to greet them?

We usually call the police.

Why didn't you this time?

How do you know we haven't?

You'd be waiting inside. Not out here with Nepal's finest.

A GUY SHOULD
GET TO KNOW
A GIRL BEFORE
HE SEES HER
GHURKAS.

DIDN'T
YOUR MOTHER
TEACH YOU THAT?

THAT'S WHY
I LIKE TO DO IT
IN THE DARK.
IT'S MORE FUN.
DIDN'T YOUR MOTHER
TEACH YOU THAT?
IT LEAVES MORE TO
THE IMAGINATION.

LET'S LEAVE IT THAT WAY.

IT SOUNDED LIKE
AN ACCIDENT.
I THOUGHT
SOMEONE
MIGHT NEED
ASSISTANCE.

Her father is Sir Murray Wells. He sat high on the board of The Bank at one time. Before the crash of '87. He's currently out of town with Lady Wells, spending other people's money.

In the cold light of the kitchen it's clear that young women of such birth, living in a quiet country-house and attending a village church no larger than a parlour, regard frippery as the ambition of a huckster's daughter.

Toshimi Wells is returning to a design course in London in a few weeks. I'm not sure who's in charge of the curriculum there but, from where I sit, she should be the design course. A core unit, at the very least. Skin like white honey. Lips full and firm across a wide mouth. Dentists must love her. Why she's home alone is one of life's mysteries. The men in this town should be ashamed.

Mei eats a sandwich while our hostess devours my story.

Liu Pang called about a job. Turned out there was more to it. He'd fallen off The White Path Between Two Rivers and was being blackmailed. He had to recover the sapphire or Marriage Five was deep-six. He'd lose his place in *Jōdo*. I was conscripted to accompany him and the money. We drove. We pulled over. I took Mei to the little girl's room. We heard cars. The kill shot. And we were left with one incomplete philanthropist, raconteur and patron of the arts.

She finds the whole thing terribly exciting. Eyes wide and encouraging, as if listening to a friend recounting sordid details of a wild night out.

Uniformed police arrive.

I leave Mei with her new best friend and accompany an officer to the Bentley, repeating my story as we walk. I omit the good bits. The ones that could complicate my evening and the rest of my life. He tells me I'll have to go to the station in Stanley. And he doesn't mean the bus station. It's been a good night for car accidents. There was another called in just now. Tai Tam Reservoir. Someone went off the road.

Not like this they didn't, I think to myself.

The two of us stand deep in *shima*, shrouded in night and the cacatory stench of Liu Pang's last movement. The officer walks around the vehicle. He delights in finding parts of Liu's skull, like he's discovered the corner bits of a 10,000 piece jigsaw. We're joined by a police van and a dozen officers.

I'm escorted back to the house.

I thank Miss Wells for her hospitality and encourage Mei to do the same.

Thank-you for the sandwich Mi-mi, she says, bestowing our benefactor with a traditional, twin-toned term of endearment. The double-barrelled designation might sound like a child's cry for attention but this one brandishes it like cocked hammers on a twelve gauge, locked and loaded to go out in a blaze of glory.

Any time, Mei-mei. Today was good! Today was fun!

Tomorrow is another one!

Wells shoots me a look. I usually like to know a man's name before inviting him home, she says. But I guess I'll find yours in the morning paper.

I apologize for not making formal introductions. Jack So, I say, reaching into my wallet and presenting her with a business card.

So Fuk Yu?

Advertising.

How glamorous. You're latest campaign is a killer.

Same shit, different wrapper. But thanks again.

Any port in a storm, she answers with lips that would go bump in the night.

I owe you.

You do, she agrees. There is a hint of wickedness in her eye as she turns my card in her hand. Do you think you might be willing to take on an intern?

The smile would blow the block off your Bentley.

Stanley Police Station lies on the flaccid western peninsula of the island. The British made their last stand against the Japanese on this tiny scrag of rock. They surrendered on Christmas Day, believing this would stop the torture of wounded soldiers and killing of medical staff by the invading forces. It became an internment camp for non-Chinese allies. Over a thousand were executed here. In a way it's where the Brits will make their last stand against the Chinese too. There's a garrison of Squaddies stationed down the road, next to the maximum security prison. I make an effort to avoid both, and do my best to defend that position.

We're greeted by a familiar face.

Chau. Ex-partner of Cyclops Chau, my vertically challenged nemesis on Old Bailey Street. This was his reward for participating in the passion play that had opened in my lobby last year. A promotion and a posting to the quiet side of the island. If he bears me any ill will it doesn't show.

Jack So! Whose life did you ruin this time,eh? Two in two days. What will the neighbours think?

Fuck the neighbours. What do you think?

Fuck the neighbours! agrees Mei, who is also becoming tired and emotional.

Chau arranges for a female officer to amuse her while we talk. Throw the book at me, she instructs the bemused constable as they leave the room.

I explain the story so far. He smokes his way through my monologue, nodding in a perfunctory way, like he's heard it all before. I include what I know about the extortion of Liu Pang and the half a million I accompanied to his death. I also ask about the other car accident at the reservoir. He waves it off. Joy-riders. No one was hurt. And if they were they didn't stick around. He doesn't see any connection between that and what happened at the pump house. Maybe he doesn't want to.

Liu called you this afternoon? He got your name from who?

Whom. From *whom*. A mutual friend.

Whom?

I don't think that matters, at this point.

Never mind. You don't have many friends. It will not be difficult to find out.

He's right. Except I don't care if people hate my guts. Like William Burroughs I just assume most of them do. It only matters if they're in a position to do anything about it and, in this instance, Chau is.

Why would you take a child on a journey like this, Jack So?

I didn't know it was going to be like this. I got a call from Liu. He wanted to see me. You would've gone too, if he'd asked you. He wants to show me a property? Sure. I'll see what he's put his money into.

He bought himself a piece of dirt, that's the truth.

He said he was getting stitched up. And had to drop something off on the way. Would I mind going along? I wasn't going to say no.

Not at that price.

It's not as much as you think. And I only get paid at the end of a job. You guys are the ones on retainers, getting cash in advance.

You didn't think something was wrong?

Of course I did. But he seemed like an honourable man and I'm a trusting guy. Look at a property, drop something off, make some money. No big deal.

It is a very big deal now.

Who knew it would turn out this way?

Maybe you. That's what some people will think. You take a walk and he gets shot in the face. Half a million goes missing. Sounds like a set-up.

It is. I'm the one being set up.

They let you walk away.

My kid needed to pee.

Another coincidence?

You think she's in on it too?

Maybe.

They told him not to bring anyone, Chau. Maybe they meant it.

So why not take you out as well?

Maybe they didn't know I was there. Maybe they draw the line at kids and men who travel with them. Maybe they wanted to keep it in-house. Maybe they only had one loose end to tie up and didn't need another. That's the good thing about organized crime. It's so organized.

Twice in two days, Jack. Hard to ignore. You and Bronson Chung.

It's not a crime to go to the pub. Your boys spend time in there too. And they put everything on the corporate account. You want an audit on that?

After what happened last year, this is just another twist of fate?

Maybe I'm unlucky.

Maybe you should get a good *feng shui* man, and a decent lawyer.

You know any decent ones? It's a lawyer that got me into this.

If you're going to blackmail someone you don't kill the source of revenue.

You do if the stream has run dry.

You're saying there's more to it?

You know what they say, apart from shotguns, there are two things that can destroy a man.

What are they?

Love, ambition and financial trouble.

That's three.

And there are a whole lot more. You're the detective, Detective. Detect. Can I get a lift home now?

Yes. Constable Wu can sort you out.

I'm sure she can, but what I'd really like is a lift home.

10. SITUATIONS VACANT

Mei falls asleep in my lap. The taxi takes us over Magazine Gap into Happy Valley. It would be easy to collect the Range Rover from Belleview. All things considered, however, a straight line home is best for all.

It's almost midnight.

Any hope of finding my not-so-distant relatives tucked away for the evening, or gone, is drowned by the unmistakable death knell of mahjong. I can hear it from the elevator.

It's worse than I dared to imagine.

They've corralled another band of outlaws into the fray. They're operating two tables, in Dolby Surround Sound. One is positioned between Por-por and the television. Not a place I would put myself when she's trying to watch Enjoy Yourself Tonight. She's grinding her teeth. It's audible beneath the clacking of ivory tiles. A disapproving glare is sent my way.

Toilet fixed, Gu-por tells me from behind Table #1.

That's as good as news gets around here these days. Of course it's not too late for someone to trip in the bath and break their neck.

Great, I reply with mild enthusiasm. That explains the all-nighter.

You want some duck tongue, *gweilo*?

I tell her I'm fine but thanks for thinking of me. Truth be known, I'm starving. I'm just too scared to go into the kitchen. Bing is probably curled in a fetal ball on the floor, sucking her thumb and talking to Jesus. It's a testament to Mei's somnambular strength that she remains unconscious. I tip her into Ewok pyjamas and slide her between the sheets.

I wrestle with sleep for an hour, turning over the mayhem of the last 48 hours, banging my gulliver against the turnbuckle of madness. Darkness eventually pins my shoulders to the floor and does a triple suplex with pile-driver on my consciousness.

The girl without a face is driving the Bentley. Naked. Mahjong tiles for nipples. Bronson Chung sits in the back. Liu Pang's gulliver is in his lap. He strokes Liu's hair, like Blofeld with his Persian cat. We're driving along Shek O Road. The Wan Chai doxies that chased me through last night's reverie wave from a bus stop. We round a tight corner. Toshimi Wells stands in the middle of the road, hair dyed platinum blonde. I swerve to avoid her, run over the cliff and plummet into the ocean. Kitty Ho, replete with mermaid tail, swims by. The Bentley dives deeper and deeper. I turn toward the sky. Mei looks down from the surface. She reaches for me.

Ba-ba! What's that noise?

Mei's face is three inches above mine. She leans over the side of the bed and pokes my ribs. It shakes the illusions from my mind. Reality dawns.

The mahjong tournament has made it through the night and charged into the morning. Light leaks from behind the curtains. I look at the Garfield clock on the bookshelf.

Eight-twelve.

Don't worry, Doodle-pop. It's just Gu-por, playing mahjong.

In the morning? Ba-ba, you must you must get rid of those pests.

I would but I can't, they're guests.

I'm hungry.

Then let's get dressed!

Mei is adamant she gets to choose her clothes today. No party frocks. Jeans and a t-shirt. For both of us. We look like one of those same-outfit families. National Lampoon's Canton Vacation. As much as two people can resemble a family. A sub-nuclear family. We brush our teeth. I collect Mei's ballet outfit, for her afternoon class, and put it in a plastic bag. I can't find her backpack and don't recall where I left it. I hope it wasn't in the back of the Bentley. I wouldn't want anyone looking through that on their own. The police station? Even worse. Back of the taxi? No comfort there either.

It's going to be another uneasy day.

We attempt to sneak by the mahjong massive. One table has collapsed in upon itself, legs buckled. Exhausted. Expired aunts lay scattered across vinyl gurneys. Other's have been shelved in The Room Of Pilfered Publications. Gu-por tells me the air-conditioner in her room is leaking. I am amused and terrified by her appropriation of Por-por's bedroom.

I'm sorry. I know how annoying that kind of thing can be. I'll get it fixed.

Hope it doesn't take as long to fix as the toilet, she warns.

Bing presents a welcome shot of espresso. I down it in one. It burns, in a good way.

Will you be home tonight, Sir?

It's more of a plea than anything. I can tell by the look in her eyes and the bags under them.

We hit the *dai pai dong* and make short work of fried-egg sandwiches, then knock over a bowl of macaroni in soup with ham. An order of thick toast drowning in condensed milk is surplus to needs but ordered anyway.

The breakfast of champions.

A cab takes us to Belleview. The Redhill massacre dominates the airwaves. I want to get to my car before the police and paparazzi take up residence at the Liu estate. It's a safe bet. The city isn't a morning person. It doesn't wake up until ten or eleven. Homicides can have a way of changing that but, given Liu's wife is away, there shouldn't be much life up there at all.

A striking figure in a Stygian Mao suit stands alongside a black S-class Mercedes. His habroneme hair is powder white, in the Andy Warhol style. His skin is pink.

The albino studies us as we walk from the taxi, across the drive.

Look Ba-ba, a ghost! In the daytime! In the daytime!

I ask Mei to mind her manners and not to point. Or stare. She turns away, deliberately not looking. This is worse than staring.

I open the rear passenger-door of our car and lift Mei to her seat. The albino greets us. His tone is clipped and Cantonese.

Good morning.

No one home? I ask, unsure if he is aware of Liu Pang's fate.

It appears not.

The maid's a bit deaf. Maybe she didn't hear you.

Are you friends of the family, or Liu Pang?

A business associate. He called yesterday evening. We went out. I left the car here. Just came back to pick it up.

Must have been quite a night.

Brutal. You're here about the…?

I leave it open, hoping he'll complete the sentence.

He spreads his arms wide. A gesture intended to draw attention to himself rather than his surrounds. The feng shui, he says, as if it were self-evident.

Ah. We were talking about that last night.

You don't recognize me? Io Lam. I'd be surprised if you haven't heard of me.

Not as surprised as you, I think as I shake his pink paw

Jack So, isn't it? You were involved in that thing last year, with Micki Wong? Awful business.

Io Lam. I've heard of him. Geomancer to the stars. Feng shui Master for the rich and gormless.

You're here about the feng shui, Mr Lam?

In a way. I'm consulting on products for the boutique, and some matters of a personal nature. Liu was going through a phase. Forces were conspiring against him, on domestic and business fronts. He was a big believer in the life sciences and sought to rearrange the elements that governed his existence.

A little late for that, I think and wonder how much of an expert this guy can be if he didn't foresee Liu's planets falling out of alignment last night. Maybe his powers are connected to the meter and only work when the flag is down.

Could use a little help in that department myself, I admit. I'm going through some phases of my own.

Call me, he says, reaching into his tunic and furnishing me with a card. Always happy to improve the fortune and fate of others.

I thank him for the offer, exchange cards and take my leave.

Mei looks over the bay as we peel out of Belleview. She's pretending she hasn't been watching my interaction with the ghost and marvelling at the cosmic forces that control our lives.

Lam and I have more in common than casual observation would suggest. We're mongrels of a slightly different breed. Both suffering the loss of a client. One of us, admittedly, further along the grieving process than the other.

What were the chances of our paths crossing at this point in time?

There are no coincidences nor accidents. Like William Burroughs said, nothing happens unless someone wills it to happen.

Angel's tanktop is tight across her chest. And tucked into stretch-denim jeans. Kenny at The Horse & Groom would envy her boots. Yippee ki-yay. A battered white Stetson sits low on her gulliver, obscuring the pique in her eyes. I can tell she's seen the breaking news by the way she's waving a Chinese tabloid around like a broadsheet lariat.

Care to explain this? Jeezus.

Call me Jack. I'm good, but I'm not that good. I can't resurrect the dead.

I read about your latest attempt in the local Bible. It's a radical business development strategy you're working on, Jack.

We saw a ghost!! interjects Mei.

Did you? Was it a friendly one, or a spooky one?

A creepy one.

Were you scared?

A little bit, but it was day time. Last night was scarier.

I bet it was.

Can I have a cowboy hat?

Of course you can. Here you go, Clamaity Jane.

She takes off her chapeau and drops it on Mei's head. Junior trots to her desk in the creative department. Angel shakes out her tresses like Cindy Crawford on heat. If I ever do a shampoo commercial this will be the money shot.

A ghost, Jack?

I'll explain later.

Yes, you will, she says. And hits me in the chest with the paper.

I look at the front page. It's dominated by a night-shot of the Bentley, stranded on Redhill Peninsula. A plastic sheet is draped over Liu. Next to that is a photo of the deceased in happier times, a giant cigar and show-boat smile where his gulliver used to be. A sinister shot of the house on Belleview, looking more like Bates Motel, is offset in the corner. You can just make out the Range Rover in the foreground. A collage of Liu's wives rounds out the story. All six of them. Same number as Henry XIII.

Didn't he have a couple of them beheaded?

Don't even think about asking me out, says Angel, materializing before my eyes. The way your nights end I'd feel safer riding bareback with Benny down Ladder Street.

That can be arranged, shouts Benny from the studio.

Seriously, Jack, we need to get a *feng shui* man in. Before we all end up on the front page. There's something not right about this place. Maybe it's built on a mass grave, or an ancient burial ground. Our *chi* is taking it up the ass.

One step ahead of you, Tangina. As fate would have it we met with Io Lam this morning.

The albino?

Mei's ghost, in the gleimous flesh. Not as tall as he looked in Poltergeist.

Where?

The house of the damned. He was supposed to have an appointment with Liu. Offered himself to me instead.

What did he say?

Not a lot. I was probably jamming his frequency. Something about keeping Carol Anne out of the spectral light and Mei away from the TV. The Beast is restless. He said I should call if we were having problems with the people under the stairs, or our *chi* was taking it up the ass.

It's not easy to get a consultation with him. If he makes it through today, after meeting you, take him up on it. He's supposed to be good.

I boot up the Macintosh and sign-off layouts for Flora and Wing. They keep a safe distance, like I'm an axe murderer still holding the bloody blade. Benny tries to lighten the mood by ranking Liu's ex-wives in order of hotness and why. I suggest he tone it down. He's is in the presence of minors.

Old enough to know better, and young enough to do it anyway, says a voice from the door.

Toshimi Wells.

I'm here for the internship, she says.

I didn't know we had one, replies Angel, unamused by second-hand news.

You've got the job, declares Benny, making his first and only executive decision.

She's carrying Mei's Sesame Street backpack in one hand, and a black leather portfolio bag in the other.

Mi-mi! You found it! Ba-ba, Mi-mi found my backpack!

The patron saint of lost causes. Mind your gulliver on the way in, Miss Wells.

She dips her shoulders and crosses the distance to my desk in three strides. A riled Angel Luk departs in her wake.

It's difficult to reconcile what towers before me with the nubile athlete of last night.

Eliot and I were wide of the mark when it came to her disregard for frippery. Gone is the wide-eyed naïvety, the pile of hair and Lycra leisurewear. In its place stands a youthful dame of urbane style, cultivated sex appeal and obvious confidence. Amazing the difference a pair of six-inch heels can make. The high waist of her pin-stripe pants exaggerates the length of her slender stilts. A matching three-button jacket has been tailored to follow the taper of her torso. It's unbuttoned over a white business shirt that reveals the precise blades of her collarbone. Long, lubricious hair is dissected by a sharp part and held behind her ears. Eyes are shadowed in smoky grey, with thick black liner. Her lips, shellacked in burgundy, are the centre of attention in a well-crafted presentation.

The design student gets an A+.

She hoicks Mei's backpack onto my desk with a strength that belies her willowy frame. You forgot this, she says. What do you keep in there? I can barely lift it.

School fees.

Hey Mi-mi, you want me to draw you a picture?

Sure Mei-mei. That would be nice.

Saint Fiacre save us all, whispers Benny, taking mental Polaroids at sixty frames a second.

Saint Fiacre is Benny's patron saint of choice. When not watching over him the venerated one is also responsible for cab drivers, florists, gardeners, tile makers, box makers, pewterers and hosiers. Other responsibilities, more relevant to Benny's life, include preventing haemorrhoids, sterility, syphilis and assorted venereal diseases. Benny often refers to Fiacre as Saint Fucker.

Close your mouth, Mother Fiacre, I instruct him. One is not a codfish.

This line, purloined from Mary Poppins, is more of a half-truth in the context of Benny Yu.

I came about the position, she says, parking her anterior flexure.

Did you? Benny got excited too. Maybe we should start with a closer look at your credentials.

Maybe we should get to know each other first.

I was referring to your portfolio. You bought it for a reason.

An excuse, really, to continue our conversation.

The backpack would've been enough.

I thought you might need more.

You've given me plenty to consider already. I was going to drop by this afternoon.

Miss me already, did you?

I missed Bert and Ernie. Thanks for bringing them home safe and sound.

I thought you might need the money.

The money?

In there. School fees are they? Where have you got her enrolled, Eton?

It's rude to look through a man's purse. Didn't your mother teach you that?

That and a whole lot more, but I'm a curious girl.

So you keep saying. You want to drop that habit, trust me.

I will. Did the police keep you long?

As long as they could. How about you?

A few questions.

Your Gurhka's?

Deadly, but silent.

You really want to work here?

She looks around, as if the architecture needs to be taken into account first. Even her neck is beautiful. I don't know, she says.

What do you know?

You want to know what I know?

I don't know. Do I?

I bet you do.

Miss Wells, I'm not a bored student looking for holiday thrills.

Neither am I. It wasn't me that followed a stranger down a dead end just to see how it turned out.

I followed him for forty thousand. You want to tell me how this turns out?

She studies me for a moment. I feel like I'm the one being evaluated and considered for a position.

Turns out your client was not the owner of that sapphire, she says.

His wife was, I know.

Someone else's wife.

And you know that, how?

This is the smallest big city in the world. The social world is even smaller.

How small?

Everyone, except you, knows Liu Pang was stepping out with Koko Man.

I decide to put this last statement to the test. Who was Liu Pang seeing on the side? I shout to Angel in reception.

Koko Man.

How do you know that?

Every idiot knows that.

I know that, agrees Benny.

Toshimi Wells presses her lips together. Told you. Everyone knows, Jack. You really ought to get out more.

Did Mr Man know?

Darius Man. Owner of a television station, a film studio and a lot of property. He's got boats. And casinos in Macau. The rest of us are motes of dust in the vastness of his empire. No one had told him that anyone who piles up treasure in such a manner has much to lose. Or he wasn't listening when Lao Tzu said it to the group.

To have enough is happiness. To have more than enough is harmful.

Man is an influential man. Loved, as Groucho Marx might say, with the same fervour that is reserved for leaders like Stalin, Hitler, Mao and Torquemada. He is one of the few people to have married more times than Liu Pang. They even have an ex-wife or two in common. Man's fifth was Liu's third. Or Man's third was Liu's fifth. There's a steady roster of mistresses too. At his age it's unlikely he's bedding them all, unless he's borrowing Benny's vacuum erection pump. Or has an endless supply of dried tiger penis, which he probably does.

It might be one of the reasons he's also confined to a wheelchair.

Man lives on a property in Shek O. I'd worked the perimeter at parties, around the time of wife four or five.

The old wheeler-dealer returned home from a trip last year with Koko in tow. Not a lot was known about her. She was an entertainer one of Man's cruise ships. The incumbent Mrs Man was as surprised as anyone to find her husband had remarried. The only thing more shocking, as far as society was secretly concerned, was the way Koko flaunted her extra-curricular activities.

When the main Man leaves town, Koko a go-go.

I remind Miss Wells that all happy families are the same. And each unhappy family is unhappy in its own way. She should know that, or don't they teach Tolstoy in high school anymore?

You don't have to read Anna Karenina to know Koko likes a good time, Jack.

To prove her point she retrieves an issue of Tatler from her portfolio bag at her legs, and spreads the pages.

Koko Man lies unfurled beneath me. It's a beguiling portrait of a lady, in the Jamesian sense, written in a foreign tongue with an obvious and immense curiosity about life. Staring and wondering, she only calls people rich when they meet the requirements of her imagination.

I always want to know the things one shouldn't do.

So as to do them?

So as to choose.

She's quite a dish. There's not a lot there you wouldn't eat and most of it is on display, thanks to a sheer Valentino gown. It's slit high in the thigh. A deep V plunges to her naval. Taught skin binds moderate curves, accentuating the inconsonance between the warp of her breasts and the weft of her hips. Nothing a couple of stodgy dinners wouldn't even out. A black bob of hair brackets the attenuated oval of her face. Almond eyes and aquiline nose are complimented by a small, Monroe beauty spot. It draws more attention to the smile beneath than to itself. I could see why Darius Man wanted to own her, and why it was so easy for Koko to jump the queue of women lining up for his millions.

You could do a lot of things with those legs.

I'm drawn to one picture in particular. It's not the company she's keeping, or the gown that brazenly struggles to contain her.

It's the diamond-set sapphire nesting in her décolletage.

I congratulate our dilettante detective.

So, you've solved the secret of the sapphire necklace. Well done, Daphne. Well done. Give my regards to Shaggy, Scooby and the rest of Mystery Inc. Liu was trying to get it back before the old man found out.

Or worse. What if the papers did an exposé? Cuckold a man like that in public and you lose more than a necklace and those keys to the executive washroom.

She had a point. You don't lose everything for fooling around. Men like Man expect that. He couldn't leave tributes at the altar every night. He would, however, expect her to be discreet and wary of false idols. You don't get cooked for getting caught. You do if you get caught out. The loss of the necklace wasn't as big a problem as the loss of face. Liu would've been shut out of more than his mansion too, if he'd been collared with his pants down. The men behind the Man-bush would've known all this. I'm surprised they settled for half a million. Maybe they hadn't.

Maybe that was just the beginning.

Liu should've known better, but Koko's out of her league, Jack.

She's punching above her weight?

Man's in a whole different division. She doesn't understand that. Women like her should pick on men their own size and standing. Stay within their class.

It sounds like you know her well.

I know her type.

What else do you know?

There are some things a man should learn for himself. You could still help get that sapphire back. The blackmailers will come to her now, if they haven't already. I'm sure she'd be grateful for any assistance you might give.

You're sure of a lot of things, aren't you?

You'd be saving her marriage.

Maybe it shouldn't be saved.

It's worth a little more than forty thousand, I can assure you of that.

She got you on a retainer too?

I'm want experience, Jack. You couldn't use some extra cash? Those school fees aren't going to get any cheaper.

I've had the experience, remember? And if it means meeting any more of Liu's acquaintances, I can live without the money.

She'll be disappointed. She got excited when I told her I ran into the man who was with Liu when he died. She thought you might be able to pick up where you left off and help get the necklace back.

I'm finding this hard to believe. And yet I know she isn't joking.

Why would you do tha, Miss Wellst?

How could I not? We know each other. She knows where I live. She called to find out if I saw or heard anything. The whole of society is talking about it. I didn't tell her your name.

Gee, thanks. Try not to do me any more favours. And tell society to keep it's beautifully reconstructed nose out of it.

I didn't have to tell her because she already knew. You don't think Liu told her what he was doing, with who?

Whom.

She's right, of course. Again. Curse her fancy learning. Once the police knew, everyone knew. I witnessed a murder. Two murders. I was probably a suspect for them both as well. A person of disinterest.

What if the guys who took care of Liu decide to take care of me?

Finding out whose name was on the report wouldn't be difficult. You wouldn't even have to buy it. Cyclops Chau would give it to you for free, if it meant making my life difficult. Still, it didn't make me any happier and I couldn't hide the fact that here I was again, up shit creek, with an nymphean student for a paddle.

She's pouting, like I've hurt her feelings. You can't teach that specific curl of the lip. Hong Kong girls are born with it. The Pout is like a superpower. It can be used for good or evil but all are impuissant against it.

Koko wants to meet, she says. She knows all about the affair with Micki Wong last year. You're a bit of a celebrity yourself. You're like our very own Thomas Magnum PI.

He went off-air this year. Retired.

Someone's got to fill his shorts. You could be rich. And famous.

The type of fame that comes with this I don't need, and if you're as smart as I think you are you'll walk away too.

So, no job then?

I'll call if a position becomes available.

That's too bad. I'm quite flexible, you know. I'd fit in nicely. You'd be lucky to have me.

Thanks for returning the backpack. I appreciate it.

You should find a way to show it.

She turns and leaves, tapping the Stetson on Mei's gulliver as she passes.

So long, cowgirl.

Hey! You forgot your picture!

Mei chases her into reception and out of my life.

I look at Benny.

Don't let the door hit her in the ass on the way out, he says. Be a shame to bruise a peach like that.

11. KILLING TIME

It's been quite a week. Business as unusual. A lot to take in. Professionally. Mentally. Domestically. And we still have Christmas campaigns for Chinese Arts & Crafts, Wing On and Wellcome to do.

Gu-por appears.

The air-conditioner is still broken.

I tell her the repair man is on his way, loud enough for Angel to hear and make sure the repair man is indeed on his way.

You don't have to shout, *gweilo*. I'm Chinese, not deaf. Maybe I use your bathroom while I'm here.

The one upstairs broken again?

No. There's a queue. Something we ate. Everyone *gup-si*.

I thank her for sharing that information, and wonder if this explosion of diarrhoea means we'll be seeing another run on our office ablutions.

I drive Mei into Wan Chai for dance class, dreading the disapproving lour of Sam and her mother.

It seems I've underestimated my little sister. Again. Her eyes offer more concern than scorn. We speak briefly of recent events, *con anima*

Stay and watch the lesson, she suggests.

I'd be too much of a distraction.

Stand behind the two-way mirror. The kids won't even see you.

It's not the girls I'm worried about. It's your mom.

Irina stands at the entrance to the office, hands behind her back. Her eyes are dark with disquiet, as if she's just found a bar of bum notes in Chopin's Waltz in C Sharp.

I tell Sam I'll see her in an hour and a half. She recommends I stay away from bars, and don't talk to strangers.

Bowen Road has an irregular flow of pedestrian traffic. Those blazing the trail at this hour seem to be more professional in nature. Military or law enforcement types.

Health Nazis. There's a regular parade of grandparents walking with grandchildren too. Teenagers killing time between school and home, or making appointments at Mother's Choice. Taxi drivers, on the side of the road, are cleaning their cabs or exchanging vehicles between shifts. Some take a nap, or check barrier draws in the racing guide. There doesn't appear to be any police observing 5C. Doesn't mean they're not there. I just can't identify them as I approach Sprudel's unit.

Hey good-looking, an overcooked English accent beckons.

Hazel, I say, peering down the stairwell. How's things?

Better now, she says with a smile and a snort. If you're looking for Lynne she's not there. You can wait down here with me.

I wouldn't want to intrude.

It's not like I'm beating 'em off with a stick.

Snort.

She clumsily pulls a soft pack of Marlboro from her towelling housecoat, revealing more than patented filter tips. I avert my eyes while she readjusts the robe and repackages her pendulous bosom.

Come to where the flavour is.

She offers me one. A smoke, that is. I accept and lean on the rail. She flicks her Bic. The uncommon, concentrated blast of tobacco and nicotine sends my head spinning.

You find that Kitty Ho?

She asks like she knows the answer. It catches me by surprise. I'd almost forgotten about her.

No, I exhale. I don't think we will.

I bet you don't.

Why do you say that?

She hasn't been seen for years, you said so. She did a bunk with Nifty's money. I bet she's got a lot of dissatisfied customers, if you know what I mean. Wouldn't dare show her face, I don't reckon.

How's Lynne holding up?

She's tough. You have to be to live her life. Let herself go a bit lately though.

Pot meet kettle, I think, suppressing a laugh and trying to stop the smoke from exploding out of my lungs.

How well do you know each other, Haze?

We've been neighbours for years. Shared a lot of laughs, and a few bottles. More they a few, eh? Been having quite a party we have this year.

Is that right?

Oh yeah. She came into some money.

From Nifty?

Don't be stupid. Nifty never gave her nothing but grief. No. Some chap was, quote, looking out for her interests.

Whom?

Whom, get you, Mr Interfations. A local guy. Fancy clothes. Big car. He was here yesterday. I told the police. With that guy from the paper. The one they think killed Nifty.

Is that right?

That's what I told the police.

Do you know anything about those interests that he was, quote, looking out for?

He'd give her money every now and then. And some of the good stuff.

The good stuff?

Gin. Expensive. And champers. French. Told you we've been having a bit of a party. She'd get through the money though. Don't know what she did with it.

Nifty?

He didn't know anything about it. That's why it was great. Maybe she blew it on the nags. I don't know. She'd be borrowing from me by the end of the month. Had no shame about it.

Stretch the friendship did it?

We're neighbours, not sisters.

You looked pretty close yesterday.

We were celebrating.

I thought you were in mourning.

Wouldn't waste tears on that prick. You know what they say, one man's misfortune is another woman's fortune. Snort. Lynnie didn't even have to go through with the divorce. That Chinaman served him and saved her the trouble. One whore's grief is another woman's gift. Hopefully she'll get enough to clear her debts.

Money from whom, insurance?

From the developer. Haven't you been listening to me? The one who's been looking after her, for when the divorce came through. She'd get at least half of what was Nifty's and was going to sell it to Fancy Pants.

Sell what?

Whatever he was after. Are you sure you're a lawyer? They usually pay a little more attention. I don't know too much about it, I told you. If she didn't get all of it she was going to sell him her half of whatever. She's got a lot to look forward to.

I guess she does. And so do you.

You think so? No one's knocked off my old man. They sure gave it a good go though, didn't they? Snort. I guess I should be grateful for that, shouldn't I?

Maybe I'll pop up and see if she's back. Do you mind?

Suit yourself, handsome. I don't think she's there. Unless she snuck in the back. Give me some warning next time you're coming over will you? It's embarrassing to be seen in this old thing. I'd invite you in but, well, the house is a bit of a mess too.

I ascend the stairs.

There doesn't appear to be any light or life behind Sprudel's door. I knock on the peeling paintwork.

Not a sound.

A stifled curse and the smash of glass on wood boards breaks the silence.

I knock again and test the handle on the door.

It gives. I push in, calling after the lady of the house. No verbal response. Just mattress springs adjusting to the weight of someone. I trace them across the acrid room. Empty bottles, glasses and an overflowing ashtray clutter the coffee table.

Down a short hallway.

I prod at a door with the toe of my boot.

I go to the kitchen. There's no bottled water to be found. I run the tap, rinse a filthy glass as best I can and take it to her.

She pulls herself onto one elbow. You find your girl?

You still in mourning?

Of a different kind.

How so?

I don't want to tell you and you don't want to know.

It helps to talk.

I already told you everything.

About some things, not about others.

Like what? Go on. Tell me all about my dirty little secrets.

Do you need reminding? I was with him when he died you know.

Who?

Whom.

What?

Never mind. I was with him. Your suitor.

My suitor? Get you with your *whom* and *suitor*!

Liu Pang. You know him. And whatever you had going with him, it's done. Like him. You know that too. That deal. It's blown. Like a leaf on a tree and the gulliver on his shoulders. Goodbye. So long. Farewell. Auf wiedersehen, pet. Sayonara bitch. *Zaijian.* You're going to have to find another buyer, or someone else is going to pick up where he left off. And they might not be as pleasant about it. You know that too, don't you? You've already met the Von Trapp Family Singers.

Hazel tell you that? She talks too much about things she knows too little about.

Liu told me about the deal for The Auld Ball & Chain, I lie, seeing no need to compromise the spurious relationship with her goodly neighbour and partner in quinine any further.

She looks at me out of one eye.

He had plans for Lockhart Road, that's all I know. Plans. Men and their plans. Pah.

Visions before midnight and dreams out of the ivory gate.

What?

Pie in the sky. Dreamers. Don Quixote. Walter Mitty. Reaching for the stars. Ending up with a handful of dirt.

You're probably one too. And you're making my headache worse. So unless you're going to crawl in here and give me something to take my mind off the pain, go tell it to someone who gives a flying French fuck.

You might want to keep that door locked, I advise, backing out of the room.

You threatening me?

Warning you. Whatever this is, it started with your ex-husband. Whoever takes Liu's place in the food chain might cut you out of the deal too. The same way they took care of him, Nifty and his girlfriend.

Tell your smartarse ideas to the cops. If they did their job I wouldn't have so much to worry about.

I don't know about that, I think. Her worries might have been hibernating. Or worse, breeding. Maybe she should get the *feng shui* man in too.

Back on Old Bailey Street, Oldham wants to know if I'm turning myself in.

Yeah. For the witness protection program. I've had a couple close calls. Next time I might not be so lucky. Caught any bad guys lately?

Thought we had a lead on Bronson Chung last night. Turns out it was just you working the other side of the island.

You lean any further back in that chair you'll snap its spine, and they'll want to pin that on me too. You think all these deaths are related?

Only to you. What do you think?

You should take a look at Lynne Sprudel.

Not my type.

She's got a friend. I can arrange an introduction. Sprudel's old man is gone but that's only taken care of half her problems. She had a deal with Liu.

Liu had a lot of shit in the pipe. Got his name on half a dozen leases on Lockhart Road. Were you going to tell me that next?

No, but It does add more weight to my theory. She was going to sell him The Auld Ball & Chain too.

She already did. Yesterday.

How do you know that?

We're the police, Jack. We know things and what we don't know we find out. We're good at it. Sometimes we even manage to do it without your help.

She didn't look like a millionaire when I left her half an hour ago.

She's not. The settlement, in lieu of Liu Pang, is pending. She may even have to find a new buyer.

I don't fancy her chances. She doesn't have much of a head for business.

Neither do her recent partners.

No sign of our Lion Tamer?

Invisible.

One of those things you don't know but you're going to find out?

He'll be seen when he wants to be, or when he's told to be. He could be anywhere. Guangzhou. The Walled City. Holed up in Club Volvo or Ned Kelly's. Even if we knew where he was we'd never find him.

The girl?

Dead, or she might as well be. No records. Birth, death, marriage, ID card, passport. Nothing. She cleared out her bank account and rode off into the sunset years ago.

How do you know she's on Boot Hill and not whooping it up in Rio Grande?

We don't even know if Kitty Ho was her real name. Those girls have half a dozen aliases and can change them like underwear. Fill out a couple of forms incorrectly and you could have a whole new identity. No one would know who you are. You'd probably forget yourself after a while.

When the line between legend and truth becomes blurred, print the legend.

I'm paraphrasing John Ford. Too bad we're not at The Horse & Groom. Kenny *The Cowboy* Lau would've got a kick out of it.

If she's not dead, she's a dead end. What's she guilty of anyway, Jack, trading up and out of Wan Chai?

A life of suffering and a pauper's grave, I agree, switching to Kurosawa and feudal Japanese adages. I'll probably steal something from David Lean next. Epic directors can be habit forming.

It's not a crime to look for a horse while you're riding an ox, he counters in Cantonese.

A good person will be reborn, how much more so the evil person, I reply sagely, not wanting to be outdone.

That's the career path down there, Saint Shinran. The mantra. The right of passage, scaling the greasy pole of success.

Maybe you should call Interpol.

The whole thing has been eclipsed by Liu anyway. Society darlings have more cache than expats who've gone too far up the river.

Even with his Kitty connection to land-grabs and property tracts?

Teplice is a footnote. If it's related it'll come out in the wash and we'll have a movie of the month. If not, people will soon forget about it. RIP Nifty. You'll get over it. His wife has. You got anything else you're dying to tell me?

Nothing I haven't said already. Just a couple of ideas.

That's right, I forgot. You're an ideas man.

One of them firms up, you'll know.

I'll be the last to know. I can't work out if that's because you're bad-mannered, or half-witted.

I have the same problem.

You're a clown, Jack.

We can't all be lion tamers.

I collect Mei from dance class, happy to have got through a whole day without any grisly deaths or physical incursions.

My pager kicks into gear.

I step behind the mirror, Alice through the looking glass, and dial the office.

Angel tells me I've been invited to the home of Darius Man, by the man himself. I'm expected on Prospect Point in half an hour. Afternoon tea, with the family. The Jabberwocky, The Walrus and The Carpenter.

The time has come, the Walrus said,

To talk of many things:

Of shoes and ships and sealing-wax,

Of cabbages and kings,

And why the sea is boiling hot,

And whether pigs have wings.

If the invitation had come from his charming wife I might've told Angel to send my apologies. I needed to get involved in their sordid affairs like I needed a hole in the gulliver.

But you don't say no to Darius Man.

Of course, sometimes, the only thing worse than saying no was saying yes.

A king is a bad enemy, a worse friend and a fatal relative.

That's the price of admission to the pantheon.

Still, it had been years since I'd been to Shek O. And I always did want to see inside that place.

Come on, Mei-mei. Let's hit the beach.

Why are we going there?

To see the Star-belly Sneetch.

As we climb into the car, however, it's Lewis Carroll that springs to mind once more. Like Alice, my head is filled with ideas. I just don't know what they are.

Beware the Jabberwock, my son!

The jaws that bite, the claws that catch!

Beware the Jubjub bird, and shun

The frumious Bandersnatch!

Somebody killed something. That much is clear, in any rhythm or meter.

12. OVER THE DRAGON'S BACK

Shek O lies on the southern tip of Hong Kong Island, isolated by acres of national park and a ragged spine of rock. The Dragon's Back. A verdant mesa, pock-marked with colonial estates and summer retreats. The low-lying golf course has been carved out of the stratum and scrub. Dig deep enough and you'll find thousands of corpses. The bodies of those terrorized, brutalized, raped and murdered by the Japanese in the wake of Black Christmas.

Despite its painful history, Shek O is a peaceful postcard from a simpler time. Stroked lazily by warm sands and languorous currents. The village is a farrago of spontaneously erected lean-tos and lodgings, devoid of planning, ignorant of zoning. At the centre of the ramshackle community is an empty, two-storey dwelling. A home for spirits of the dead, who venture out to haunt a lonely branch of The Bank. Disgruntled customers were on the rise since Sir Murray Wells orchestrated the crash of '87.

A sole, winding artery hugs the steep scarp, granting one-lane access to this forgotten corner. As we crawl along the narrow bridle, I recall my last trip over The Dragon's Back.

Mike Midian and I were patrolling the perimeter of a party Man was hosting, celebrating a triumph at the local film awards. We did a kilo of coke off a starlet's golden orbs, then rested on her laurels.

The past is a different place, said Hartley. They do things differently there.

Are we going to the beach? asks Mei as I reverse out of Memory Lane.

Maybe later, Karate-chop. We have to see The King in his castle.

I throw the car on the curb beside a large stone wall that separates The Mansion from intrusive eyes.

Mei and I approach the iron gates.

There's a castle in there, Ba-ba?

There's a whole different world in there, Pudding.

A stout security guard appears behind a portal in the wall. I used to do this type of thing, for less money but more laughs than this guy was taking home.

He asks what we want.

I tell him we have an appointment with Mr Man.

He leaves us standing on the pavement while he goes to see if this is true, and closes the thick door behind him. It takes a little longer than I would expect or deem socially acceptable.

He invited me! I shout over the wall.

The threshold re-opens to reveal a bookish woman, closer to thirty than twenty. Smart business attire. Sensible shoes. Flesh-coloured stockings. Gray skirt. Matching jacket over a crisp white blouse. Large bow erupting from the collar. Thin eyes sit deep on a thin face, behind the wire frames of her glasses. Her hair flows from a centre-part, pinned and prised into a bun. She strikes me as someone that wouldn't miss much, even if she was blindfolded. Ruthlessly efficient. The type that would fit you in between appointments.

Sorry to keep you waiting. Security, you understand. I am Misuki, Mr Man's Personal Assistant.

Misuki Man. Personal Assistant and daughter of Darius Man.

Missy, isn't it?

She looks at me as if that term of endearment is reserved for family, close friends and paparazzi. You will follow me, she insists. Mr Man is waiting.

Is that The Queen? whispers Mei.

One day, Shutter-bug. More like The Princess, for now.

Missy stops. She turns, looks at Mei and then to me.

This is Mei, I explain. My daughter. And Personal Assistant.

She gives a sharp, flat smile. Pivots on her heels and continues across the manicured grounds. We follow her up the garden path.

The salt air should have made a mockery of the flora. Old, windswept trees have evolved to accommodate the breezes that howl off the shipping lanes. Half a dozen expensive cars are parked in the far corner. Rolls Royce. Bentley. Ferrari. Two black Mercedes. Range Rover. Porsche. A Toyota mini-bus completes the vehicular comedy.

The house is wide. Oriental style. The multiple peaks of the roof would not be out of place in The Forbidden City. Two storeys high on this side. Three or four on the other, facing the beach, if I remember correctly. Although it looks as if the new Madame has overseen some renovations.

In my father's house there are many rooms, I remark, a little too loudly.

Pardon? snaps the headmistress, as if dealing with an impertinent teen.

Oh, nothing. I like what you've done with the place. Early Tang Dynasty is it? Later Han?

You've been here before, Mr So?

Yes. Undercover of night, so to speak. Probably when you were about Mei's age. Event security. I didn't get a peak behind your curtains though. It's exciting to be invited in.

It's like a Chinese castle! decides Mei.

The geometry of Missy's cheeks alter upon hearing this. Was that the hint of a smile? It should be. Mei has this effect on most women.

We're led through large double doors buttressed by ornate, dragon-wrapped pillars. The short hall is lined with enough vases and Chinese paintings to give Christies a thrombosis. Darius Man was so old he probably liberated them from the Summer Palace himself, before the Brits burned it to the ground during the Taiping insurgence of the 1860s. There's even an Oscar that was awarded to Bertolucci for The Last Emperor on display.

We descend into a wide room that runs the width of the house.

If seven maids with seven mops

Swept it for half a year,

Do you suppose, the Walrus said,

That they could get it clear?

I doubt it, said the Carpenter,

And shed a bitter tear.

Across an acre of shagpile, floor-to-ceiling windows look over an immaculate lawn to the open sea. Any closer to the ocean and you'd be pulling prawns from your pants and clams from your drawers. Waves crash against rocks, sending explosions of spray across the grass. I'm pretty sure John Woo filmed a few scenes of The Killer here.

Mr So, and his daughter, Mei, announces Missy.

The room is occupied yet bereft of life. I've known funerals with more buoyancy and sparkle. Henry James observed that, under certain circumstances, there were few hours in life more agreeable than the hour dedicated to afternoon tea. You didn't have to read leaves to know this journey into The Temple Of The Golden Pavilion would not be one of them.

Mi-mi! squeals Mei.

The eager intern sits primly on the edge of a large white sofa, dressed as she was this morning. Her conniving hands cupped around a tumbler.

Hello Mei-mei, she says with a subdued smile, then shifts her attention to me. She winks and tips a healthy measure of brown liquor down her throat, taking a moment to savour the whiskey, or the moment. Maybe both.

Darius Man sits in his wheelchair on the window side of the sofa, at a forty-five degree angle. Like he's torn between the view outside and the women inside. A rich charcoal suit still manages to look immaculate, despite his vertically challenged status.

Missy walks to him and turns the chair to face us.

Is that The King? asks Mei, *sotto voce*.

Before I can answer there is a shift in the spatial currents.

The air has been electrified.

A broad emerges from the long end of the room. Sparks fly from her heels as they chip into the marble. She burns a path through the carpet, singeing the shagpile.

This High Priestess is a piquant *carte de visite*.

I am a camera with shutter wide open. Passive. Recording. Not thinking. I am Isherwood. Goodbye To Berlin.

The photos in Tatler don't do her justice.

There is no flash to flatten her features or turn her complexion to paste. In the warm light of the afternoon Koko takes on a new dimension. There is an enigmatic quality beyond sophistication and sex appeal. And everyone in the room knows it.

Especially Koko.

There's no puppies pulling her sedan chair. Jet-black hair still frames the tapered oval of her face. Now, however, I'm aware of subtle cheekbones. The lustre of her eyes. They're gems straight out of the mines and polished for prime position in the store window, cut by Rene Lalique himself, highlighted by a thin stroke of eyeliner. Lips, when not stretched in a vainglorious smile, sit fuller on her wide mouth, below a sharp sculptured nose. Tear-drop diamonds, suspended on short links, swing from each curvilinear lobe. High breasts amuse themselves, jaunty beneath the improcerous brilliance of a Mary Quant frock. The thews of her thighs lead to slender calves and continue to narrow ankles. Six-inches of Jimmy Choo push her gaunt frame beyond average height. She almost teeters off one heel as she approaches the sofa.

That tumbler of whiskey in her hand may not be her first.

The fluidity of her recovery suggests she's recently filled a prescription for Prozac and is self-medicating on the other side of caution.

Is that The Queen? asks Mei.

Koko flashes her celebrated smile. I like to think so, she says. Although I'm sure some would take issue with that. Wouldn't they, Suki?

She's endowed her daughter-in-law with her own term of affection, yet barely deigns her worthy of a sideways glance.

Mr So, says Missy, may I introduce Horoko. My father's wife.

She sizes me up. Her eyes are searching and not as welcoming as her lips.

They're wary. Assessing. Evaluating. As cold, empty and wanting as a bachelor's refrigerator. A contrast to the warm English tones of her voice.

Call me Koko. All my friends do.

I take her cultivated hand in mine. Soft of touch, firm of grip. As she withdraws her clasp, manicured nails caress my wrist and palm, seductively stroking my libido as they slip away.

Nice to meet you, is all I can manage.

I'm sure it is, she replies. I hear you're lucky to be alive.

She looks at Toshimi as if they're two schoolgirls with a secret.

Aren't we all? I say, and realise such comments might be construed as inappropriate in the presence of Darius Man. I decide to walk over, throw myself at his feet, and seek his forgiveness.

Jack So, I say, presenting my paw in the time-honoured custom. Thank you for inviting me into your home.

Man looks me in the eye. He declines the formal greeting. Either he can't, or can't be bothered. He returns his gaze to the view, and the cold dark sea that waits for him. For us all. There is a quiet dignity in his mien, in a shrinking wittol kind of way. I get the feeling he's a man of few words. The women in his life probably do most of the talking, with his permission.

Please take a seat, suggests Missy.

Yes, why don't you sit down? says Koko, indicating a place on the sofa not far from her. Suki can get you a drink. Can't you, Suki?

Don't go to any trouble.

It's no trouble. Is it, Suki? What would you like? Whiskey? Champagne?

Water will be fine.

And for your delightful daughter?

Mei is still at the bottom of the stairs. I call her to me. Say hello to Mr Man, Pudding-pop. And Mrs Man.

She meekly says hello, curtsies, and skirts by the wheelchair. Her ballet outfit briefly gains the patriarch's attention, almost garnering a smile. She offers Koko the same, and skips by Toshimi Wells with an excited wave, then sits beside me.

She'll be fine, I affirm.

Nonsense, disagrees Koko. Milo? Would you like a Milo? Suki, make the adorable thing some Milo.

Missy eyeballs her stepmother. The amarulence is obvious as she leaves the room.

Where is your wife? asks Man.

She passed some years ago.

He considers this. The room is silent, as if a great portent is upon us. Koko may even be holding her breath.

An ice cube loses its nerve in Toshimi's tumbler.

My condolences. It is a sad thing to lose a good woman, he susurrates, before returning his attention to life beyond these walls.

You know Miss Wells, Koko reminds me, regaining control of the room.

We've had the pleasure.

Not yet we haven't, Toshimi fires back.

The schoolgirls exchange lewd grins, like they've shared more than a couple of cocktails. They're drunk. Elegantly drunk. Seductively and pugnaciously drunk. Elmer Gantry in panties.

Missy returns with a large plastic cup upon a silver tray. She places a lace doily on the antique coffee table and sets the drink down. Mei leaps to liberate the Milo.

Careful, Sweetheart. Two hands.

Missy stands at her father's side. We're told you might be able to help retrieve a family heirloom, she says, as if reviewing minutes from the last board meeting.

Well, that's that out in the open, I think. No messing about with her. Straight to the point.

I'd like to help, Ms Man. I'm just not sure I can. You may have been misled.

I would be very grateful, implores Koko, in a tone that promises more than cordial gratuity. Such a manner, I would've thought, was inappropriate in this situation. In front of one's husband, with one's clothes on. Maybe she's been doing it so long she forgets she's doing it. Maybe her confidence overrides her common sense.

She crosses one leg over and around the other. I sway defensively. I could lose an eye on one of those six-inch, patent leather spikes.

I don't really know anything. I was along for the ride, if you'll pardon the expression. Liu told me little. Things transpired incredibly fast.

Darius Man sighs, looking from me to his wife and then out the window, as if what was out there held more answers.

The shock of the events must have scrambled your memory, suggests Koko.

My mind's been muddied, I want to say, by events of the last fifteen minutes.

Perhaps you can tell us what Liu Pang said, proposes Missy.

Koko waves her stepdaughter off. Do not pressure our guest, Suki. He's here to assist us, if he can. Maybe he needs some time and encouragement.

The two women observe each other for a month and a half.

Perhaps, agrees Missy.

I'm sure my husband has more important things to attend to than this unpleasant business. Perhaps, Suki, you can assist him with those? All this talk of murder and criminals is hardly worth his time. It is beneath him.

And you are not? snipes Missy.

Her father reins her in with a gentle hand to her thigh. The jewels have sentimental value, he says with conviction. If you can assist with their retrieval I will be indebted to you. If you cannot, then I thank you for your time. You shall be compensated.

His vultuous eyes rest upon mine. An ocular bond. A guarantee of his words and a sign of his desire to take no further part in proceedings.

Missy wheels him from the room. Like Jude The Obscure we watch their departure in silence.

The school master was leaving the village, and everybody seemed sorry.

Bye-bye Mr Man, calls Mei, remembering her manners.

Koko fixes me with a gaze. So, she exhales. What can you tell us?

Probably no more than your girlfriend here has told you already. In fact, I think Miss Wells knows more about it that I ever will.

You're a fast learner, observes Koko.

She drains her glass. It signals a sizeable shift in character. As if all pretence has been shed. I'm getting a glimpse of the real Koko Man. The naked Horoko Kitajima. School's out. Recess is in. Let's compare notes and see what we gleaned from our lessons.

She pushes up from the sofa and strides to the bar.

I figured you for someone who likes it straight up, like me, she says, dropping a glass of liquor in my hand. Two strands of diamonds laze around her delicate wrist. Rings embolden her fingers.

Can I go outside, Ba-ba?

That's a good idea Mei-mei, agrees Koko. Take Toshimi with you too. You girls can play together out there, and the grown-ups can get down to business in here.

Can we Ba-ba, pleeease?

Of course you can Mei-mei, says Toshimi. Come on.

There's a swing-set and playground at the side, Koko reminds her.

There's one here too, I think.

The two girls leave through a sliding glass door. Mei runs onto the grass. Toshimi departs with a furtive glance in my direction.

And then there were two, says Koko.

I miss them already.

Toshimi is a sweet girl. I know her father.

I'm sure you do.

She was shocked by the events of last night.

She'll get over it.

I'm not sure I ever will.

I'm beginning to feel she already has. There's just this one unpleasant detail lingering, and the need to maintain some semblance of propriety.

You'll find a way, Mrs Man, I'm sure.

A vote of confidence. How endearing.

Her smile goes from alluring to leering with a prurient twitch of her lip. It is the anaesthetized simper of the inebriated.

Yes, I suppose it can. Poor Liu. I shall miss him.

Yes, poor Liu. I weep for him. Was it his past he couldn't outrun, or his future?

What are you implying?

Tell me how you explained your part in his fate to your husband. I hope you did it a little better than that last performance.

I told him the truth. I was at the nightclub. Liu Pang drove me home. We were set upon. The jewels were stolen. You don't believe me?

I believe what you told him. It's what you didn't tell him that I need to know. Why did Pang have to give you a ride? Where was your driver?

A woman in my position sometimes dismisses the staff, at her discretion. It's called benevolence.

It's been called a lot of things. That's the first time I've heard it called benevolence.

What would you like to call it? she says, turning her body to confront me.

I could think of a few things, but I don't think we're talking about your munificence anymore, are we?

She throws her gulliver back and laughs.

Munificence! I have no idea what you're talking about, but I love it. I'll show you my munificence if you show me yours.

I stand.

Mei and I have better things to do than amuse mollycoddled tai-tais, Mrs Man. Thank-you for welcoming us into your home. I think, however, you know everything you need to know about my involvement with your dear friend Liu Pang. Whatever that is, I can assure you, it has been greatly exaggerated.

Please sit, she says softly, sliding closer. She takes my hand and gives it a gentle squeeze. Please. It's a difficult and confusing time. Forgive me if I am not myself.

Who are you then? I ask, sitting beside her.

See, we can be friends. Now, what did Pang tell you?

About the robbery?

Let's start there, she confirms, and I wonder who is interrogating whom.

There were men, in a car. They were waiting at his house, on Belleview.

It was on Belleview, but not in the grounds. Not at first.

From the top then, Mrs Man, please.

Let's dispense with the Mrs, shall we, Jack?

From the top then, Koko.

She smiles, claiming another small victory.

I had dismissed the driver earlier, she recounts. I often do. Pang was to give me a lift home, as he often did. He liked to drive at night. He said it gave him freedom. I soon realized, however, he was driving over Magazine Gap.

Instead of up the expressway, to Chai Wan, and on to Shek O.

He was keen to pursue the night elsewhere.

Did you often pursue it with him, and how far were you willing to go?

He was into flirting, Jack, not fucking.

I'm surprised by the sudden burst of crassness.

Maybe he had other ideas that night, I suggest. He had hold of the deer, maybe he wanted the horns.

Most men I meet have other ideas. I'd be worried if they didn't. You've had one or two yourself since sitting down, haven't you?

We were talking about Liu.

His wife was away. He was quite insistent that I come to his place and that we should party into the night, as we often did.

You agreed?

Something didn't feel right. I told him it wouldn't bode well for a woman of my profile to be caught in a compromising position.

Her use of *bode* is almost as distracting as her profile. It's hard to imagine her in anything but compromising positions, with a bodey like that. The sudden surge of blood in my veins was probably audible throughout the mansion.

Missy appears out of nowhere.

I feel like I've been caught with one hand in the cookie jar. Guilty of a thought-crime, I shift in my seat and attempt to inch down the sofa. Koko Man's spell has been broken. She is not amused.

Suki, why don't you check on Miss Wells and Miss So?

Missy studies the portrait on the couch before acquiescing to the command. She locates the girls in the far corner of the grass deck and walks to them.

Koko wrinkles her nose and sticks out her tongue.

You were taking the long way home? I remind her.

A car pushed us to the side of the road. I thought it was photographers. They are forever hounding me.

I've long admired their work, but they ride motorcycles. You know that.

It was late. We'd been drinking. I didn't have time to think. It was a black Mercedes. They had guns. One of them had a shotgun.

Serious accessories, for a robbery.

What were they supposed to have?

It was an observation, not a criticism.

They seemed very professional.

In your experience.

In my observation. They didn't bother with rings or wallets.

Just the good stuff, I say, indicating the area beneath her chin. She smiles. I blush. I was referring to the necklace, Koko.

I know, but you were looking at my breasts when you said it.

We were talking about the men who accosted you. They weren't your idea of common thieves.

They could've been from the mainland. We've had nothing but problems since the British signed the city away. They slip over the border looking for quick cash.

In a Mercedes?

Yes, I see what you mean. I've heard triads are competing for space too and, since the crash, they're not the only ones looking for ways to make easy money. I shouldn't have to tell you that.

Entrepreneurs, you think?

I don't know. I'm just saying it could be any one of a number of things.

They must have been watching you for quite some time, to know you'd be wearing that necklace. To know when you were leaving and when you were on your way home. The route your were taking.

I like to go out, she offers, as if that explains everything.

You're not really a homebody, are you? You're spread quite liberally across Tatler, I'll say that. You put on a good show.

What do you mean?

You dress well.

I'm lucky I can afford to adorn my body, she admits, prebitioning her form for my assessment. I like to be seen at my best. That's not a crime.

Sometimes it ought to be. You gave your driver the night off. You trust him?

He's worked for my husband many years. I trust him as much as I trust any man. Or woman.

You don't trust me?

I don't know you, but I'm sure you can be counted on for many things.

What's your point?

I don't have one. I'm trying to work out the point of all this.

And what have you worked out so far?

You're testing more than my patience. You're testing my knowledge. Finding out what I know and how much that might contradict your version of events.

I'm interested to know what Pang might've said. Of course I am and, naturally, I want to it to be the same. I want it to coincide with yours too. It must, if we're all telling the truth. That is what I have to know. So, was it?

Same, but different. You're both pulling the cat's tail, just in opposite directions. Maybe he was scared and confused.

He was. I spoke to him that evening. He was in a frightful state.

You should have seen him by the end of it. A complete mess.

She giggles, then realizes that's as ill-suited as my comment. She lifts a hand to her mouth in embarrassment. Either that or she has gas.

Was there anyone that wanted to compromise him in some way?

You think he was set up?

Who would've known what you were wearing that night?

Everyone at the club. Anyone in the bedroom with me when I dressed.

She smirks, pulls at the halter of her dress, puffs her cheeks and exhales.

Is it hot in here, or is it just me?

It's you, Koko. Look, hire me or fire me. Or this is as far as we go.

Maybe we should go somewhere else.

In my father's house there are many rooms.

Pardon?

Nothing.

Something biblical?

Is that an offer, or another sterling observation? Stop shipping tangerines around the shopfront, Mrs Man. It's tiresome. You either want to find your irreplaceable jewels and save your precious marriage, or you don't. You want to find out who killed your dear friend, or you don't. What you don't want to do is waste more of my time.

What do you want from me?

More than you've given, not as much as you're tendering now.

You want the night in full?

Top to bottom.

Blow by blow?

Mei runs by the window, chasing a ball. Toshimi chases her. Mei kicks it back, out of view. They both run after it.

When did you realize it was no longer a simple robbery and turning into blackmail, or something bigger?

When they took more than the necklace.

What did they take?

Pictures. Not the kind you see in Tatler.

Family portraits?

This is embarrassing enough, Mr So. I would asks you not to pudify me with attempts at humour. I have been humiliated and violated.

Her words fade away. It's a convincing performance, if it is one. This dame is harder to read than Anna Karenina, and there's not a lot of self-respect covering the empty place where love used to be.

They said they had photos of us leaving the club. Images of us, together.

Cavorting?

Fooling around.

Like school friends?

That would depend on where you did your schooling. It was innocent enough. Sometimes all a man wants is a taste. And that's enough. Sometimes it's the best way to get past a difficult moment. A lot of women will tell you that.

Difficult is climbing a wall that's leaning in while trying to kiss a girl who's leaning out. Winston Churchill will tell you that.

Have you never engaged in a moment of reckless passion?

The way she asks makes it sound like an invitation. It's easy to see how quickly she could get into trouble.

They drove us to the house. They forced me to remove my clothes.

She pauses, judging my response to this information.

What choice did I have? Part of me thought it was just a perverted thrill. Who wouldn't want to see me naked?

I'm amazed she can find the temerity to throw a gourd under these circumstances. How hard it must be for her to contain that pride, vanity and attendant deadly sins.

There was three of them. Standing. Watching. There may have been another in the car. It was dark. I thought I heard a fourth voice.

You understood what they were saying?

Yes.

What language?

Cantonese.

So, not Mainlanders.

They could've been from Guangzhou. Maybe I heard both. The night was a blur. It's hard to pick accents when all you can hear is crude grunts and snide laughter. Their preferred language was not high on my list of things to be concerned about.

She draws deep and throws whiskey down her breathtaking neck.

I'm sorry. You're doing well.

I'm putting on a brave face.

She putting something on, that's obvious. The brave face is only part of it. There's a lot of kinks in this yarn. And it's about to get kinkier.

They took their pictures and left with the sapphire?

They splayed me on the hood of the car. Liu was told to stand between my legs. He fumbled with his belt. I closed my eyes. I don't know how long it went on.

I don't know how you did it, I admit, stunned by the deadpan delivery.

The trick, Mr So, is not minding that it hurts.

She lights a mental matchstick and extinguishes the burning head between the fingers of her faculties.

We had to act as if we were enjoying it, while they recorded. They said they'd kill the worst performer if we didn't impress them.

Recorded?

Video. They took us inside, to the stairs. Then the living room. Liu was having trouble. Performance anxiety. He couldn't. He was crying. A weak man. They gave him something to drink. They made him watch while others, while the others enjoyed themselves.

You saw who they were?

They had masks. Did I not mention that? Like a fancy dress ball. Black masks across their eyes. Like Kato and The Green Hornet. One of them, I called him that when he took me. The Green Hornet. He was half a man, I said. He had a small-

Stinger. Mrs Man, I think you-

They all smelled of cheap cologne.

She inhales deeply and searches my eyes.

At least now I know why she's so unhinged and why Liu went outside the circle of trust. Why they were unable to employ Man's covert resources to recover the jewels. He had connections to triads. Most businessman did, one way or another. They could achieve things no legal process could begin to attempt. If they were engaged, however, the full extent of Koko's degradation would be exposed. They might even be part of it.

How much of this did Eric Tsoi know when he gave Liu my name?

It didn't really matter.

By pulling the cat's tail, and playing half a dozen ends against the middle, Liu Pang and Horoko Man had fucked us all.

Liu insisted we deal with it ourselves, she continues. We were desperate. He spoke to a lawyer who knew someone. You.

The way she says it makes me feel like Han Solo to her Leia, and I'm momentarily unglued by an image of her in a metal bikini.

Did her husband and his daughter know the sordid details of her defilement?

Of course not.

You don't think he would be a little sympathetic? You were raped.

He would not understand it that way. He'd believe it was my fault. He often cautions me with regard to social activities. He says I invite much unwanted attention. He has been vindicated. I have shamed and embarrassed him.

At least he still has his health.

Don't let appearances fool you, she replies, misunderstanding my jocose allusion to her husband's frailty. She could smote him with one squeeze of her thighs.

How's your medical condition? I ask. Has there been any, shall we say, sequelae from the attack? The men who had their way with you may not have been the most hygienic. And sex can be quite the killer these days.

I was somewhat tender for a while, as you might imagine.

I'm trying not to. My mind is more concerned with diseases of a venereal nature. AIDS in particular. I'd had a close encounter with this latest scourge of the world's underpants last year. The fear of the virus and stigma of the test was nothing compared to the anxieties that festered while waiting for the results.

I am clean, Jack. If that is what you are asking.

I turn the conversation back to her husband's knowledge of her exploits. He'd expressed concern before and yet he allowed her to continue with her wild nights.

Wild nights are the price of a relationship with me. He was partial to my inhibitions. He encouraged them, when his feeble body permitted.

Geri-active participation aside, Koko, public cuckolding would sting a bit. Being made to look the fool at The Jockey Club would hurt. A warrior can be dispatched but not dishonoured. A gentleman can be eliminated but not humiliated.

And a woman can die, but she cannot be defiled. I know the rules of engagement, Jack. This is not my first battle. We all know the wages of the eternal war.

How did you get to know Darius Man.

How does one get to know any man?

Stalking? Cavorting?

I courted him.

Courting? You didn't strike me as the Jane Austen type. Get all Elizabeth on his Mr Darcy, did you?

I got his attention, the old fashioned way.

You climbed the corporate ladder in your silk stockings.

As you say, Jack, if you're going after a deer you have to grab the horns.

The hunter stands and gathers another round of single malts.

I was introduced to him on Bellatrix, she says, circling the sofa.

Bellatrix is an infamous luxury cruise ship and floating casino. The ideal place for women to try their luck and men to risk theirs. It is the largest of vessels in the Man flotilla, which includes two private yachts.

Canis Major and Canis Minor.

Men his age are always looking for something special, says the face that could launch a thousand ships. Helen of Hoi Polloi.

Yes. It is a truth universally acknowledged that a man in possession of a good fortune must be in want of a wife.

She ruckles her nose. The literary reference is beyond her.

Jane Austen, I add for her benefit.

Again with Jane Austen. Where is she from?

England.

What has she been in?

Pride And Prejudice.

I would like to meet her.

She's not with us anymore.

That's too bad. She sounds like fun.

She was a hoot.

She was right, except for the bit about wanting a woman.

Men with money don't want women?

They want young women.

Better to satisfy a young woman's curiosity, than to disappoint a widow.

Jane Austen?

Fred Allen.

He probably wanted something to lord over his friends as well.

You don't mind being a trophy, Koko?

As long as I'm kept polished and not in the back room on the lower shelves, with the plaques and certificates.

Next to the old Barbra Streisand records. What about Liu Pang?

He was a big fan of Barbra Streisand. He liked show tunes.

He didn't see you as a trophy?

I was more of a must-have accessory.

How did you meet him?

We rotate through the same circles. I guess society threw us together in a way. A type of gravity.

Society does make for some strange bedfellows. Any other common interests? Investments?

I'm invested in this, she says with a wave of her arm. It's either a reference to the house, or her body. Or both.

I'm surprised your weren't more careful with your assets.

I won't make the same mistake again.

Not with Liu.

Are you always this cold, Jack? I thought you were warming to me.

I feel the burn of blood on my cheeks.

I'm following the example of Lao Tzu, I tell her. Ridding myself of desire, the habit of flattery and excessive ambition. Those who know that enough is enough will always have enough.

There are times when even the Buddha gets inflamed.

Was there something else of yours that fuelled his burning passions and desires? Did he plumb your line? Whose mazuma was lost on Redhill? Did you lend him any readies?

He had ways of getting money out of people.

He put the fun in funding. What do they say, evil is the root of all money?

She ponders this, smiles and reminds me Liu was married six times.

A man in possession of a good fortune must be in want of a wife.

He wasn't as interested in women as you might think. He lived off them. Wealthy divorcees. They funded his ventures. He was involved in many things. His personal stake, however, was limited. He wanted to change that.

With you? Was he planning on some kind of nubile takeover?

I doubt it. What I get out of this estate I won't be sharing. We were friends because we weren't interested in each other. It's what made that night so awkward. I thought we played the same game, albeit in different leagues. You never had a female friend you didn't fuck, Jack?

I'm from the When Harry Met Sally school of relationships.

I'll bear that in mind, should we become friends.

I'll bear in mind what happens to your friends. You don't think he might've been part of the extortion? Why was he so eager to play along?

If this came out he would lose his wife. His whole livelihood.

His cash cow.

He was running out of lives, and wives. He'd been ploughing the same field for many years. It would be much easier for me to find someone to satiate my needs, financially. What was it you said? Better to fuck a young woman and satisfy her curiosity than to disappoint a widow? Maybe Pang had become a disappointment.

Double jeopardy.

What does that mean?

Usually it means you can't prosecute a person twice for the same offense.

What does it mean in this instance?

Getting fucked from two ends, to use your parlance. Whoever caught this yellow-legged chicken chose well. You're damned if you do and doomed if you don't. Have the photos surfaced?

I've seen a sample.

Can I see them?

She slaps me. I shouldn't have smiled when I said it.

I meant that from a professional point of view. There might be something that could identify where they were developed, or who might've been involved.

Her eyes narrow. A lip curls.

I could get my doctor to take some pictures, Jack. Then you can look at me from inside as well. But if it's a real Kodak moment you want, I'll give you one.

I am a camera.
Shutter wide open.
Recording. Not thinking.

Her wanton, triumphant smile is warped in Baccarat crystal. My surprise, fear and embarrassment engorge her lubency. The broad is certifiable.

She could pessundate us all.

What does that tell you? she demands to know, coolly observing the heat of the moment. Had enough, Jack, or do you want some more?

I'm not sure. I'll look into it and get back to you.

Don't leave it too long. The offer might expire.

So might I.

Doesn't she know that the Tao values stillness and idleness? All haste, passion and frenzy arouse only distaste. They're symptoms of bad upbringing and a lack of refinement. She seems incapable of curbing her *jing*. The Dalai Lama would struggle to keep his *de* away from her *wu wei*, and his *yin* out of her *yang*.

Did you keep the photos? I ask, praying for The Pure Ones to return.

We burnt them. If anyone were to see them, even if they believed we were forced into it, I could never show my face.

There's her pride and prejudice resurfacing again. It's not the act that concerns her, just getting caught. And maybe who she gets caught with.

Outside, the light is fading.

Mei, Toshimi and Missy file across the lawn.

Koko straightens her dress. I have more for you, she says. Meet me at eleven. Disco Disco. There's a booth at the back. Get a baby-sitter.

You think you'll need one?

Mei bursts through the door and runs toward me.

Ba-ba! The house is so big! We should come here all the time. Can we come again? Can we? It's so much fun!

Oh, it's a blast, I reply, avoiding eye contact with any adults in the room.

We'll have to see what happens, Sweet-cheeks. We don't want to wear out our welcome.

I thank the Mans for their hospitality. Koko authors another lascivious grin. Missy must be wondering what transpired in her absence.

I'm still trying to work it out.

Toshimi Wells is keen for an upload too.

Could bother you for a ride, Jack? It's on the way.

Don't trouble Mr So, cautions Koko. My driver will run you back.

It's okay, I want Jack to take me.

I bet you do, she replies. And they share that schoolgirl joke again.

Missy hands me her card. She tells me to contact her directly. I can let her know my rates and how I wish to be compensated for my time.

My charges are reasonable. It's the expenses that can really add up. Sometimes they keep running after the work has stopped too. Small leaks can sink great ships, but someone has to pay to have the piano tuned.

If you're unable or unwilling to help, we will understand. My father has instructed us to lend you any assistance, financial, legal or otherwise, should the actions of his wife or her associates cause you further inconvenience.

It's a shame he's not here. I'd like to say good-bye to him.

Who wouldn't? moots Koko, under her breath.

I tell Misuki, in Cantonese, that I respect her father's generosity. Hopefully the matter will be concluded with the greatest satisfaction and least embarrassment, and the sapphire will be returned. A precious jewel does not belong in the hands of those who cannot appreciate it. The deeper meaning of this is not lost on her. I have no idea if it registered with Koko.

Anything could be lurking behind that smile.

13. THE LONG WAY HOME

The Range Rover climbs out of the village. My rear-view mirror struggles to frame the zaftig lips of Toshimi Wells. All mouth, no trousers.

Objects in the mirror are closer than they appear.

Don't be angry, Jack.

I'm too old to be angry.

You're not too old, Ba-ba..

But you still wish I'd kept my mouth shut, says Wells.

I think that's difficult for women like you.

What kind of women are women like me?

Overindulged.

What did you think of Koko Man?

Overindulged.

Is that all?

She earns her keep, plus interest.

When I grow up I want a big house like that, declares Mei.

No you don't. Not like that.

She pouts.

Wells sulks too. She tells me she was just trying to help.

There's no helping her. Man's life is powerless, brief and dark. It's impossible to make her happy. And I can't afford to try.

That's deep.

That's TS Eliot.

He was a bit before my time.

Most things are.

Think of it as a financial proposition. Missy was instructed to open the cheque book. A lot of people would pay to be in your position.

A lot of them already have. A cheque is not much good if you're not around to cash it.

Is that what you told Koko?

Not in so many words.

Read your lips, did she? Looks like you gave her quite a firm *no* there.

She passes a tissue and suggests I take a good look at myself in the mirror.

Mrs Man has dignorated my mouth with a rouge smear of approval. I wipe her tell-tale signature away.

She was just showing her appreciation, I posit.

She was showing more than that when we left.

We contemplate this retina-scarring portrait of a lady in silence for the duration of the journey. Crossing Tai Tam Reservoir, I recall Eliot's Waste Land. He knew a thing or two about over-indulged women.

The awful daring of a moment's surrender,

Which an age of prudence can never retract

By this, and this only, we have existed,

Which is not to be found in our obituaries.

Mei never cared for Eliot. She feels his quatrains are laboured and lack a natural cadence. It's not surprising she's asleep by the time we arrive on Redhill. Wells offers to have the guards watch over her, if I want to work on a couplet and see some poetry in motion. I decline. She pretends to be disappointed and makes a comment about equal opportunity employers as she closes the door.

Angel is sitting at my desk. I tell her the executive position suits her. She checks to see if Mei is asleep on my shoulder. I'd take any position tonight, she says. I haven't flushed the pipes in weeks.

I know someone who might be able to help you with that. He's got an industrial strength pump. Your pipes won't know what hit them. One minute it'll be all Nights In White Satin and then pow. Cross-eyed. He could flush them all the way to next Tuesday.

She lifts a box-knife from the table, extends the blade and threatens to perform inoperable surgery.

How was Shek O?

I give her an expurgated version of events, up to Mr Man's four-wheeled exit, then recount Koko's version of the hold-up and how she had to cast her pearls before swine, spread on the hood of the car.

They fucked her with a corn cob?

I don't think they are the type of people who read Faulkner. Let's just say there was no possibility of taking a walk that day.

More into Brontë were they?

Well there was three of them. Seems they wandered in the leafless shrubbery for an hour, until the cold winter wind brought with it a rain so penetrating, further out-door exercise was out of the question. So they took her inside the cottage and went all Heathcliffe on her moors.

Sex is the poor man's opera, Jack. Theatre for the masses.

What does that make oral sex?

The fancy liquor you swill before.

What are you still doing here, Jane Eyre?

Waiting for you, Godot. Isn't that reason enough?

Were you worried I wasn't going to come back at all?

You can't blame me for considering the possibility. I was waiting for Mei, actually, to make sure you didn't take her with you to Kowloon. You're going to see Io Lam.

I didn't know I had an appointment.

He made one for you. Better get your skates on. Curtain goes up at eight.

You should've paged me. It's going to take an hour to get through the tunnel.

She tosses my pager to me. You should've taken it with you. I had to make sure Mei came home anyway. Albinio's orders. No kids.

Why would I go?

You want to know what he was really doing at Belleview, and more about his relationship to Liu Pang. And, in case you haven't been paying attention, we really need someone to look at the *feng shui* here.

She hands me a sheet of paper.

Here's a layout of the office, Jack. He'll want to see it. I wrote Benny's birthday on the back. Mine too. And yours, in case you've forgotten that as well.

What are you going to do while I'm with The Great Pink Hope?

I'll tell Por-por we're having a girl's night in. You can pick Mei up from my place on your way home.

She's right, on all counts. Mei's got more chance of getting a regular night on Ladder Street than in the Happy Valley Mahjong Lounge & Hostel For Itinerant Swallow Wranglers. She stirs briefly as I hand her over but quickly finds comfort on Angel's shoulder.

I love it when you take charge, I tell her.

I wear the pants. And I'll take them off when I'm good and ready.

She calls me a taxi. There's no way I'll find Dumbarton Street on my own. Kowloon Tong might as well be another planet as far as I'm concerned.

Cross-harbor traffic is thick. Crawling through the tunnel gives me time to think about the situation. The opportunity to get out with honour, courage and expectation had passed, if it had ever existed. I was up to my neck in this from the moment Liu Pang called.

I might as well haul myself out of it with some coin, plus expenses.

What to make of the cavalier Koko? Horoko Kitajima. Mrs Man-eater. The intrigues of her family were as offbeat as her relationship with Liu Pang. Then there was his association with Lynne Sprudel. The three-way intersection with Bronson Chung. And Kitty Ho at the centre of it all. Dead or alive she was the only one to get out of this with her reputation intact. Maybe Lam could shed some geomantric light on her fate too. He could look into my prospects for later this evening while he's there.

Should I keep my date with Mrs Man? That was the $64,000 question.

The radio queries the motives of hungerstrikers at the New China News Agency. Another group is burning copies of the Basic Law, contesting their right to pursue a more democratic society post-1997.

The taxi exits the tunnel and moves freely into Waterloo Road. A plastic Garfield clings desperately to my window. Beyond him a 747 approaches Kai Tak, about to take the top off a couple of buildings and paste itself across Checkerboard Hill.

Over Prince Edward and Boundary Street, past The Walled City.

Fifty dollars there would get you a bucket of Blue Girl and someone to take the top off your bottle, with change for cigarettes and a ride home. Like the past it was a foreign country. They do things differently there.

Waterloo Road dives straight into Kowloon Tong.

A sprawling labyrinth of schools, hospitals and one-hour love motels dominates the landscape. The vital pillars of any community.

The driver swings two laps of La Salle before locating Dumbarton. Narrow and dark, the building we're looking for resides in a blind alley.

Lam's black Mercedes occupies two parking bays. A pensioner, in singlet and pyjama pants, wanders between vehicles. A cigarette is stuck to his lower lip. He gives me a disinterested glance and disappears into a small room. He's probably been living there since the liberation of the colony. Security is not a high priority in older buildings. Random acts of violence and domestic burglaries are relatively uncommon. The same cannot be said for domestic violence and daylight robbery. It's a dichotomy that distinguishes Hong Kong from a lot of cities, and makes the whole Liu-Man affair so extraordinary.

I ride the ancient elevator to the sixth floor. It stops with a jolt. I slide the iron gate open and advance on the lair of the white worm.

There should be four apartments on this dimly lit corridor. Yet each security grill tells me to *Please Use Main Entry*. Io Lam must occupy the whole floor. He's done well, for a snake-oil salesman. People with more money than sense must pay through the nose for a little practical judgment and fortune-cookie wisdom.

I ring the bell beside a clean white door.

A CCTV camera observes me from above. The electronic buzz and snap of a lock tells me to push the heavy door.

It feels like there's inches of steel beneath the wooden veneer.

The clinically waxen room is wide and deep. Against the back wall, behind a small antique writing desk, a chubby man squats on a round stool. He's clad in a charcoal gray Mao suit. Bald and epalpebrate, his fat round face looks empty. Tiny eyes struggle to be seen behind round glasses perched on the conical snub of his nose, above a puckered cat's-bum mouth. His hands are clasped on the surface of the altar, a pad of paper and sharpened pencil within reach. Nothing else. Not even a telephone.

The door shuts behind me with a foreboding clunk.

You are Jack So?

I am.

You are late.

I am? I mean yes, I am.

A narrow moat bisects the room. I step upon a broad, flat stone and cross the great divide. Koi swim beneath my feet, *agitato*. To my left a granite obelisk rises from the inky shallows. It supports a small basin. Water cascades down the miniature mountain within. A quartz sphere spins at the peak. Its quiet trickle echoes off the walls.

You are coming with me, please, Mr Jack So.

Where? I wonder. There are no doors on his side of the Rubicon.

I follow his portly path to a corner. Another camera is wedged into its apex. He presses the wall. A two-meter panel swings in.

He leads me from one large, ghostly room in the Korova Milk Bar to another.

Io Lam sits beside a low, antique painting table. Pu Yi probably signed his life away atop its rich, lacquered Rosewood. It is a barren plane, devoid of standard business tokens and essomenic chattels, save for a small ceramic pot and two cups.

Great. Another tea ceremony. Henry James must be out there, somewhere, pissing himself at the diuretic agreeableness of it all.

The windows behind Lam are black. In daylight they would offer panoramic views of West Kowloon Park. Tonight they are a thick swathe of ink amongst the white parchment of walls. He motions to a pair of Huanghuali chairs.

So simple, so refined. So expensive.

I'm in a nouveau Imperial chamber. Lam completes the picture. A caricature in black silk Mandarin-collar tunic, fastened with elegant knots and loops. The usual good fortune and longevity symbols are embroidered upon it along with, atypically, a number of bats. Go figure. No doubt they have the power to amplify prosperity and turn the kismet up to eleven.

He studies my face as I approach. I return the compliment.

He's older than I thought. Closer to sixty than forty. The albedineity of his skin matches the walls. His pink eyes are calm and project a certain serenity. He has a cultivated, knowledgeable countenance.

This probably means he's a mess of insecurities and anxiety.

Lam places a cup before me, and I recall the last time I accepted *cha* from a stranger. I remind myself to sip politely from it. Once, and once only. Until I'm sure there are no artificial sweeteners or sinister motives to Mr Lam's invitation.

THANK-YOU FOR JOINING ME.

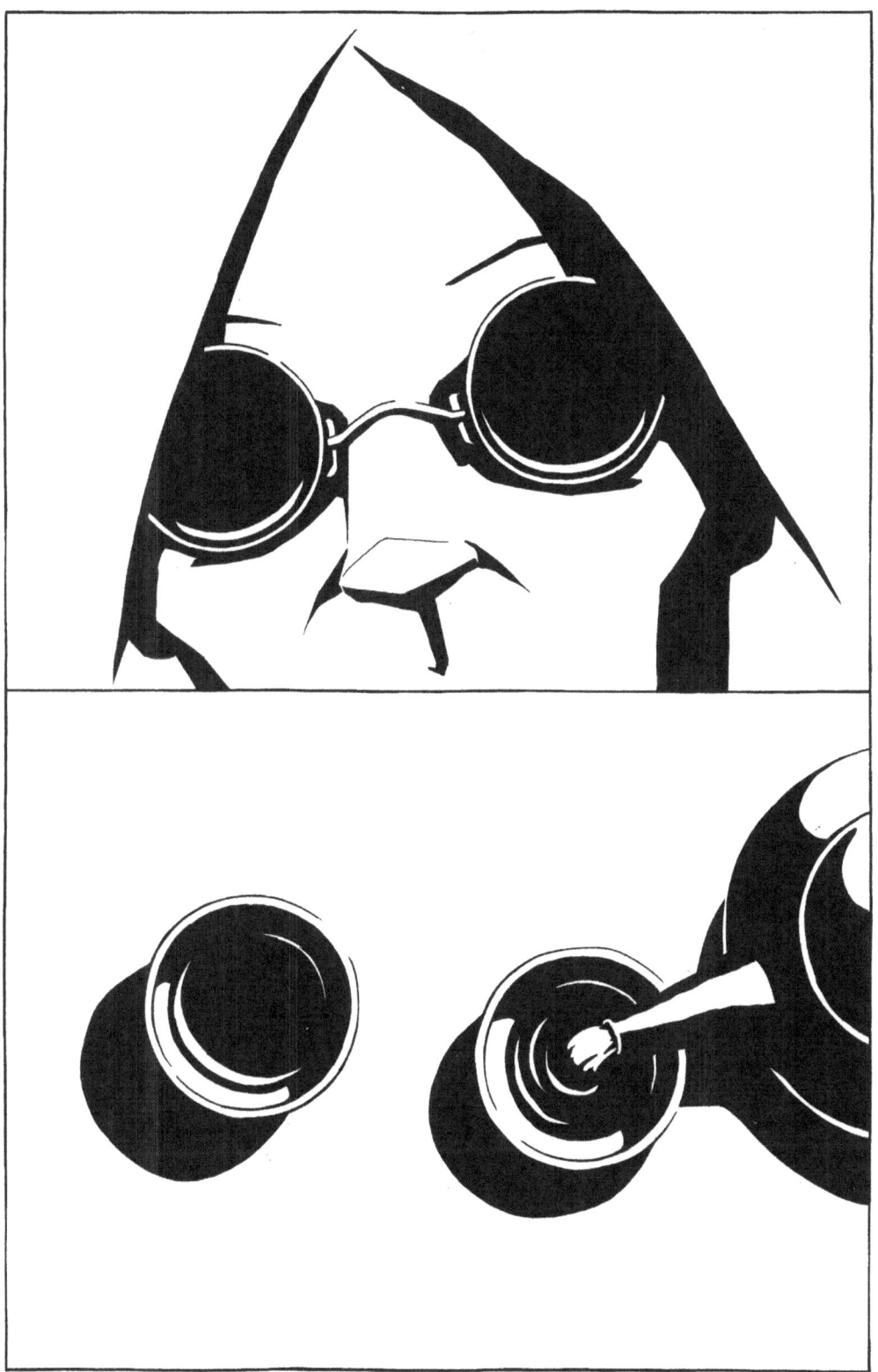

No, thank *you*. I know how busy you must be. And how fortunate I am to have secured a consultation.

He smiles, a flat line of acknowledgement.

I ask if the meter is running. Do I have to pay extra for the tea? I didn't really order it.

He doesn't appreciate this as much as he enjoyed the fawning.

Perhaps we can start with your birthday, Mr So?

February seventeen.

What year?

Every year.

He is not amused. I pull Angel's schematic from my pocket and present it to him. Here's one I prepared earlier.

His blonde eyebrows continue to disapprove. He takes a sharpened pencil from a hidden draw in the lip of the table and makes notes upon the paper.

It has not been a good year for you, he says.

You don't know half of it. Actually, you probably do, if you're half as good as they say you are. I bet you know all of it. How's the year ahead looking?

It will be difficult for the remainder of The Dragon. For you and your family. There are things you can do to improve your outlook. The Year Of The Snake bodes well for those on the cusp of The Chicken and The Dog.

And for the word *bode* it seems. It's really *de rigueur* these days. Could you narrow it down a bit? Be a little more specific? On a scale of one to ten, with ten being the sole winner of Mark Six and one being Liu Pang, how well does The Snake bode?

He scrutinizes me, and places his pencil on the table.

Did you come here to discuss your fate, or Liu Pang's?

You invited me, remember?

I was extending a professional courtesy. Perhaps you could reciprocate.

Okay, professionally speaking, was it Liu Pang's fate or a *fait accompli*? Did you see it coming? I know he didn't.

I don't discuss my clients.

You don't seem too worried by the grisly demise of them either.

Perhaps if he had listened more.

You sound angry.

I am upset.

With him for not listening, or me for asking?

With you both. It grieves me when people have opportunities to avoid misfortune or unpleasant situations and choose not to take them.

It would've taken quite something to avoid the twelve guages of ruin Dame Fortune broadsided him with that night.

Sometimes all you have to do is heed the words of another.

If he'd moved his bed, changed the colour of a rug, installed water features, put a golden ox in the corner of the house and kept a pig in his pocket, would he still be here?

We'll never know. And, now, I think your attitude signals an end to any help I may have been willing to offer. My clients have personal issues and private concerns. It would be unprofessional to broach them. I'm not sure how it works in your business, Mr So, but in mine one does not pull up the planks after crossing the bridge.

Go on. It's not going to make any difference to Liu Pang. He's already gone to the other side and isn't looking to come back.

I have many clients. If I were to betray their confidence…

It wouldn't bode well for you. I get it. You don't want to eat from their bowl and turn it over. But I also have clients with concerns related to Liu's recent activities.

His family are welcome to contact me. You are neither kindred, friend nor associate as far as I am aware.

He was my client. I was hired to protect him for the evening, perhaps from something you warned him about or, quite possibly, from you.

If you'll pardon my frankness, Mr So, you didn't do a very good job protecting him from anything. You should look into your handling of said affairs, rather than the deeds of others. Any obligation I have to divulge information regarding Liu will be a matter for the police to decide, not you.

I can arrange that, if you like. They'd be interested in what you were doing there the morning of his murder, and what the two of you were working on.

How well did you know Liu Pang, Mr So?

Like a brother.

He never mentioned you.

More like a Catholic Brother. I kept him at arm's length. We were close in the spiritual sense. I was the last person to see his soul as it disappeared into the ether. If you're unwilling to talk about him perhaps you can tell me if you know Koko Man.

Of course.

Did you know she knew Liu, intimately?

I don't think I am betraying anyone when I say that the depth of their friendship was common knowledge.

They have you in common too.

And you, it seems. All too common.

I'm not sure where to go from here. Home might be nice. I decide to adopt a bit of Mao Theory and see where that takes me instead.

The best tactic in the struggle against a prevailing enemy, is an adroit elasticity and ceaseless tormenting of the opponent.

I think Liu ate rice in his slippers, I tell him. He lived off women, the same way Koko Man lives off men. Someone wanted to compromise their relationship. Probably to leverage her or, more likely, her husband. And I think your angle is as predatory as theirs. Or, at the very least, it operates on the same business model. I don't know what this session is going to cost me but I doubt it will cover your overhead and meet your margins. I'm a small businessman too and I bet you need another stream of revenue to make it through the year. I've got a child, mother-in-law and two barmaids to support. What are you propping up?

Lam presses his thin lips together and stands.

I hear the tranquil waft of the door opening behind me. Roly-poly's crassulent frame is reflected in the windows.

Unless that's Sammo Hung stitched into that outfit, Lam, you're going to need a little more than Totoro here to throw me out.

Another hidden door opens to my right. Three large orientals, bedecked in gray Mao suits, enter.

That's more like it.

I brace myself for The Hidari Brothers.

Plegnic hits beneath my ribs remove all air from my lungs. I'm on the verge of losing consciousness and I haven't even managed to upset a chair.

The albino leaves through the tradesman's entrance.

Come back here, I gurgle, gallant in defeat like Monty Python's Black Knight. The flow of my *chi* is being severely restricted. You're still on the clock, I croak. This is where you can really earn your money! Come on! Dazzle me!

I'm not sure if I've passed out or merely closed my eyes for an extended period. As the darkness lifts I find I'm in much the same position, and pain.

Lam has returned. He's flanked by two solid enforcers. With all this extra beefcake in the room it's starting to feel like a gay nightclub. The standard issue haircuts on these two suggest they're police officers. Detectives. The Drebin and Nordberg of local law enforcement. An unremarkable pair. Average height. Average weight. Average intelligence. I assume the latter from the way they tilt their gullivers to one side, like confused Shih Tzu, as the albino relates his version of events. It's actually quite accurate, albeit a little skewed to his point of view. Still, as they say, history is written by the winners.

You got here just in time, I say. These men are detaining me against my will.

Nordberg can almost see the funny side of this. His sense of duty is all that prevents him.

It has been suggested you became aggressive during a consultation and had to be restrained, he says. There is an audio-visual recording to corroborate this.

VHS, Beta or laser-disc?

Mr Lam has decided not to press charges. He understands you have been in some distressing situations recently and believes you may be acting out of character.

I wonder if the albino and Koko get their munificence from the same place. In the spirit of the occasion, I decide not to make a formal complaint.

Lam's hands are clasped within the baggy sleeves of his tunic. He declares our business at an end and asks the detectives to ensure I leave the premises. There will be no charge for the consultation, he adds, as I'm frog-marched to the door.

Descending in the elevator, Nordberg wants to know what I was doing there.

I had an appointment. What were you doing there?

Lam called. We were informed a man associated with the Teplice and Liu murders was in his office. And his behaviour was becoming aggressive. We've seen a section of the tape. It looks and sounds like you were threatening him.

He records everything? Isn't that a little strange?

A man has to protect his interests.

You just happened to be in the neighbourhood? Was it an official visit, or a courtesy call? Not everyone has Peelers on-demand. You must be freelancing. And that's okay. We all have to make ends meet. Do you charge by the hour, the size of the job, or do you get a percentage of profits?

Where can we drop you? says Nordberg, opening the rear door of a Toyota.

What time is it?

Bed time.

A hand slides across my face. Darkness swallows me and, with all the abruptness of a dozen martinis on an empty stomach, I labascate into the night.

14. KOWLOON TONG

I'm in a miasmatic fugue. Like Gregor Samsa in Kafka's Metamorphosis I find myself atop a bed, transformed into a giant insect. Nostrils ablaze. Fetor. Cigarette maladour. Aporrhoea. Lights pop and flash. Naked silhouettes. Faceless women. Cold, musky skin. Giggling. Throaty laughter. Lights. I'm lying down. I try to turn, to see something. Anything. My arms are heavy. A silky Cantonese voice tells me to relax. I struggle against the cheap perfume. That's enough, says a familiar tone. I seek it out. My eyes sting. My lungs burn.

If this is a dream, what is this blackness I'm fading into now?

There's light under the door. My mouth is dry. My eyes creak and itch. I sit up in a small windowless room, naked. An air-conditioner hums a pointless tune. The oubliette is heavy with the mephitic fetor of moral degradation and the murmur of spiritual putrefaction. Sticky. Odorous. Odious. It is dark, dirty and deathly still.

A bottle of water sits on the bedside table. I drain it.

I squeeze life into a small lamp. The globe goes supernova and temporarily blinds me. The sensory overload bites my brain and punches me in the throat. I gag, double over and slaughter the white crane, regurgitating water on stained carpet. Burns, blood and bodily fluids.

The interior design is from the Early Nothing period. Faded wallpaper has been perspiring without relief for years. The lumpy mattress lies uncomfortably on a base of wood-boxes. Emaciated sheets, once white, are now yellow. Soiled.

I look at my watch. Three thirty-three. Angel will be out of her mind.

My clothes have been thrown over an old chair. Wallet, check. Pager, check. Half a dozen messages, check. It's still the same night so, technically, I'm not a completely missing person. I just don't know where I am. Only a handful of people do and at least two of them are police.

A small bathroom *en suite*. The opposite of posh.

I take a piss, not bothering to lift the seat. From the look of the boot marks on it, neither did Han Xin when he squatted there.

I wash my face.

There's a complimentary toothbrush. Gee, they've thought of everything. I brush my teeth. Twice. Three times. It's like they've been roasting garlic in my mouth. I see a swab of gauze by the wastebasket. I wave it under my nose. It burns. I almost feint and have to steady myself on the frame of the door.

Chloroform? Ether? Some kind of flurane? Durian?

I wobble to the bed and sit, until I feel confident enough to stand, summoning the energy to kick this situation out of neutral.

Beyond the walls, a muffled radio or television argues with the early hours. Further out, cars. Minibuses shift gears. A jet passes low in the sky. I gingerly approach the door and slowly turn the handle. Whoever is in charge of security will have some explaining to do in the morning. Through a narrow crack in the cheap timber I see a long, jaundiced passage. I know this type of set-up. It's a by-the-hour hotel. A love motel.

Time to check-out.

A pudgy man in dirty slacks and faux Versace shirt dozes in a chair by the door. Beneath him, a bloated ashtray and an untidy collection of San Miguel cans. I retreat into the room and pick the gauze from the waste basket. Taking it in one hand, and the red badge of courage in the other, I return to the sleeping sentinel.

He struggles briefly as I hold the cotton swabs over his nose. He soon becomes a dead weight and I drag him into the room.

The cold pressed reluctantly from the earth, and the retiring fogs revealed an army stretched out on the hills, resting.

I sidle quietly, almost comically, down the hall. John Belushi. Animal House. The mission into Dean Wormer's office.

There's a half-open door on my left. Low voices compete with the gogglebox. Maybe it's the bridal suite. Whatever they're watching it doesn't sound like scheduled late-night programming. Over-zealous moans, squeaks and slurps suggest Swedish adult videos.

Kärlekens Språk. Language Of Love.

The only way out of here is across Pornographers Gap. I inch toward it. My field of vision expands. The dank interior in panorama. Cinemascope. More Kafka-esque than Kafka. Metamorphosis. The beast with two backs has its backs to me.

A thin mirror frames a lean Mong Kok mistress, hair frazzled by a full-length perm. She's on all fours at the edge of a bed. Back hollow, neck extended, eyes closed in the throes of faux passion. She grinds, coos and hyperventilates without conviction. Penetrating her, pants around his knees, is Bronson *Lion Tamer* Chung. The emperor's naked army marches on, *allegrissimo*. Eyes glued to a television in the corner, his rhythm tells me I don't have a lot of time to play with. Completing the perversion, a large video camera has been mounted on a tripod to monitor his tardy tryst. Misery makes the strangest bedfellows.

I step across the void.

Mong Kok's Marilyn Chambers opens her eyes, seeking a horse while riding an ox. The bored, ocular strips nail me. Her thin lips part. A small tongue performs sickly lambitions, her interpretation of wanton carnality. More derisible than desirable. She closes her eyes and works her grindstone with an overcooked groan. Perhaps her life is complicated enough. Or maybe her privileged upbringing and notions of etiquette dictate an over-riding, single-minded commitment to those in her immediate orbit.

A hearty sexuality inspires both to the right estimation of the faculties and qualities of each other.

I put the teterrimous scene behind me and move quickly down the corridor, careening into a man who has chosen the wrong time to enter the hall.

He's as surprised by my appearance as I am by his.

I don't normally assault people who are drawing a pension, let alone push their nose out the back of their skull. In my defence, however, I only become aware of his age as he drops to the patchy carpet.

The walls are too thin to mask this dramatic increase in activity.

Chung shouts a couple of names, demanding attention. I bolt down a flight of stairs, across the foyer, into an empty carpark. A malnourished lad approaches. I deal with this *asigaru*, the lowest of the foot soldiers, in the same way I Travis-Bickled the veteran upstairs. Swiftly, with extreme prejudice.

I burst onto the street.

All the animals come out at night. Whores, skunk pussies, buggers, queens, fairies, dopers, junkies, sick, venal. Someday a real rain will come and wash all this scum off the streets.

The pillar at the entrance says 41 Cumberland Road.

I turn left for no reason other than I remember Batman once told Robin that when you're in a maze you should always make left turns. I make another at Rutland and run into the path of a green Public Light Bus. One of these took my wife. Now it's going to save my life. I force the driver to make an unscheduled stop and claim a seat next to an old woman. Her smile says she knows what I've been up to, at this hour of night in this part of town. My musky odour confirms her suspicions.

I'm going to need another AIDS test, aren't I?

We cross Cumberland and pull onto the main artery, within walking distance of Io Lam's funhouse. It's on the opposite side of Waterloo Road.

I drop a dollar into the fare collection box.

Amazing what you can get for a buck these days.

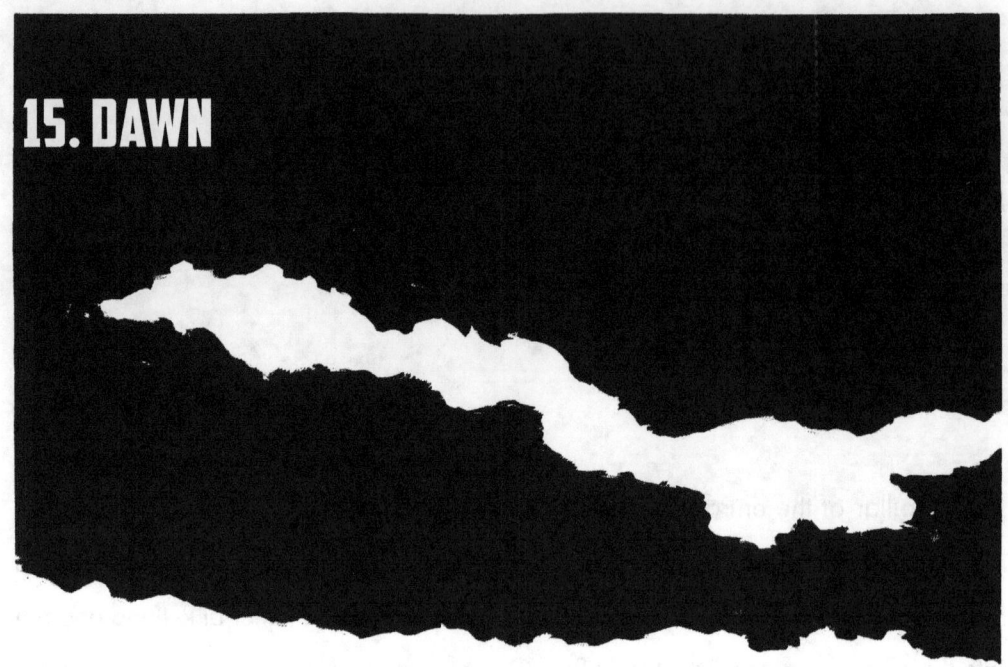

15. DAWN

The bus terminates at the Peninsula Hotel. This was where General Isogai established his command during the Japanese occupation. The capitulation of Hong Kong was signed here on Boxing Day, 1941. The teppanyaki has been great ever since. If I was going to subject a detained terrain to martial law I'd do it from an illustrious five-star hotel as well. It's not like I'd have to pick up the tab on my way out.

Our soldiers are not overburdened with money, not because they have distaste for riches. If their lives are not unduly long, it is not because they are disinclined to longevity.

The doorman hails a cab. The driver is dressed for covert operations deep behind the bamboo curtain. Beret. Aviator sunglasses. Camouflage jacket. A golf glove on his left hand. I question him about it. The glove. He says it's because he is a driver, and a passenger once told him that golf gloves and drivers go hand in hand.

I can't decide if this is a golf joke, or a taxi joke. Both have their own peculiar brand of humour.

He's been waiting all night for me to turn up, so he can discuss this and George Bush's victory in the US elections. He thinks it's amazing that Michael Jackson came so close to being elected President.

I explain that Jesse Jackson and Michael Jackson are not the same person.

Bah! Those Jacksons all look the same, he says. They were in the same band. Five of them, right? What were there names?

Michael, Tito, Jermaine, Jesse and... I can never remember the other one.

No one can! So sad for him, to be the fifth brother!

I exit the taxi at the temple on Hollywood Road. And not a moment too soon. A Canto-pop version of Kokomo came within seconds of destroying my will to live.

I'm grateful for the support of the handrail as I navigate the path on Ladder Street. I can feel every crack and pore in the concrete as I ascend the three flights of Dante's stairs to Angel's apartment.

It's almost four-thirty by the time she opens the door.

Her aging t-shirt barely makes it past her thighs. FRANKIE SAYS RELAX it shouts at me. This is ironic, given the worry on her brow and agitated state of her breasts. Her eyes offer a brief glimpse of relief before concern paves the way for anger. She says nothing. Only when she stands aside do I know I have permission to enter.

I try to squeeze by without coming into contact with her extremities.

It's a small, carefully appointed room. Clean to the eye, fresh on the nose. There's an underlying scent of baby powder, although that could be coming from my host's skin. A lamp lights the corner, next to pots of leafy plants. Posters of classic French films hang on the walls. Le Samouraï. La Belle et La Bête. Les Quatre Cents Coups. I remember when she lent Benny a copy of her Truffaut, and how disappointed he was to find out The 400 Blows had nothing to do with oral sex.

The glow of Betty Blue 37º2 Le Matin from the television reveals the callipygian curves beneath Angel's nightshirt as she walks to the kitchen.

It occurs to me this is the first time I've seen her sans pony-tail, hair cascading over those resolute, redoubtable shoulders. There's no diamond studs adorning her ears either. She looks naked without them. I blush at the thought of her unbridled genetic advantage and lobes *au naturel.*

Water, or something else? she calls from the scullery.

Water, gallons of it. Cold. Just throw a bucket of it over me.

I sit on the floor, against the burgundy love-lounge, beneath a grainy Alain Delon.

How you doing, Costello? Got nothing to say? Killed anyone lately?

Angel places a jug of iced water and small glasses on the coffee table.

Mei-mei's in my bed.

I couldn't think of a better place to be. For her, I mean. For me, too. Bed is where we should both be, is what I was trying to say. At home. You know what I mean. What did you guys get up to?

Movie night. Totoro, again. She drops a cushion on the floor and lowers herself to the lotus position. How about you, Jack? I hope Lam wasn't charging by the hour.

That consultation could bankrupt us. Or did you accept Mrs Man's invitation to see The Sleeping Princess In The Devil's Castle as well?

That would've been the smart thing to do, I say, chasing shots of water with shots of water. I had a night out with the boys instead, on Cumberland.

Cumberland Road? Not in one of those-

41.

41 Cumberland Road?

You know it? I didn't imagine you as a by-the-hour proposition.

How did you imagine me? Everyone knows it, Jack. That's Bruce Lee's house. Whose idea was it to go there?

Not mine. Lam may have had a hand in it. I doubt the cops that gang-banged me would've had the initiative or inclination.

Police? What happened?

I went to see Lam. He didn't like the cut of my jib and had a couple of his boys show me the way of the dragon. I came-to at Chez Kato. Free but lost. A non-writing writer, a monster courting insanity. Kafka's afflatus and all that.

Urgh, nightmare. I never finished The Castle.

Neither did Kafka.

It must've been awful.

Metamorphosis was worse, ask anyone.

You smell worse, I can tell you that.

She reaches beneath the coffee table, retrieves a small cigarette case and pulls out a Camberwell Carrot. She lights it, draws a healthy lungful and deals me an ace. If copping a bomber means getting rid of the cat turd in my mouth, I'll try anything. It's not like I haven't earned it.

What are you going to do about your new friends, Jack?

Friends like that I don't need.

You think they'll just drop it? Leave you and the rest of us alone?

I'm beginning to think I've nudged the mighty mezz enough for now. Her shirt is starting to blend with the milk of her thighs. I can feel another metamorphosis coming on.

Why put you into storage, Jack? Is Lam in the Man-Liu triangle?

Two people is not a triangle.

It would be if he were in it.

He might set them up, I just can't see him knocking them down. I guess all their paths would have to cross at some point.

Maybe they collided. The past comes unbidden or not at all.

Maybe they did, I agree, wondering when she found the time to interrogate Proust. And wishing she hadn't.

Maybe he framed Roger Rabbit, and arranged the photo shoot on Belleview.

Now I'm distracted by thoughts of her dressed as Jessica Rabbit.

I'm not bad. I'm just drawn that way.

These words, combined with all the airmail from Mazatlan, trigger a flashback.

I see the writhing nymph with the cheap perfume on Cumberland. The strobing blasts of light. Lam's predilection for audio-visual recordings.

Maybe I can expect a few doctor shots of my own. They'll expose me if I expose them. Maybe it's not money they want. They're buying silence. Compromising is better than killing. They own me.

Another yellow-legged chicken caught and stuffed.

The best soldier does not attack, the superior fighter succeeds without violence and the greatest conqueror wins without struggle.

So why kill Liu? I beseech the Tao Te Fuk.

Maybe it's not a triangle. Maybe it's a square.

Don't let the geometry distract you.

Maybe that's part of their cunting plan.

Cunning, I correct her.

They sound like a bunch of cunts to me.

This cracks me up. I laugh until I dehydrate and my lips stick to my teeth. I stave off the dry horrors with a shot of water, and get the dialectic back on track.

Koko is connected to Liu, and Liu is connected to Lam. And I don't think there was too much love lost between them.

So many two-headed snakes in this nest of vipers.

Maybe Liu Pang had rubbed others the wrong way too. He's got a string of disgruntled ex-wives.

In love and revenge a woman is more barbaric than man, she says, getting all Nietzschean in her perspectivism.

I've learned that the hard way, I admit, feeling positively nihilistic and rapidly losing the will to power.

Every man does. It's Herodotus' eternal law of retribution and reprisal, Jack. An eye for an eye. Don't underestimate the obligation. It's as important as Face. You don't follow up on it, you and your family can be cursed forever.

I was just going to suggest that one of his cash cows had grown weary of him feeding off her finances, I say, wishing she'd stuck with Proust.

What's a cash cow? asks a sleepy voice from across the room.

Mei stands in the half-light of the door to Angel's bedroom. She's clutching a Care Bear. It's time we all made a move.

Herodotus was right about that too.

Human happiness never remains long in the same place.

16. GOSSIP & INNUENDO

The early morning machinations of the gypsy insurgents ensures my bizarre sleep deprivation experiment continues. The *jigoku-tabi* marches on.

Mei remains undisturbed by the overzealous chatter and clatter.

I pull a stiff pair of jeans up and attempt to drag a starched t-shirt down, and discover a whole new set of tenellous muscles in the process. It's like I've been water-skiing, played two halves of rugby and engaged in a rigorous bout of sexual activity. Experience tells me the pain will be figuring-on-biggering by this time tomorrow.

So, you know, I have that to look forward to.

I brush my teeth and wonder if I'm ever going to get that fetid dryness from the inside of my cheeks. I scrub and rinse again. And again. It's not helping but it is therapeutic all the same.

Looks of disapproval are in season in the living room, something I don't want or need in the sanctity of my own home. I get enough of it at the office, for free.

Gu-por thinks Mei should spend the day with her family. I thank her for the offer and suggest we see what Mei feels like doing when she wakes.

Bing presents me with a double espresso. It scolds my lips, singes my tongue, cauterizes the phantom cat turd within and neutralizes the olfactory receptors.

I might just make it to the elevator.

In an unnerving coincidence, Angel has also opted for blue jeans and a white t-shirt. I wish I looked half as good in mine. She throws on a weary smile as I approach.

Oldham and Cyclops Chau have decided to join our morning work-in-progress meeting. They're wearing matching outfits too. Oldham's suit is Bobby Kennedy blue. Chau's is Jack Ruby brown, flecked with dandruff and struggling to contain the critical mass of its occupant.

Oh look, it's Jake and The Fat Man. Why aren't you on Nathan Road arresting whoever fitted you for those bags of fruit.

Have a good time last night, Jack?

I don't know what your idea of a good time is but it wasn't mine.

Anyone we know?

Depends on the company you're keeping.

The same company as you, it seems. Police business. Ring any bells?

Funny business, police business.

No funnier than yours.

At least I don't come around to your office and criticize you for doing it.

We got a call.

You wait by the phone for long enough and it will eventually ring.

Officers in Kowloon say they had a run-in with you.

Is that what they called it? I guess one man's run-in is another man's cold-cocking and kidnapping.

They had to escort you from a building.

They didn't have to. I was about to leave when they stepped in and brought the meeting to a rapid conclusion.

Seems to be the way a lot of things end with you these days.

What's this got to do with you, Oldham? Kowloon's not your beat.

I'm involved because you, and others with more influence in my career, are getting involved. I'm trying to do half a dozen people a favour, including you.

Sorry, I don't get it.

Why did you go see lo Lam?

You don't think my luck could use a little upward momentum?

Fortune comes in many guises.

What are you saying?

There's a theory Liu was not an unwilling participant in the extortion. And now you're looking to carry on from where he departed. To clean up where he fucked up.

Like it paid off for him?

I move to walk away.

Chau takes a step toward me.

Oldham raises an arm, diffusing the explosive possibilities of the moment.

I've read the reports, Jack. What Liu and Horoko Man got up to behind their spouses backs is not new. Neither are dirty pictures and blackmail.

How many people get killed for them?

We were told you tried to implicate Lam in Liu Pang's murder.

Did they tell you why they left me to fester in Bruce Lee's living room?

They said they followed you there.

Sure, me and Jimmy Swaggart. I bet they've got the pictures to prove it. Can you get doubles of the prints when they drop off the film? I want a set for the family album.

They thought you had a date there. It's a popular spot for discreet couples.

And threesomes. It can't be that discreet if everyone knows about it.

Is there something you want to tell me?

I told you all I know. Maybe there's something I'm missing. Connect your dots for me. See if we end up with the same picture of Dorian Gray. I bet you know more than you think you know, and less than you want to.

Liu lived off women, although probably not for women.

They were the means to a stipend.

And Koko was cut from the same cloth.

Except when a woman marries again it's because she detested her first husband. When a man marries again it's because he adored his first wife.

Optimism over experience.

Women try their luck, men risk theirs.

Liu was trying to put together a property deal. A couple of deals. He got creative with the financing. Produced an art film. Someone wanted in on his action, or him out of theirs. A botched pay-off for some unsavoury snaps with the wife of an esteemed business leader makes it all make sense. Finding someone who's actually saddened by his death is quite difficult. The list of people with motives is growing exponentially.

NEVER
DISAPPOINT
A WIDOW.

WHAT DO
YOU MEAN
BY THAT?

SOMETHING FROM
A CONVERSATION
WITH HOROKO MAN,
ABOUT THE DIFFERENCE
BETWEEN BEDDING
SOMEONE'S MOTHER
OR THEIR DAUGHTER.

Or it collided head-on with someone else's future.

Liu knew something was coming.

That's why he called me at the last minute.

How did he know to call you, Jack?

How does anyone know? How do you know?

We have a history.

So do I. It's no secret. It's well documented too. Nothing illegal, of course.

You've never been caught. Doesn't mean you haven't done anything wrong.

I could say the same thing to you.

But you wouldn't.

You're an officer of the law, Oldham. An incorruptible pillar of society. The thought is inconceivable.

You, on the other hand, were privy to a homicide in Wan Chai and seen in the company of the only suspect. You're also the sole witness of another murder and were conspiring with the victim, a celebrated humanitarian, in the hours prior to his brutal demise. You've been observed visiting spouses, intimate acquaintances and business associates of both the deceased. Now we have reports of you disappearing into a motel known to be a front for triad activities and frequented by prostitutes. And that's just this week.

I clap slowly.

Well done. All you need now is the link between me and the missing girl. You'll have this whole basket of crabs wrangled, trussed up and locked away.

Missing girl?

It's where this started, remember? Come on. I know Chau's only got one eye, but what's your excuse?

A man looking for a hooker? That's every night of the week. Kitty Ho is everywhere and nowhere. We don't even know what she looks like.

Yes you do.

Those pictures of yours are five years old, maybe more.

You saw her. Worth killing for?

Men have killed for a whole lot less, but you and Bronson Chung are the only ones with hard-ons for Kitty Ho. Him, I can understand. You? I don't get it.

It's the Madonna-whore thing. I'm looking for redemption. Absolution. Where men love they have no desire, where they desire they cannot love. And all that crap.

Is that what aroused your interest in the affairs of the late Liu Pang? You see it in Koko Man? That I can understand.

She more your type, is she?

I couldn't afford her on my salary. You flashy advertising types, however.

I'm a cheap date. You've seen the places I hang out in.

What were you doing there last night? Cumberland Road?

It wasn't my idea to go molrowing, if that's what you're asking. Caterwauling with disease-ridden strumpets is not my idea of night out.

What happened?

I don't really know, but if you guys have been observing it then maybe you should look a little harder. You might see a certain sought-after suspect slipping in and out. And I mean that in every possible way.

Chau checks his pager. Lynne Sprudel is dead, he says.

Oldham looks at me. I raise my hands, a show of innocence. For the first time in days I can honestly say I know nothing about it.

Maybe my luck is changing.

17. NINE LIVES

Oldham doesn't waste time getting me to Old Bailey. Sprudel's death is one coincidence too many.

I have an alibi, I protest. It'll probably be available on video by tomorrow.

We know what time you went in to forty-one Cumberland. We don't know when you came out.

Ask your colleagues in Kowloon. I bet they know.

I'm standing by a window at the top of Central Station, looking into the street. An old man struggles to carry a cane basket, laden with offal, from the back of his push-bike to a small restaurant. The base of the basket gives way. Guts and vital organs spew onto the pavement. He ponders his situation, puts the basket sideways on the pavement and sweeps the offal back into it with his foot. It's takes a couple of trips to complete the delivery. He continues his mission as best he can, hoping no one notices yet not caring if anyone does.

The restaurant staff are of a similar persuasion.

Inside the station others grapple with their role in the food chain. At least I'm not the only one with a crime wave breaking around me.

A triad gang attacked a hairdresser at the 7-11. Stabbed him to death with barbecue forks. There's been three armed holdups across the island in the last twelve hours. Masked bandits got away with millions.

Oldham enters the room and throws a manila folder on the table.

What kind of person kills cats?

I know the answer to his question but decline to answer. It sounded rhetorical.

Someone has caved in Lynne Sprudel's gulliver with a bottle of gin. The expensive stuff. Then they went Ivan The Terrible on the feline population. Hazel heard rowdy behaviour coming from upstairs and called the police. She went to check on her good friend and neighbour.

Sprudel was irredivivous amongst the kitty litter.

I ask Oldham if this gives him license to pay an official visit to the motel on Cumberland.

You said it yourself, Jack. It's not my beat. I could suggest someone take a look but what would be the point?

Finding the perpetrator of a double homicide?

We don't know it was Chung.

Who killed all those cats? I wonder who that could've been?

If we send someone in they'll know we're coming before we get out of the carpark. My sphere of influence stops at the tunnel. I go over there I have to pay the toll like everyone else. I get something or someone that says Chung was in that house on Bowen Road, and that he's banging whores in Bruce Lee's lounge room, they have to listen. That's all they have to do. I can't crash a fuckpad unless there's a legitimate complaint. And you're not going to file one, are you? There isn't a law against sex. Not even bad sex. So go back to work and we'll take care of the rest.

Don't look back or I'll fall down the stairs. I get it, Rudyard. What am I going to tell the Man family?

Why do you have to tell them anything?

They're a client.

Koko Man is advertising her wares now?

Women like that don't need to advertise. Plenty of business comes her way.

I hear they're lining up. You at the front of the queue?

At Darius Man's request, with Missy's blessing. They asked me to look into the death of a beloved friend and help retrieve a priceless family heirloom.

Your obligation to them stops where the murders begin. What I can tell you, officially, is that has nothing to do with this.

Nothing to do with it? Like the bits of Liu's left brain have nothing to do with his right? Like they're obviously part of the same thing, just not in a way you can piece together? Liu had a deal with Sprudel regarding her husband's pub. And they're all dead.

We know, Jack. The wheels turn, no matter how slow. Don't let your curiosity and Boy Scout creed override your self-preservation. Don't let your relationship with me embolden your confidence.

You'll have me up for Chico Mendes and Lockerbie by next week.

All I'm saying is you're not above the law.

That's a privilege reserved for your mob.

And your new friends in The Forbidden City on Prospect Point. Don't forget that, Jack. The rest of us have to abide.

Or end up like Liu? Like Nifty and Lynne Sprudel? I'm the only one involved in this who doesn't think they're above it all. Present company excluded, of course.

You going to make a deal of the discrepancy between your version of last night and the official one?

Are they going to make a deal out of it? Are they looking for a deal? What kind of deal?

Nothing's been filed. Like I said, calls were made. In everyone's best interests.

Who gets Nifty's estate now? Who's interest is that in? Liu had a deal with Sprudel. Signed, sealed and undelivered. Who's his beneficiary? Who's hers?

The body's not even cold, Jack. We'll find out.

Someone has hung up a goat's head and they're selling dog meat, Oldham. And it's not me.

I look out the window. Down in the street the old delivery man stands by his bicycle, ruptured basket in hand. He stares into it, through the hole.

Taxis are thin on the ground but I don't have to wait for a ride. Oldham pulls up in his war-issue Land Cruiser.

Get in. I'll drop you back at the office.

I'm sure you've got better things to do. Crimes to solve. Hawkers to arrest. Murders to ignore.

Keeping you off the streets is part of our latest crime prevention initiative. We've noticed Jack-related deaths decline when we know where you are. Besides, you paid for a round trip. What would your mother-in-law think of me if I didn't bring you home before midnight?

I climb in. He tells me to buckle up. I put on the seat-belt.

See. I've already stopped one person from breaking the law. And I'm not even out of first gear.

Inspired by Senna's win over Prost at the Japanese Grand Prix, Oldham bullies his way through midday traffic. We power down Cotton Tree Drive. He misses the turn to Queen's Road East. We're heading for the cross-harbour tunnel.

Taking the long way home, Inspector? I don't put-out on first dates.

It's not our first date. And I felt there were matters you might want to discuss, unofficially. Maybe there's a couple of things I can explain a little better, when we're not on government property, that will help you select the right path.

And what path would that be?

Apathy. You shouldn't care too much about this one, Jack.

Which one?

Teplice. Liu. Sprudel.

That's three.

And there are a whole lot more. More than you want to know. They're drawing attention and my political masters are being pressured to solve it, fast. And fast means the path of least resistance. The shoe that fits best. It doesn't have to be a perfect fit.

Too many irresistible forces meeting immovable objects?

So you understand?

Just so you understand, I'm trying to extricate myself from this not get embedded in it. But every time I try to do the right thing it goes wrong.

Stop trying to do the right thing. Sometimes nothing is the right thing to do. By letting go it all gets done. The world is won by those who let it go. When you try and try and keep on trying, the world is beyond the winning.

Get you, Mo Tzu. I met with Io Lam last night. I asked about Liu and Koko Man. The next thing I know two of your boys have Shanghaied me and I'm in slumberland on Cumberland. Does that sound right?

Maybe it was a warning. You said it yourself. Maybe Lam thinks you're trying to leverage him and he had them stitch you up to make sure you couldn't.

We exit the tunnel and drive toward the airport.

It's a different country over here, Jack. I don't have to tell you that. There are places we don't go without an invitation and even then we take Special Forces. There are things we just pretend don't exist and, soon, they won't.

He's talking about the impenetrable, rogue precinct on our right. The Walled City. Hong Kong's very own Mos Eisley spaceport. A wretched hive of scum, villainy and bargain-basement oral sex. Salman Rushdie could be hiding in there with Lestor Piggott, Noriega and the Ninja Turtles. No one would know. Many of the Gangjiu and Dongjiang resistance fighters settled there too, when they finished waging a guerilla war against the Japanese in the New Territories. Like a lot of things this hotbed of vice and sedition had been tagged for extinction before the 1997 handover.

My pager bursts into life.

I ask Oldham if I can borrow his portable phone to call a client.

Sure, as long as it's local. And legitimate business.

I dial Koko's number and apologize for not making our appointment the night before. I was way-laid.

Lucky you. I've been cooped up for sooo long.

I'm trying to make this sound work-related, for Oldham's all-hearing ears. A client making last-minute changes. It's not easy. Darius Man is leaving town this evening and his wife is trying to arrange a clandestine encounter. Funny business, monkey business.

Will you be needing anything else?

I need to satisfy my curiosity, Jack. You're working for me now. And working for me can be more fun than fun.

Let's have a status update at the office, later tonight. I'll get back to you with a time. I need to check my schedule.

I've cleared mine to fit you in. Opportunities like this don't come along every day, or night. I might not be widow, yet, but who knows what tomorrow will bring? You wouldn't want to disappoint me again.

She hangs up.

I feel dirty. Guilty. Like I just got caught giving Whistler's Mother a Turkish snow cone. Oldham has been eying me throughout the call. He's seen rapists in the dock that look more innocent than I do right now.

Unreasonable client?

I've never met a reasonable one.

Dissatisfied?

Insatiable.

We're behind The Walled City, circling West Kowloon Park. The albino's neighbourhood. I ask Oldham if he thinks I should go and apologize.

Jack, have you heard anything I've said?

You said you wouldn't go into The Walled City without an armed escort, which actually works on a number of levels when you consider some of the working girls in there.

Armed escorts. The weapons they carry?

I was thinking of the amputees.

Kinky.

Irony. See, it works on so many levels.

Like this city, Jack. It's demarcated horizontally and vertically.

He takes a moment to wax lyrical on triad societies. 14K. Sun Yee On. Wo Hop To. Wo Shing Wo. Their influence and how the colony is divvied up between them.

That's the thing about organized crime, Oldham. It's so organized.

They're better regimented than we are.

No law, more order.

It's getting complicated. Mainland gangs are after a piece of the pie-chart. The locals don't like to share. One group wants a deal, the other doesn't know how to give one. It's a hostile takeover and they're battling for the assets.

Valet parking. Mini-bus schedules.

Prostitution, gambling, entertainment and property. It's not just Hong Kong. Macau is on the block too. There's a lot to command and conquer.

And to protect. Someone has to look out for the public interest occasionally.

We do that in our spare time. And by we I don't mean me. Most Peelers are in the service of their superiors. A conscience doesn't really have a place in the life of a law enforcer, on any side of society. It will have even less in the years to come. But you already knew that. You experienced it first-hand last night. Lam and his unofficial officials. Just sign on the thin blue line.

Amazing what you can get for a buck these days. What do you know about those two conscripts?

They're on leave for the rest of the week.

Personal tragedy or professional development.

Medical.

Gee, I hope it's noting terminal.

They'll be okay. They've got insurance, remember.

I wish I could get some.

Hard to say. When there are too many policeman, there can be no liberty. When there are too many soldiers there can be no peace.

And when there are too many lawyers there can be no justice.

There'll be some new players and a few new rules. But the sun's still going to come up every day.

And when one chicken dies another will crow.

We're all just trying to escape the plough.

Speaking of cocks and hoes, I say, grabbing the analogy by the balls. He was in there.

We've turned down Cumberland and are approaching number 41. Jailbaits Motel. It looks innocuous in this light.

Who's in there? asks Oldham, hitting the brakes and gawking like a tourist.

The dingo that ate Azaria Chamberlain. Who do you think? Chung. He was putting it to someone in the room down the hall from mine.

That works on so many levels. Think about it. They have you in his company, twice, tearing up bars and cavorting in love motels. Known criminals. Murder. Prostitution. How's that shoe fit now? Would you like to see it in another colour?

Why would they do that?

If you don't know, don't try to find out. Maybe they don't know why either. Maybe they were just doing what they were told.

Our is not to reason why.

Ours is but to do.

Or die.

You got out, Jack. Leave it at that.

They didn't let me out.

They would've. They might've even given you an explanation, if you'd let them. Fear the office more than the officials. A cop can lop the head off a snake but the administration can torch the whole fucking trogle.

Never has a person who's bent been able to make others straight.

People enjoy making money out of other people's misery. You know that, you're in advertising.

So who stands to make the most?

I'm not paid to think about things like that.

Koko Man?

She has more to lose than gain, don't you think?

I thought you said you weren't paid to think about things like that.

I can't afford to think about things like that. I don't know why you would either. Why go out for *chutoro* when you've got *otoro* at home?

They're more Barracuda than Blue Fin at my place. Is it Angel, Por-por or Bing you fancy the most?

It's not too late to have you arrested.

But it is getting late. Are you planning to take me home soon, or are you going to talk tuna for the rest of the night? If I'm not back by bedtime my *otoro* goes off.

We've ended up on the other side of Kai Tak, by the fetid nullah. The stench from this toxic canal by the tarmac invades the vehicle and kills the conversation.

A plane waits until the last minute to avoid colliding with Lion Rock and prematurely commencing demolition of the Walled City. The jet banks late and is almost blown into Victoria Harbour by a temerarious gust. It struggles to right itself and arrive nose-first. A magical puff of screeching rubber eventually signals its desperate grip on terra firma.

I think about how easy it is to get blown off course, to get dragged across the tarmac, to crash and burn, unless you know exactly what you're doing. Even then there's no predicting wind-shear. Your autopilot could be finely tuned but you'd still end up in the wreckage at Ramstein.

Nifty and Liu.

Lynne Sprudel.

The disposable Kitty Ho.

The drop-dead gorgeous mess that is Horoko Kitajima and Koko Man.

Bronson Chung and me, for that matter.

We're all on the same path, all victims of the same existence. None of us any better than the other. None of us are getting out of here alive.

A simple trip to Wan Chai, if there was such a thing, could blow you off the map. One day you could wake and find yourself so far up the river you've terminated your own command.

The airstrip plunges like a dagger into the seething chaos of tortured water that nourishes the city. Cruise ships, container boats, ferries, yachts and sampans are all on collision courses in Victoria Harbour. It's another of Hong Kong's separate states. If people knew what was really happening they'd sleep with their lights on. Drugs, guns, money, people. If it can be shipped, trafficked, venundated or exchanged, it's out there.

Bellatrix, the jewel in Man's aquatic crown, lies otiose off North Point, unworried by the winds of change and shifting currents that harry Hong Kong. Soon it will create a whole new reality for its fevered occupants. It will take them for a ride, one way or the other.

One way and then the other.

There is a tide in the affairs of men.

Which, taken at the flood, leads on to fortune;

Omitted, all the voyage of their life

Is bound in shallows and in miseries.
On such a full sea are we now afloat,
And we must take the current when it serves,
Or lose our ventures.

The cards are dealt before we reach the table. What does it matter if we know when to hold 'em and when to fold 'em? Even if we knew when to walk away there was nowhere to run. Hong Kong is the smallest big city in the world. And everyone punches above their weight. We bet contrary to the odds stacked against us. The house always wins. It doesn't matter. It's the only chance we have to challenge our fate and change our destiny. We'll always chance our arm and more chasing down the orgastic future that, year by year, recedes before us. Pursuing Gatsby's green light.

Tomorrow we will run faster, stretch our arms farther.

It's no coincidence there's a race track at the topographic heart of the island. Not a church or a temple, a museum or a gallery, a parliament or a governing body. A racetrack is all of these things, and more.

A sure haven and sovereign vessel in a sea of uncertainty.

So we beat on, as Fitzgerald observed, boats against the current, borne ceaselessly into the past.

Time and tide wait for no man. Not even Koko Man.

18. ÉTUDES & MYTHS IN C MINOR

Por-por, Gu-por and The Guilin Seven have taken Mei to dance class. It's part of our new equal opportunity, joint custody agreement. She hasn't spent enough time with them. They think I'm hiding her from them. Maybe I am, subconsciously. I remind myself how important family can be, no matter what you think of it or how much it imposes. Family is a source of incalculable strength and a point of incurable weakness. It is not the fittest who survive, but those who best manage change by whatever means necessary.

Natura non facit saltum.

This is easy for me to say. I've never really had a family of my own. Not a complete one. I've only ever had what's left of one. Bits of those that belong to others. Darwin's displaced grab-bag of humanity. Descent of modification. Complex creatures from simplistic incestors. The process of unnatural selection.

Nature is prodigal in variation yet niggard in innovation. Taking advantage of slight successive variations, she can never make a great and sudden leap, but must advance though short, sure and slow steps.

Benny, in his effort to move further along the evolutionary trail, is attending his weekly physiotherapy session. He has a thing for his therapist. She can't keep her hands off him, he says. It's probably the closest he gets to a sexual experience these days. He left the picture of Kitty Ho on my keyboard, and stuck a note to it.

Let me know if you find her. I'll pick her up and drive her home!

It's accompanied by a caricature of Kitty gyrating in his lap. Naked. Eyes wide and tongue panting as Benny burns rubber, vigorously spinning his wheels beneath her. Harry Crumb. Fritz The Cat.

Keep on truckin'.

I dial Koko's number, flicking through the copy of Tatler that Toshimi Wells left on my desk. The pictures are impossible to ignore and hard to syncretize with the duplicitous, unsightly contradictions that lie in the mattress of her smile. They seep from the plush tones in her voice as she suspires concupiscently and drips honey in my ear.

I HOPE YOU'RE
NOT CALLING
TO CANCEL.

She tells me she's been abandoned. Her husband and step-daughter will be aboard Bellatrix tonight, celebrating the launch of a new venture. In the morning they set sail with a select few on a three-day cruise. The coast is clear.

I ask her why she's not on the guest list.

It's invitation-only. I wasn't invited. I shouldn't be seen enjoying myself, in the wake of the tragedy surrounding my good friend. I've been instructed to lay low.

That's not a bad idea, I think. I have a new set of images coming together in my mind's eye and they're not pretty.

We could lay low together, Jack. No one said I had to do it alone, at home. Fancy a room with a view?

Of the harbour?

Of me.

So much for not being seen.

We'll keep the curtains drawn and the lights low. No prying eyes. No distractions. I have a friend at The Hilton who can arrange it. He's very discreet.

She doesn't have to tell me who that is. Mike Midian has been leveraging his position there to provide all manner of inconspicuous services to Hong Kong's wanton echelons. He's not as tight-lipped as she thinks. We trade favours. He introduced So Fuk Yu to the Hilton's marketing department. We still owe them a Christmas ad.

The Hilton is covered in Holiday spirit.

I tell her I have to put Mei to bed first, and then finish up a few things at the office. A couple of them might interest her. They concern the necklace. She should come by later. I'll fill her in and we can go to The Hilton from here.

Is your place fun?

It can be, depending on your idea of fun. Was it you or Noel Coward that said work is more fun than fun?

I can be pretty wild.

We'll make it a come-as-you-are party then. I'll put away the good china. You can throw all the gourds you like.

It's not bragging if it's true. Why don't you just fill me in at The Hilton?

There's stuff we should go through here. And I'm expecting a call.

You're working overtime?

Certain clients demand it. They will not be denied. Like time and tide they wait for no man.

Your beloved Jane Austen again?

Geoffrey Chaucer.

He probably never met a woman worth waiting for.

The Wife Of Bath may beg to differ.

The Wife Of Bath sounds like an old maid that lived on her knees. Men throw themselves at my feet.

Forbid us something, and that thing we desire.

I always get what I want.

Whatever the price.

Does OT cost extra?

Nothing you can't afford, Koko. Maybe a pound of flesh.

I'll give you two.

I can hardly wait.

When do you want to get dividend?

After ten? Eleven? Are you allowed out that late?

That's early. How long have you been shut away? Thing's don't heat up until midnight, Cinderella.

I guess I'm starting to show my age.

You're as old as you feel. A couple of hours with me will make you young again. I have that affect on men. You'll be up all night.

Now I'm feeling old and frightened.

Exciting isn't it?

It's a lot of things, I think. Exciting isn't one of them.

I hang up and find Wing is waiting with a brace of layouts for Clinique, Bella

Facial and Ultima II. I tell him to leave them on my desk. I'll check them when I get back this evening. I'll mount them on hardboard for tomorrow's presentation.

That's all you better be mounting in here, says Angel, making me wonder how much of my conversation with Mrs Man she might've heard.

No fear of that. You wore me out last night. I don't know if I've even got the strength to get the blade of the Stanley Trimmer up.

If you need a hand with your tool, Jack.

I'll call if it arises. Finish up here. I'm going to collect Mei and her maternal massive from Wan Chai.

Sam puts a protégé through her paces, *scherzando*. Mei waves to me and is swiftly reminded where to direct her attention.

Irina stands at the door to the office.

Chopin? I inquire, lifting my eyes to the delicate notes drifting by.

Étude Number Twelve. C Minor.

She tells me Gu-por and her troupe have gone to get foot massages.

Great, I think. More women with the world at their feet.

They were evicted for making too much noise, she adds.

I apologise. Apart from that, how are things going?

They could always be better. But Mei is progressing well. She has talent. She is developing into a charming, determined young lady.

I thank her for the compliment.

You are doing a good job, she continues. It is difficult to raise a daughter on your own. You have to be there for them. Always. That is the challenge.

Woody Allen said eighty-percent of success was just showing up. He probably wasn't talking about children but I'd always felt the principle applied.

Irina steps into the office.

Her intense eyes, locked on mine, draw me in. We stand behind the two-way mirror, observing the class. Watching over our daughters.

You can be proud, I say in Cantonese. Asami is a strong, independent woman.

That is a tribute to her, not me. I have failed her many times. And you. The promises I made to your mother. She entrusted me.

You have failed no-

Please. I have judged you to be a man of honesty and integrity. Do not have me question that now, after all these years, and attempt to conciliate an old woman with the sins of her past. I have failed her. As I failed Kitty.

I'm surprised by this declaration. I turn to face her.

Irina Wang is looking through the mirror, and through time. She asks what I know about Kitty Ho.

Not much, I admit. Her parents were killed in a plane crash. She was raised by the Sisters at Po Leung Kuk. They tried, unsuccessfully, to place her in a number of homes. She always ran away. She became a hostess, and came under your care not long after she came of age.

Her parent's did not die in a plane crash, Jack. It was a story. An invention to save her from the shame of the truth.

This is quite a revelation. Legend had it her parents perished when the plane carrying them, and the United States Figure Skating Team, ploughed into Belgium's Zaventem Airport in 1961. It added to the tragic mystique of Kitty Ho. It was one of the ways she endeared herself to some, and why others were quick to forgive her malefactions. Like many things, she played it to her advantage. Now, with the unfolding of this fable, it seems Kitty's whole life was based on a lie.

What is the truth?

Kitty's mother worked at the Japanese Consulate. She had a relationship, outside her marriage, with a prominent Hong Kong businessman. There was speculation she may have been raped, on more than one occasion. She became pregnant. The true paternity of the child was never revealed. Years after her birth, the car in which the family were travelling went off the cliffs at Shek O. It was a miracle Kitty survived. Some say the husband had learned the child was not his and wanted to kill them all.

THAT MAN
WAS ALSO
ASAMI'S
FATHER.

Irina pauses. She draws breath and chooses her next words carefully.

There is disconsolation, relief and ignominy in her confession. She turns away, head low, her proud shoulders rounded in defeat. That's something else Woody Allen was right about. Life is full of misery, loneliness, and suffering, and it's all over much too soon.

He was a patron of the club where I worked with your mother, Jack. We, I, entertained him from time to time.

Now I understand her pain when it came to Kitty Wong. And it explains why Irina felt obligated to adopt her. Like sex it raises a host of questions too, none of which I have the courage to ask.

Did Sam know she had a half-sister? Who was Kitty's biological father? What did Irina know about mine?

Of course Asami doesn't know, she says, reading my mind. She mustn't. I was not aware of the connection until Kitty arrived at the club. I heard the story about her parents. The plane crash. It happened the same week her family, my client, died on the cliff. Both were big stories. I didn't recall any mention made of Hong Kong people being on the plane. For two children to lose both parents, with no relatives to care for them, in the same week, didn't seem possible. I spoke to a housemother at Po Leung Kuk. Many of our girls had left children there over the years. The Sisters had decided to tell Kitty the story of the plane crash. They felt she had suffered enough without knowing the truth about her parents, her birth and her life.

Mei and Sam walk toward us, *pizzicato*.

Irina's stoic demeanour returns. She reminds me how important discipline is and that I must not forget what she has told me. It is a warning as much as it is advice. I'm overcome by a sudden urge to hug her. Perhaps she senses it and leaves.

Another lecture from Ma-ma?

Nothing I don't deserve.

What we were you talking about?

You.

Before she can question me any further I sweep Mei off her feet and head towards the door.

Sam watches us leave and then kills the lights. Through the glass I see her silhouette rehearse a gentle *pas de bourrée* and *brisé* for her mother's approval.

There but for the grace of The Fates go we.

As Mei and I walk as one, into the twilight, I wonder who is clinging to whom.

19. A BET EACH WAY

I drop Mei and the Xiufeng footsoldiers home. They tumble out of the car, complaining about the price and quality of massages in Hong Kong. The new-car smell of the cabin is defeated, vanquished by a cloud of Tiger Balm and Imada Red Flower Oil. It will linger for weeks.

To compound the headache, my mind is swimming with images.

Irina and Sam. Kitty. Bronson Chung and Nifty. Kitty. Lynne Sprudel, Liu Pang and Io Lam. Rent-a-cops. Chung. Hookers and cameras. Necklaces. Koko and Darius Man. Missy. My mother even makes an appearance. I'd go home and sleep except Toshimi Wells might turn up in a dream and blow the back of my head off.

I need some fresh air.

The sun is setting on the harbour as I trawl the expressway.

Bellatrix strains at its mid-harbour mooring, eager to break free of its shackles, cast off and furnish the coffers.

I'm going to see if Mike Midian can get me aboard and into tonight's event. Missy couldn't be reached. I need a parley with the head of the Man clan before they set sail. Mike can clear up a few questions surrounding Horoko Man while we're at it.

He's between shifts when I arrive at the Hilton. I don't know if that means the end or the beginning of one but it doesn't seem to matter. Mike unofficially runs the joint. As head of security he can do as he pleases. And he aims to please.

Mike's always been one for a bit of adventure.

A few years ago, the girls in Wan Chai had a recurring problem with an abusive Corporal of The Black Guard. He'd often made life difficult for us too, violently objecting to closing times and last orders. We decided to meter out a little corporal punishment and seconded him for an unofficial naval sortie. We spirited him through the thalassic border between Hong Kong and China. We sedated, stripped and stranded him on the beach of a small fishing village. It would give him time to think about his trespasses, and allow him to test his survival skills in his quest to make it back to base before revelry.

Midian knows me well enough not to ask about the scaevity of my association with Nifty and Liu. He knows I'll tell him when I can. Still, he can't ignore the subject completely.

Hey Pale Rider. I didn't recognize you without the other Horsemen of the Apocalypse. How are Pestilence, War and Famine? You here about the Christmas ad campaign?

It's coming.

So is Christmas.

We discuss a more extant wish to board Bellatrix uninvited. He doesn't question the wisdom of this, just the suitability of my attire. You've been out of the game too long, Jack. The first rule of crashing a party is looking like you belong there.

We head to housekeeping.

Mike unshackles a suit destined for dry-cleaning. I look at the label.

What happens if Mr Higgins wants his bag of fruit back.

We won't be hearing from The Hurricane. He came to the end of a record, near-fatal break in the bar this afternoon. His cue is well and truly in the rack for the night.

At the embarkation point in Causeway Bay it becomes obvious we'll need to find an alternative point of entry. If we had invitations we'd know passports are to be presented prior to departure. Neither of us are carrying ours. Even if we were, these customs inspectors would deny us entry.

Drebin and Nordberg are moonlighting as part of the security detail.

We seek out Ah-fung at the North Point pier. The old sea dog co-ordinates activities here, legal and entrepreneurial. You want to get something on or off a boat, he's your man. No one knows the underlying currents of the city or life as well as Ah-fung. He is the TS Eliot of the pelagic wasteland that girts our island home.

The harbour sweats

Oil and tar

The barges drift

With the turning tide

Red sails

Wide

To leeward, swing on the heavy spar.

The barges wash

Drifting logs

Down Victoria reach

Past the Isle of Dogs.

Ah-fung recognizes me right away.

Here he is! The only man with more women troubles than Ah-fung! What is it tonight, Jack So! You are not dressed for fishing! Or is it fish of a different kind, hmm?

We wish to board Bellatrix, Ah-fung, but seem to have lost our invitations.

Gambling? You would have more luck finding fish in this harbour than money on those tables. This I know. Look at Ah-fung. Always gambling. Mahjong and women. My fortune never changes. Always lose. You cannot change your fate. You can run and hide but you cannot escape. Always it will find you

He should get together with Angel for a Proustean mind-meld. They could discuss why mankind insists on paying back evil with good.

I thank him for the advice and tell him I'm resigned to my fate. It is the fortunes of another that are at stake tonight.

Only one thing more futile than trying to change the course of your own destiny, Jack So, and that is to interfere with another. You know this.

I'm trying to figure out a way to navigate this metaphysical impasse when Midian Intercedes. He asks if five hundred dollars would bring balance to the predetermined order of the universe, and secure dark passage for a couple of fate-fucking phantoms in search of the great whale.

You have money you can make a ghost push a millstone, Ah-fung concludes. One thousand get you round trip and complimentary beverage!

We walk to a barge being loaded with bounty of every variety. He points to a dozen girls huddled between the pallets of our Pequod.

You go first class!

Most pleasure craft have a crew of able-bodied women and men to pump the biological bilges. Ishmaels, Ahabs and Queequegs seeking their Moby Dicks. Those who fish the floor come in the front door as glamorous passengers. Those who dive upon the rooms use the tradesman's entrance. We should be able to slip on unmolested. People at that end of the boat have seen stranger things than two guys in suits being piped aboard.

The wheelhouse is instructed to deliver us. All care taken, no responsibility accepted. He'll make his return trip at nine-thirty, if we need it.

To take my mind off the anxiety this mode of transport induces I ask Mike what he knows about Koko Man.

She's a sphinx. A piece of work. I don't know where Man found her but you can bet it wasn't Saint Stephen's. What do they say? You take the girl out of the game but you can't take the game out of the girl. She's quite a dancer, if you know what I mean. Good set of pipes on her too. You don't get lips like that from sucking lemons. She whistles while she works.

Can she play the flute?

Like a pro. I set her up with a suite from time to time. She'll be over tonight, in fact. I thought she'd be playing to the stalls out here but someone's getting a private performance instead.

You strike up the band for her? She shake your leg?

Not as often as I'd like. Her dance card is kinda full. You don't get many invitations to trip her light fantastic. Is this about her? You cutting the old man's rug in his own ballroom? Probably the kind of thing that would turn her on. Thought you'd have a little more respect for him than that.

He asked me to look into something.

So why don't we just go in the front door?

I have to be discreet and I don't know the width of Man's circle of trust.

I can tell you the diameter of Mrs Man's.

We're being discreet, remember?

The cargo bay of the luxury liner draws near.

Sea air has restored the *chi* to my mind's *feng shui*. The fog of images in my head has lifted. The ghost has taken her hands from my eyes and I'm not liking what I see. The foul play surrounding the sapphire necklace has too many layers to be simple robbery and extortion.

It has to be part of a grander scheme.

Liu and his property pipe-dreams? Exposing Koko Man? Compromising her and co-opting Darius Man?

The albino is a minor *daimyo*. A feudal lord, but still a supplier. A vendor. Services for hire. Geomancy and whatever else. Like Chung he's part of the *bushi* warrior class. He may have something personal at stake but he's still on someone's payroll.

Man wouldn't be involved in this.

Why would he set up his own wife? If he wanted to send her or anyone else a message there were less public channels. He could save himself the embarrassment by just having her and the whole affair disappear. Paid-off or laid-off. People in his position can create more illusions than Copperfield.

Maybe he was trying to. And someone else stepped in.

If the blackmailers arrived late, who was in the other car?

Maybe there's more than one hand being played. The immovable object and irresistible force may not be directly opposed or related. There could be two or three insoluble truths operating independently, in a vacuum of deceit and subterfuge.

The barge ties up. We help the ladies astern. Midian whistles.

Hi-ho, Hi-ho it's off to work we go.

The receiving crew are surprised to see us amongst the skirts but know better than to question anything at this end of the ship. Midian barks commands in Cantonese, like we're supposed to be here, tightening security for all the VIPs in attendance tonight.

We find our way through the lower decks.

On a narrow, exterior passageway we encounter a watchdog, smoking. I ask for a cigarette. He reaches into his jacket. Mike arrests him quickly, quietly. A sleeper hold. I take the pistol from the flunkey's belt.

So much for discretion, Mike, and the better part of valour.

That was discreet. And chivalrous. The little guy is still alive.

We enter the main reception area. Guests are arriving. They're being greeted by Captain Stubing, Julie McCoy and Doc.

The Love Boat soon will be making another run,

The Love Boat promises something for everyone.

I set a course for adventure and tell Mike he can cast-off any time. It wouldn't bode well for a person in his position to be seen crashing exclusive parties with the likes of me. He should keep his reputation in tact, so it doesn't end up like mine.

His says he doesn't need my permission to do anything, and questions my use of the word *bode*.

I tell him everyone's using it these days.

Toshimi Wells,
in all her fecundated frippery.
The isangeious highlight of the evening.
Phalerated by diamonds, she hovers among
the Star-belly Sneetches.

Before she can cut across the crowd I step into the high-rollers enclave, and close the door behind me. Mike must have drifted off as I entered.

Two solid security men approach.

This section for VIPs only, Sir.

I tell them Mr Man invited me, personally.

Half of Hong Kong's business elite, and their mistresses, have turned to see my transgression. I recognize Tony *The Wizard* Khou, he's good at making things disappear. *Dirty* Harry Wong was a Peeler and now has most of them on his payroll. Elwyn *HK Electric* Tsang is unmistakable with his Don King hair. There's enough ill-gotten gains floating around to keep ghosts at grindstones until we're way beyond The Handover. I see a couple of Kobayashi, a baker's dozen of Desai and copious cadres.

They part like the Red Sea.

Darius Man is wheeled across the room. Missy is at his side, in smart business attire. The lady really know how to unwind. She dismisses the guards, apologizes to the guests and orders them to return to their evening. She pours scorn upon me.

Mr So. Come.

I follow, half a step behind.

The fat, dark Terry *Idi Amin* Fung smiles at me. A ridiculously youthful Miriam *The Baby* Lam turns away, searching for someone to burp her.

Technically speaking, gambling isn't permitted until the boat is in open water, but who would dare to poop the party? Certainly not the Chief Of Police. He's too busy ogling the winner of the Eurovision Song Contest. Besides, no money is actually changing hands and a good percentage of proceeds are going to charity. The buying of influence and peddling of privilege in a post-97 Pearl Of The Orient is probably on the cards as well.

Is that what we're celebrating tonight?

Judging by the faces in the room, mutually beneficial agreements regarding the horizontal and vertical integration of diverse interests have been reached. The Year Of The Dragon is an auspicious time for births of every kind. Maybe we don't have to wait until the return to sovereignty. The territory has already been divided and conquered.

Missy enters a leeward ante room. I follow. She closes the door.

Darius Man has vanished, along with the two security officers that were tailing us. The room is hers, in every sense. There'll be no stepmother sending her for beverages or making patronising remarks. I'm even thinking it would be inappropriate to call her Missy.

She walks to a cabinet stocked with decanters of rusty liquor, selects one, and pours three fingers into crystal tumblers. Her eyes point to sturdy leather chairs by the wall. She hands me a glass. Her dark, attentive eyes regard me with marked curiosity. I wait for her to sit before taking my place. Her poise and aplomb as impressive as the whiskey.

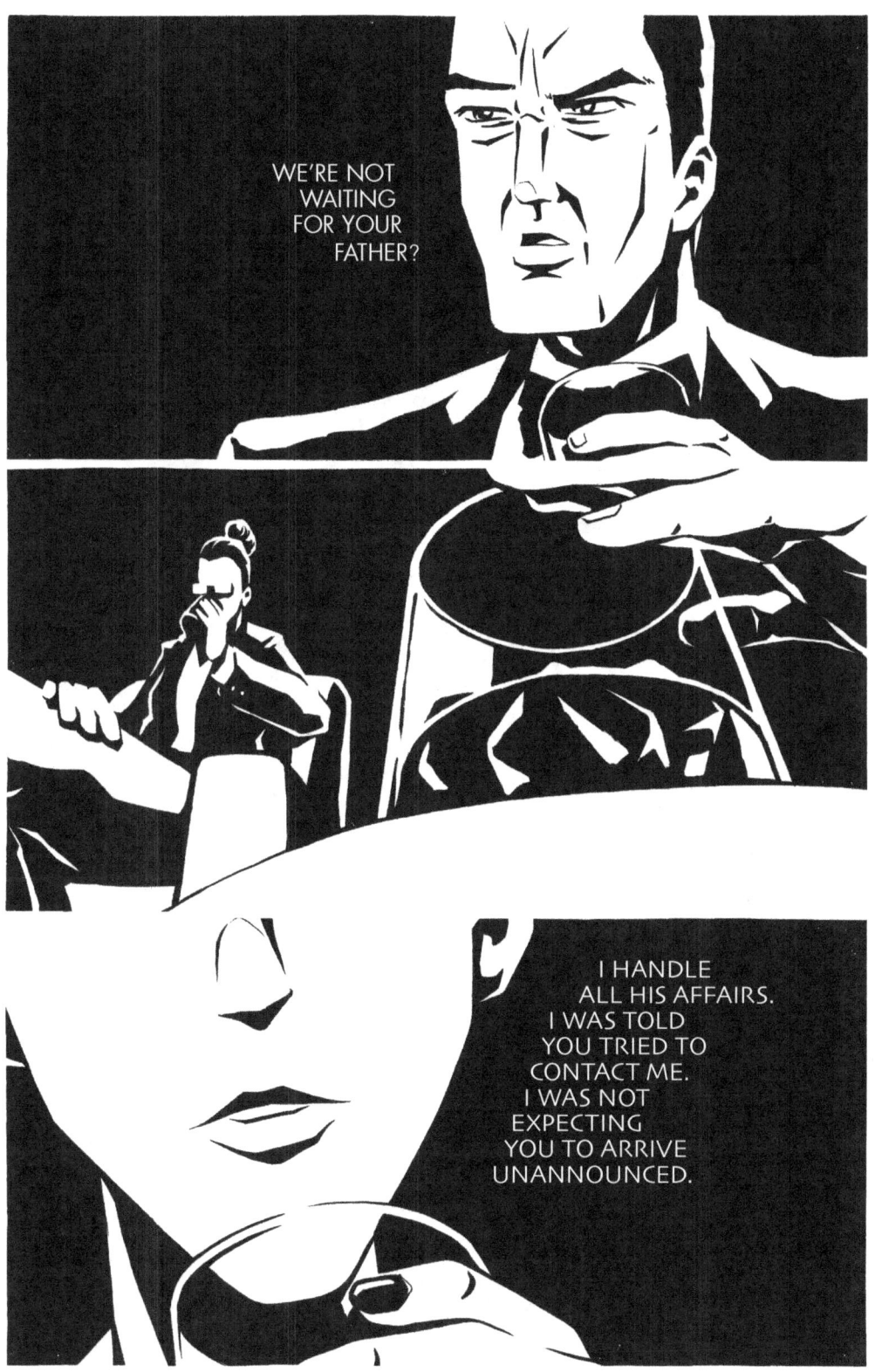

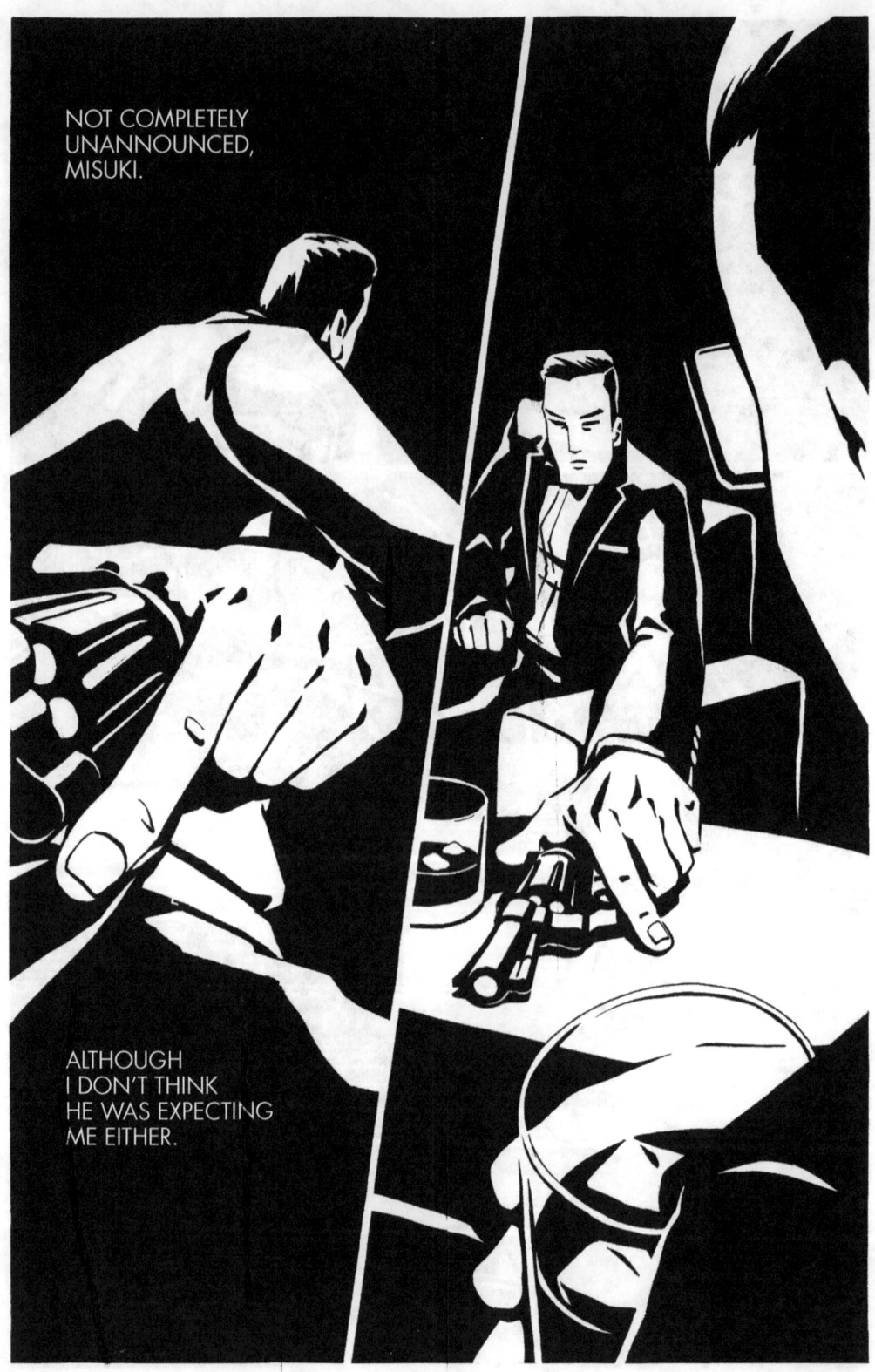

I know someone who may be better suited to the task. Congratulations on your promotion.

My promotion?

You seem to be in a more executive position than when last we met.

I handle all my father's affairs. I have for quite some time. I'm disappointed in you, Mr So. You do not think a woman can perform such duties?

I apologize for any inference I may have-

You think we would allow a half-caste to control the family business? Or we would permit a whore to ruin and dishonour everything my father has achieved?

The venom in her remarks is sharp and deadly, a flying sword of superiority forged from anger.

I mean no offense, I reply in Cantonese. I'm surprised, not shocked. There seemed to be a matriarchal hegemony at your family home. I am sorry.

I give more than lip service to The Eight Virtues. If my step-mother were more cultured she would too. Piety, respect, loyalty, honesty, duty, peace, modesty, shame. If she knew one of these she would not find herself in such opprobrious situations, the topic of gossip and innuendo. Her lack of dignity has brought disgrace to our family.

All happy families are alike, I remind her, wondering if she's studied the classics. Each unhappy family is unhappy in its own way.

She takes a measure of single malt and rolls it across her tongue. Is she savouring it, or trying to rinse an unpleasant taste from her mouth? It could be the lingering bitterness of Koko, or simply the thought of Tolstoy.

Why don't you tell me what you really think, Misuki?

A smile softens her features. There's an attractive woman prowling somewhere beneath that crisp exterior.

Tell me why you are here, Mr So. I have guests. It would not be appropriate for me to leave them unattended.

I want to get a message to Bronson Chung, I say, taking a punt that even the high-rollers next door would think foolhardy.

I meet her eyes with unblinking conviction. There is a knock on the door. Without shifting her focus she tells whoever it is to leave us be. After what seems like an exceptionally long roll of the dice she dryly accuses of me of further insulting her, daring to associate her with criminals and expecting her to function as a messenger.

I mean no disrespect. The matter is urgent and pertains to the request your father made of me. Chung could be anywhere. Guangzhou, The Walled City or Cumberland Road. He could be at the RSPCA, helping dispose of strays in a humane manner. He could even be here and neither of us would know. You're the most influential person I have access to. And while you, personally, would have no way of contacting such a figure, you might be able to delegate the task to someone who might know someone, who might be in a position to get a message to him.

And what might this message be?

One word is all I have for her. But sometimes one word is enough. One word is all it takes. One word. I'm betting the farm on one word.

She must think I'm insane.

You have no reason to trust me, Misuki, but trust me when I tell you it is very important he gets that message. Tonight. Within the next couple of hours. If I'm wrong I'll apologize for wasting your time. If I'm right this business can come to an end and your family can begin to reclaim its dignity.

She evaluates my words and my worth. Are my stocks rising or falling?

I've judged you to be a man of good character, Mr So. I hope I've been correct in my assessment. You have made enemies of late. Trust *me* when I say you do not want to add my family to that list. If this is as important as you say, and it means an end to the embarrassment we endure, then perhaps we can help your family feel more secure. Your daughter should not have to wonder if her father is going to come home every night. I will determine what can be done. My men will see you to the departure point.

She stands and scrutinizes me for a final moment, pondering her investment in my future. I feel like a minor shareholder in my own life, someone who's just exercised his last options.

A security guard escorts me from the room. We cross the VIP lounge.

Toshimi Wells breaks from conversation with Andrew *The Angel* Yuen, who's been certified dead, twice. The overindulged design student walks as swiftly as her gown, heels and the occasion will permit.

Whatever are you doing here, Jack, in there with Missy?

Liquor in the front, poker in the rear.

My official escort is irritated by Toshimi's interloping and the attention it is garnering. I look beyond her and catch a glimpse of Io Lam, his welmish skin patent amongst the glowing edifice of society.

It will be the topic of the evening, Toshimi continues. If I'd known you were invited we could've come together. You're leaving now?

My ship has sailed.

I was going to be your lucky charm.

You've done enough for me already.

I could do more, she whispers in my air, then kisses me on the cheek.

What was that for?

For luck. Rub some cards with me, Jack. You might hit the jackpot.

I've just taken my last roll of the dice. You'll have to get someone else to cash your chips tonight.

Mike Midian rejoins me as I cross reception.

Who do I have to blow to get off this bathtub, Jack?

Stick with me. I'll show you the ropes. We're pulling the pick now.

We're ferried to Causeway Bay in over-decorated sampan. There's a dragon climbing along the roof and lanterns swinging from the rafters. A strong breeze pitches and rolls the vessel. I'm feeling queasy by the time we get dockside.

The swell is not the only thing churning in my guts.

On the pier a pair of moonlighting police officers recognize me. They charter a course for confrontation.

Mike steps into the breach and suggests they save their energy.

I recommend they start looking for a new employer.

What was the point of that? Mike asks, *en route* to The Hilton.

We'll have to wait and see. The returns could be huge, but it's one of those all-or-nothing bets.

I hope it pays off

I'm worried about who comes to collect.

Like Odysseus and Jason before me, I was sailing a ship between monsters. To fall into the hands of either would be my fatal *moment décisif.*

All is quiet on the south-eastern front. As quiet as it can be with a herd of gypsies in the living room.

Gu-por tells me I should wear a suit more often. I look very smart.

Don't let appearances fool you, Gu-por. I've just added one of the stupidest things ever to my long and inglorious list.

Captured Erythmanthian Boar.

Cleaned Stables Of Augeas.

Acquired Apples Of Hesperides.

Liberated Girdle Of Hippolyte.

Slaughtered Nemean Lion.

Got out of bed this morning.

I tell The Guilin Seven I'll be down in the office, finishing up some work. There are ideas to conceive, layouts to handle and clients to mount.

Wing has left a dozen concepts on my desk. Everything is where it should be. The copy sits comfortably with the visual. I trim the edges. Then glue the layouts on thick cardboard. It's a rum collection of public notices. Cosmetics. Personal transformation is a growth industry but the beauty business is pretty ugly.

No one is happy with who they are.

Clinique For Men. *In just two minutes, this man's face will look terrific!* Bella Facial Care. *The four unsightly hair zones.* Ultima II. *The art of creating beautiful faces.*

I take a moment to ponder my upper lip, armpits, bikini line and legs.

An almost imperceptible swing of the glass door whispers in reception. The lock gently clicks into place. Someone is standing behind me. I'm expecting a concupiscent Koko Man.

You're early. Bored, or just eager to get down to business?

I came as soon as I got your message, my friend.

Bronson Chung looms large. Be careful what you wish for, I think.

He's well dressed, for a psychopath. Dark suit. A swirly Versace shirt unbuttoned to the middle of his chest. His perm has been recalibrated. Maybe he has a date.

Brother Chung. I almost didn't recognize you with your clothes on.

I could say the same to you, Brother So. You work late too, huh? Only people like us keep these hours.

By *us* I hope he isn't lumping me in with his gangster brethren. Although we have been ploughing a lot of common ground lately. I tell him I couldn't sleep.

I can give you something for that.

Not for what I got.

What have you got, Brother So?

Women troubles.

I could help you with those.

Even you might struggle with these. There's nine or ten of them upstairs.

You don't know how many there are?

See the trouble I'm in? Can I get you a drink? It won't solve our problems but it might give a fresh perspective on them.

He seems weary of helctic conversation already, and is probably remembering what happened the last time I bought us a round.

I want what you promised me, he says. What were you doing on the boat?

I was looking for answers.

What were the questions?

Why do all these people end up dead, before or after they meet you?

Teplice had it coming from many directions. It could've been anyone.

But it was you. What about his wife?

His wife?

Did she have it coming?

What did she get?

I can't tell if he's unaware of Sprudel's grizzly end, or is unsure which of Nifty's wives I'm talking about.

I was also trying to find out who was hiding you in plain sight. Why didn't the police pick you up when they knew where you were, and how come I didn't end up keeping Teplice and Liu company in the departure lounge?

Why do you need the answers to these questions? They make no difference.

Personal interest. Self-preservation. Maybe you're right, maybe they mean nothing. Maybe they'll help some dame get her jewellery and wayward life back. Maybe I get money for helping with that. Mostly, though, it's just curiosity. I have an inquiring mind, driven by restless and unfocused compulsions. It continuously generates thousands of questions and gives me no peace. I can't sleep until I know why.

He is untroubled by my existential angst. He wants to know how I knew he would be on the boat.

I didn't, but I knew someone there would be able to get you a message.

I got it. Here I am. Don't waste my time with your pointless questions.

There's a short rap on the door in reception. Chung gives me a vicious glare. I raise my hands innocently and motion for him to wait in the washroom.

Who would come here now?

I don't know, Brother Chung. You did. My clients keep strange hours. We're like a Circle-K. It could be one of my troublesome women from upstairs. Please, no one need know you are here. Wait in there. I will send them away.

He reluctantly agrees to make himself scarce.

Reception is cloaked in darkness but there's no mistaking Koko Man, or derogating her luminescence. The blue-black sheen of hair. The incandescent, pearly skin and lustrous eyes. The twin mattresses of her lips. The eminent smile. The noscible curves lurking beneath sheer hues of black silk. Matching gloves run the slender length of her arms to her elbows. Six-inch heels put us eye-to-eye. Her raven baby-doll ensemble suggests we're in for a bumpy night.

Jack So. Look at you.

I step back to give her a full view of the suit. What, this old thing?

Look at you looking at me, is what I meant. But your outfit is nice too.

I bring her into the office. She sits on the stool by my desk, opens a metallic clutch-bag and pulls out a packet of Marlboro.

Cigarette?

I didn't know you smoked, Mrs Man.

I've been known to burst into flames.

Hold that thought. I've got a couple of things to finish up and then we can get down to business.

I pour her a snifter of cognac from the bottle Benny keeps in his desk. She tells me she doesn't like to drink alone. I take it from her, whet my whistle and hand the glass back. No insult in drinking, I toast, borrowing a Japanese maxim.

When the cup's passed around there's no upper class and no lower class, no modesty and no rudeness, she responds, picking up my adage and running with it.

I return to the studio table and trim the last of the layouts.

I like a man who's good with his hands, Jack. You said you have news, of the necklace?

In a way.

What way?

Liu.

Not a great subject if you're looking to stimulate my interest.

It's hard to talk about one without embracing the other. I don't think he set you up. He was involved, obviously. Intimately. But I think, if you'll pardon my expression, it was you that fucked him.

I didn't have a lot of choice. They were standing over us, with guns.

You fucked him six ways, Koko. Royally. The sapphire, like so many things in your life, is incidental. A prop. A maguffin. A red-herring. Superfluous to the plot. An unfortunate means to his prescribed end.

Thin cracks appear in her confident veneer.

Why would anyone kill Liu?

Only one person benefited from his death. And he wasn't the only one marked for extinction that night either.

Only one other person was there. You.

And Mei. But you wouldn't have known she was along for the ride.

What are you talking about?

You didn't think it through, or talk numbers. Maybe it lost something in translation. You probably told them to kill whoever was there. They wouldn't know I'd gone for a walk. They were supposed to be there, waiting, but they got there late. They killed whoever was in the car, as instructed. He wasn't surprised when they turned up, only when they turned on him. He was expecting bagmen not assassins. And even if they knew there was another target, before they could consider witnesses, the blackmailers arrive. They saved my life. Well, them and Mei's bladder. It saved both our lives.

Why would I kill Liu? Why would I kill you and your daughter?

You didn't know about Mei. And if you did you're a much nastier piece of work than I imagined.

I hired you to find out who-

You hired me to find out *what* I knew. I found out *who* in the process.

Who what?

Who you really are. That's why you wanted me dead. The same reason you were happy to see Nifty and Liu gone. The same reason you had Lynne Sprudel killed, if you didn't kill her yourself.

I don't know what you're talking about.

Neither did I until I got carpet-bombed with Angel. She gave me a new perspectivism. In love and revenge a woman is more barbaric than man.

Fear is turning to anger now, and not just because I'm quoting Nietzsche.

Koko slips off the chair and prepares to march out. I grab her forearm and inadvertently draw the long cuff of her glove down.

Scratch marks.

Catfight? Got something against felines, Mrs Man, or were you trying to make it look like the work of someone who does? Stick around, Toots. You don't want to miss the best part of my presentation.

I push her against the workbench.

This makes no sense, Jack.

That's what I thought. Everyone's looking at you, Liu and the blackmailers. It's Io The Albino Lam, by the way, although I'm still not sure who he's colluding with. But let's try to stay *en pointe*, shall we? Everyone kept saying that death was following *me* around. Being paranoid, and starting to believe it, I un-thought it. And that's when it all made sense.

What does this have to do with you?

I'm like Bronson Chung, Nifty and Lynne Sprudel. I'm like Liu Pang.

I don't see the link.

Maybe the Buddha Amitabha will ring a few bells. A good person will be reborn, how much more so the evil person. No? Go and look in the mirror then. You'll see it as plain as the mole on your face. Really. Look in the mirror. You're the link. We all have you in common. We all know who you really are, Kitty.

I shove her toward the bathroom.

Take a good look at yourself and see what thou hast wrought, Kitty Ho. Kitajima, Horoko. Koko. Parents killed in a plane crash, were they? I don't think so. The Sisters at Po Leung Kuk localized your name when they gave you that story. Or did you came up with that yourself, as part of your stunning re-invention and privately funded Human Genome Project?

Jack, you don't know. You can't know what it's like.

I think I can. I child could work it out. Today you are you, that's truer than true. There's no one alive who is you-er than you.

No.

Maybe she doesn't like Dr Seuss. It's probably too common. I should've tried something a little more sophisticated, like TS Eliot.

And last, the rending pain of re-enactment of all that you have done, and been; the shame of motives revealed, the awareness of things ill done and done to others' harm.

Let me run this up your flagpole and see if you salute, Kitty. Big Spender gives you a taste of the good life at the expense of others. You try to leave your past behind. Rewrite yourself. Control the past, control the future. Leap-frog out of your fate on the shoulders of a few men. Unfortunately, one is connected. He doesn't want to let go. Then you see an opportunity for the law and geography to work in your favour. You get Nifty to drop a dime on Chung and have The Ministry Of Truth put him away, out of your way. Room 101. But Nifty is too small a step up the food chain. So you take what you can and recreate yourself. You get a bit of remodelling done to your grill. Put a little extra in the chassis. Add some new bumpers. How am I doing?

She stares through me, at the past, like Dorian Gray upon his picture.

I gather the issue of Tatler and open it. A polaroid marking the page.

How sad it will be, Mrs Man. You'll grow old, horrible and dreadful but this portrait will always remain young.

You've shed a bit of weight, and the heels give you extra inches. I guess a two thousand dollar hair-do helps. The flare of the flash in this one almost hides the beauty spot. I'm surprised you didn't have it taken care of when they did your nose. I'm amazed I didn't see it earlier. I mean, it's not like we're talking about Danny Devito and Schwarzenegger. You and Kitty are hardly dizygotic twins. How many women are there that men would kill or die for? It'd have to be one hell of a broad. And no one embodies, flaunts or flouts The Eight Virtues quite like you. You've got the big four in spades. Fidelity, physical charm, propriety and diligent needle work. Stick that in your eye, Ban Zhou.

She doesn't respond. I'm on a roll. I continue. This could get philippic.

The new you needed a new name, so you returned to your roots. The name on your passport. Kitajima. That gets you aboard Bellatrix, where you pole vault to the top of the food pyramid. Straight into Darius Man's lap. No one is any wiser. No one alive. Until Chung goes looking for the love of his life and the cause of his strife. The headlines wig you out. And then the grapevine kicks in. There was a man with Chung. He knows about Kitty. He's on Bowen Road. He's got photos of Kitty. I'm betting Liu Pang knew your secret identity, Wonder Woman. That's the gravity that kept you in orbit of each other. Maybe he was in it with The Albino and, well, whoever. For leverage. Maybe on your husband. Or you. So when the blackmail began, and the hand-off came, you saw another opportunity. You could make it all go away. There'd be a little humiliation, but this too would come to pass. High society can be very forgiving. You got Liu to call Eric Tsoi, knowing he'd recommend me. Then you sent a couple of shooters to join the party, to eliminate Liu. And me. To keep Kitty Ho buried. Except, *ku-blammo*, that didn't go according to plan. Never mind. You get me over to see what I know. It looks like nothing. And it was, then. That just leaves the bitter old tart on Bowen Road. She's been talking to Liu. Maybe they put two and two together and came up with whore. You go to get the pictures and kill her. You hang up a goat's head while you're there and peddle a little dog meat too. Except your canine is feline. You throttle the cats to make it look like Chung because you know he's out there, looking for you, and he doesn't give up. He's The Terminator. He can't be bargained or reasoned with. He doesn't feel pity, remorse or fear. He will not stop, ever. He'll be back. Sprudel's death will amplify the search for him and that'll tidy up your last loose end. It might not be 1984 but Orwell's maxim has never been more mantic. Who controls the past controls the future. Who controls the present controls the past. Everything is falling into place. Everything, except me.

Except you, Jack. What do you want?

Nothing. I just want to know if I'm right. I have a bet with a friend. The illicit photos, the sapphire, the blackmail, the property in Wan Chai and Redhill, and Liu's ex-wives. Everything on your litany of villainy. I'm betting it all pales compared to what you stand to lose should Darius Man and the Vicious Circle at the Algonquin Round Table find out who you really are.

A bet with who?

Whom. Not *who*. Whom. A bet with *whom*.

Whom? she asks through perfect teeth. Dyspeptic veins corrupt the elegant arc of her neck.

Bronson Chung exits the bathroom and looms darkly behind his Lolita.

Kitty? Kitty, why?

She's not surprised to see him. If she is it doesn't show. She responds with as much regard for her Humbert's feelings as she holds for Nabokov.

Why do you think? Why would I want you?

Vladimir was right. There is nothing more atrociously cruel than an adored child. And this one has no idea the reason the gods offer prosperity and riches in abundance is that it really boosts the ratings when they utterly destroy them later.

Kitty, why did you change your beautiful face?

Chung is like a kid who just found all his crayons broken. This, however, is probably not what Mencius had in mind when he said the great man is he who does not lose his child's heart.

She pushes him away and turns to me.

You can't prove a thing, Jack.

I'm not trying to. I'm just telling a client what I've found out and concluding an unprofitable relationship. Fulfilling a promise to a friend. Collecting on a bet.

I could make it worth your while. Both of you. Nobody has to know.

The Queen! shouts Mei from the doorway, cutting through the moment like a fart in elevator. I told you, Gu-por! I met The Queen!

Gu-por and her flock of gypsy insurgents move silently across the room, like Rod Taylor and Tippi Hedren in The Birds. Slowly. All eyes upon them, and their pyjamas.

Mei runs to me.

Hey Bingle-bug. What're you doing here?

Going to the toilet, replies Gu-por on her behalf. Upstairs is broken, again.

She disappears into the washroom with her incontinent kin.

Mei lags behind.

What are you doing, Ba-ba?

Just finishing up, Doodle-pop. Didn't you say you had to go to skip to my loo, my darling?

Fly in the buttermilk, shoo fly shoo! she sings as she disappears.

Koko stands at the work table, absently inspecting layouts. With any luck that nursery rhyme has become an earworm and is now drilling into her brain.

I've lost my partner, what'll I do? I've lost my partner, what'll I do?

The toilet flushes.

Chung steps toward his ex-lover. I raise my hands. Wait.

The toilet flushes.

Stay there. Until the tourists have gone. Please.

The toilet flushes.

Pennies spent, the grockles walk through our Bodega Bay.

Everyone in Hong Kong work so late? asks Gu-por. She looks at Koko. You want bird nest?

I'll get her some later. We're nearly done here, Gu-por. Sorry about the toilet.

Next time we stay at hotel. You too much trouble.

Normally I'd delight in such words. Under the circumstances all I can muster is another apology, and tell Mei I'll be up in a minute. She leaves with the rest of the party-crashers, chirruping all the way to the elevator.

Fly in the buttermilk, shoo fly shoo! Fly in the buttermilk, shoo fly shoo!

I lock the door and return to the Mexi-Canton stand-off.

I hear the immediate, ossifragant collapse of the cartilage in her exquisitely sculpted nose. Somewhere in Bangkok a surgeon weeps.

Eyes wild with *sakki*, the death lust, she drops her *kaiken* blade to hold her battered face in her hands. Even Ultima II will have problems rectifying the damage.

Crimson gushes.

I jump to intervene. Chung throws me across the room.

Seizing the distraction, Koko finds a hidden reservoir of vehemence. She bashes him across the gulliver with a heavy tape dispenser.

Humbolt falls. The tip of his tongue takes more than a trip of three steps down the palate to tap at three of his teeth.

Lo. Lee. Ta.

She sinks onto his chest, knees crushing the air from him. It almost seems to temporarily revive him, only to give her the sole satisfaction of finishing him for good. She bludgeons his head with the sanguinary stationery.

I kick her away.

My boot shatters her cheekbone.

Chung's blood-soaked dial is painted with a deathly grin. The Flute of The Falling Tiger keens from his severed pipes in the key of AB-.

This does not bode well for him.

A lugent Kitty bleeds against the wall. I approach. She swipes at my leg with the cutter. It slices open my knee. I drop.

Great. Now I owe Hurricane Higgins a pair of pants.

The vitiated *onna-bugeisha* collects herself and crawls to Chung. She plunges the knife into his eye like Excalibur in the stone.

She pushes herself up and stumbles to the door, leaving a smear of claret across the floor, then disappears into the darkness.

I hear her staggering down the stairs toward her own private *meifumado*.

No general can pass up a beautiful woman, I think, recalling a pearl of my mother's wisdom.

A hero prostrates himself before feminine charms.

I'm curled on the floor, lain with the slain Lion Tamer. Ain't we a pair. Desire and desperation does indeed make for strange bedfellows. He's brutalized beyond recognition. There's not a lot I or the Clinique range of men's products can do for him. I let him rest. A host, after all, must be nice to his guest.

Today is gone. Today is done. Tomorrow is another one.

I consider Angel's reaction to what transpired tonight.

It won't be pleasant.

This is the second bloodletting we've had here in the last twelve months.

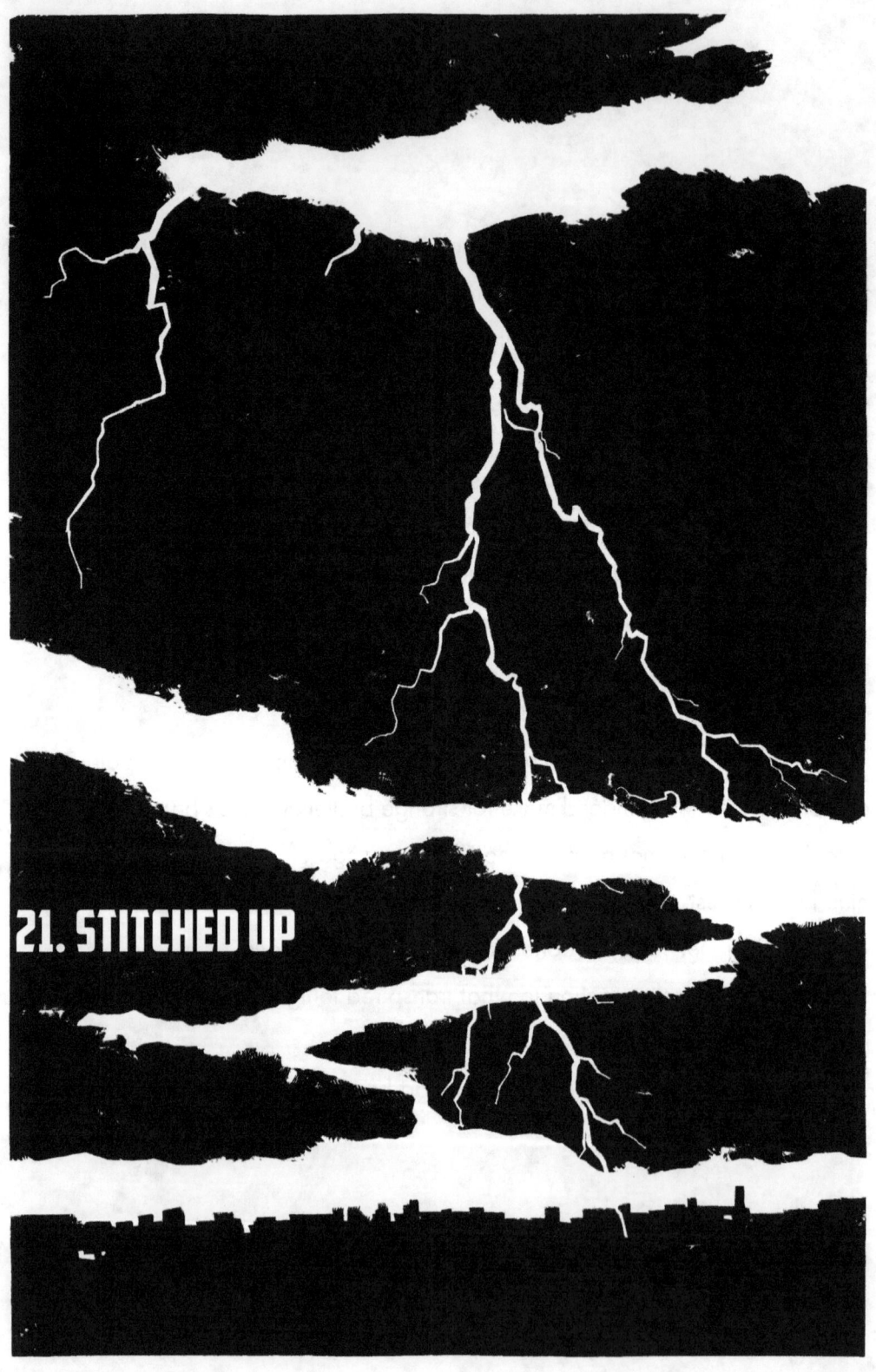

21. STITCHED UP

All this happened, more or less. The Peelers arrived five minutes after the bloodied and battered Koko Man fled Slaughterhouse Five. Oldham had checked the number I punched into his portable. He figured I was arranging a vespertine briefing and had planned to drop by. He thought it might be interesting. It had to be something for me to be in the office that late.

All part of my cunning plan, Inspector Poirot.

Was that laceration on your leg part of the plan too?

Occupational hazard.

And how about the abattoir?

Business expansion. Horizontal and vertical integration.

You got a health plan too?

Oldham accompanied me to the hospital. I told him how the nocturnal knackering had gone down. How quickly it all went south.

I look forward to another of your official statements, Jack. They're required reading at The Academy now. People are requesting personal copies. You could have your own shelf in the bookshop.

Fiction or Non-fiction?

I limped home in the wee hours.

The vacationers were packing up the mahjong table. They'd had enough. They were leaving in the morning. Gu-por asked what happened to my leg. I told her I had an accident at work, with the box cutter. They might have to go to the *dai pai dong* if they want a toilet. It's backed up down there. They've sealed off the whole office. Something about toxic waste.

What did you guys have for dinner?

This building is falling down, she complains. British plumbing is rubbish. The *feng shui* is very bad. Do not wait for China to fix everything in ninety-seven.

I rang Angel. She didn't work Saturdays anyway but if she found out what happened from the papers, again, fifteen stitches in my leg would be the least of my problems. A little professional courtesy goes a long way.

She offered to bring me some recreational drugs, for medicinal purposes, to help me through this difficult period.

We went up to the roof and discussed The Transformation Of Things.

There was a Taoist in the Zhou Dynasty. Chuang Tzu. He dreamed he was a butterfly, flitting about. He was pretty happy with himself, doing as he pleased. He didn't know he was Chuang Tzu, until he woke up and was confronted by the solid, unmistakable reality of being Chuang Tzu. And there was the rub. Had he, as Chuang Tzu, dreamed he was a butterfly? Or was he a butterfly dreaming he was Chuang Tzu?

I had no idea. Chuang Tzu was not the only one having trouble distinguishing between two states of being. On the back of Angel's skunkweed I would've thought a brain tumour was a birthday present.

Floating on the finger-lidded fog of firewood and flowertops, she chased the metamorphosis metaphor down the rabbit hole.

The caterpillar does all the work, Jack. But it's the butterfly that gets all the hype. In the natural order of things beauty is kind of taboo. Koko Man should've known that. Look at the moon. As soon as it becomes a full, perfect circle it starts to erode and decay. Fruit ripens on the tree then it's manhandled and bruised, or falls to the ground and rots. A proportion of imperfection and deficiency is vital if things are to have lasting appeal. You can see it everywhere. I like to think that's why one of my boobs is slightly bigger than the other.

It took me the rest of the weekend to get over her profundity.

I made a few calls and looked into the archives of the South China Morning Post. The full tragedy of Horoko Kitajima was laid bare. Not only did she survive the murder-suicide of her parents but it turned out, with a high degree of certainty, that she married the man who raped her mother.

Darius Man.

Horoko's husband was also her paternal father.

Forget it, Jack. It's Chinatown.

I was grateful it had all come to an end, and Angel was quoting from something Benny could almost relate to. He was worried literacy, intellect, sophistication and style were going to be mandatory aspects of life.

Irina and Sam were devastated.

It wasn't going to be so easy for them to consign Kitty to history. No one had seen her, or Koko, since that night.

Or rather, there was no one that would admit to it.

When trouble comes close ranks, wrote Rhys in Wide Sargasso Sea. And so the Man family did. Kitty would not be allowed to disappear and emerge in a different guise again. Yet neither was she the type to throw herself under a train at Obiralovka station while waiting for Vronsky.

Toshimi Wells called, to get the scoop straight from the horses mouth. I told her I felt more like an ass.

Is it true what they're saying, Jack? Did she really kill those people?

Ask her yourself next time you see her.

You're not worried?

About what? Everyone left alive knows I'm not a liability.

Such a strange bunch of coincidences.

Not really. Just one. When Bronson Chung walked into the Irina Wang School Of Dance. Everything *balloned* and *chasséd* out of that chance encounter. If he hadn't gone looking for his girl…

T'was beauty that sleighed the beast.

T'was beauty that t'was the beast, Miss Wells.

I wonder t'what happened to the necklace?

Koko Man resurfaced. Off the coast of Big Wave Bay. Her body swimming with a lethal cocktail of drugs and alcohol. Face barely recognizable. She'd fallen into the Wide Sargasso Sea at Prospect Point and drowned. Family and staff said they hadn't seen her since the Bellatrix soirée.

There were rumours of a suicide note.

Namu amida butsu.

That's all she wrote. A short prayer. A call for mercy in the world to come.

Darius Man suffered a fatal stroke that afternoon. Some say he died of a broken heart. Others believe it was chronic shame. When photos of Koko and Liu Pang engaged in graphic sex began to circulate, everyone except the coroner agreed it was a case of terminal chagrin. A variant of the strain that killed his wife.

Funerals for the prurient pair were awkward and shamelessly well-attended. The commendaces had been scripted by someone with a flair for melodrama and overstatement. The weather was biblical. All his surviving wives wept like open wounds.

No more to build on there. And they, since they

Were not the one dead, turned to their affairs.

The Trausians had it right, declared Angel, ignoring my Frost. When a child was born they'd gather to grieve for all the troubles and suffering the kid would endure on its journey through life. When people died they'd have a big party. Everyone at the funeral would be so happy for the dead. They'd escaped all the crap of life and were in the best place anyone could hope to be.

Remember that, Angel. When my time comes.

A month later, the gentrification of Wan Chai began. The velvet curtain was brought down on many of the bars. Up-market meat markets would soon take their place. Same shit, different wrapper, to invoke advertising parlance.

I was getting a shave and a haircut at The Mandarin, while I waited for Mei to finish dance class. Thumbing through the latest issue of Tatler I saw a striking image.

Missy Man, leaving a Central nightclub.

She had Mike Midian in tow, yet this was not the surprising thing. I'd heard he was now in charge of her personal security arrangements.

It was Missy.

Gone was the conservative bun, studious glasses, officious twin-set and sensible shoes. A vivacious woman stood in their place, draped in a revealing Chanel gown. Her full lips were drawn back across brilliant teeth. Long hair swept across proud shoulders. Eyes wide with fire.

It was her and it was not her.

It was what she wore around her neck.

A blazing sapphire, set among a string of diamonds.

I got my person to call her person and arrange a meeting. There were some outstanding invoices to clear up, expenses to settle and an account to close.

I was told to visit her at the house in Shek O.

Afternoon tea, again.

Are we going to the castle? asks Mei as we slide down The Dragon's Back to the village. Are we going to see the King and the Queen?

There's a new Queen.

What happened to the old one?

She forsook the crown, Princess, and all that should be to a woman worth possessing, wherein sparkling shone the sacred gems of chastity and modesty.

Huh?

She went on a holiday.

Did she take the swings with her? Will the new Queen let me play on the swings? I really like the swings. And the playground. There's no other kids to boss you. I hope she lets me. Do you think she'll let me?

I'm sure she will, Bar-ba-loot. I'm sure she will.

Ba-ba ba-loot!

Up canyon, off cliff! Over wild rocky trail!

Up gully, through gulch!

And down slippery sluice, again.

It's hard to believe this is the same no-nonsense Nazi who officiated at previous encounters. Beneath the tussled locks, makeup, form-defining blouse and Armani slacks, however, it's still business as usual.

Thank you for coming.

Mei is dispatched to the great outdoors. She races across the lawn, giving the Gurkha charged with her safety a good run for his money.

Missy hands me an envelope. Nonsequential bills. Tax-free US Dollars.

I trust that will appease your finance department, Mr So.

You may have over-compensated.

We pay our dues and honour debts. I don't like open endings. You've earned it. What was it you really came here for? A drink perhaps?

She raises a sculpted eyebrow, then walks to the end of the room. Her steps are measured. There is a deliberate sway in her hips. It's a few degrees shy of a swivel.

Ice is dropped into tumblers and drowned in bourbon. Sprigs of mint are crushed and plunged into the liquor.

Refreshing, she says, handing me a glass. It reminds me of Kentucky.

It reminds me of peas.

Peace?

Peas. It's one of the things I remember about my mother. She put chopped mint on top of peas. We hardly ever had peas but when we did there was always mint on top.

Angel and Proust were right, I think. Our memory is not ours to command. The past comes unbidden, or not at all.

In Chinese we have a saying, Mr So. When eating bamboo sprouts remember the person that planted them.

The conversation is taking a sibylline turn, and I wheel with it.

I saw you in Tatler.

An unfortunate consequence of tragic events. With my father and stepmother gone the media has turned its attention to me. I'll shall miss the anonymity.

I wish I could pronounce it. Stunning piece, by the way. The sapphire.

She issues a long, intense stare. Swirls her glass. Drinks.

It was my mother's. I never really liked the pearls and had the gemstones reset. Would you like to see it?

Don't go to any trouble.

It's no trouble. Not any more.

Missy takes her leave, ascending the stairs.

I look out the window. Waves crash over the rocks where Koko completed her journey down The Six Paths. Shuffling off the *shaba*, she slipped into the cold, dark sea and set sail for the *meido*. The land after death.

A life of suffering and a pauper's grave.

How did the sapphire find its way home? Did Missy pay a ransom for its return? Was it repatriated willingly, or retrieved forcefully?

War is of men, not castles. War lies in attack, not defence. Lay down your corpses to be your walls. Lay down your corpses to bridge the moat. Attack your enemies on the corpses of your comrades and victory will be yours.

Missy returns, black velvet case and manila envelope in hand.

She passes me the case and I admire the jewels within. The gems here rival and surpass even the best of those in my larcenous library, stashed behind a copy of Breakfast At Tiffany's. I've never seen a sapphire. It's heavier than I imagined. The polished surface pulsates.

I'd want it back too.

My host fixes another round of Mint Juleps. Then primes a pair of Cohibas. She offers one to me and I accept, seeing how we're celebrating. It would be rude not to.

I thought you might like to see these as well, Jack.

She passes the yellow envelope. I look at her manicured nails and wonder what hand she had in harvesting the crop of images that tumble from within.

There's half a dozen glossy, five-by-four prints. In most of them, a naked minx crouches upon my semi-conscious Cumberland sausage.

Made it, Ma! Top of the world!

White heat of different kind, but no less explosive. So much for sex and pornography being the poor man's theatre. Did Missy's mother approve of her daughter's viewing habits?

They're the only copies, Jack.

I don't know what to say. It's not just me I'm seeing in a whole new light.

We weren't sure if you were working for us, or with her. My family thanks you.

What's left of it.

What?

I know what it's like to lose close family members, suddenly. To lose two, in a such a short period, at the same time, is inconceivable.

She was never part of this family, Jack. None of them were. The women that came after my mother. None mattered to him, or meant anything to me.

She watches the smoke from her Cohiba run to the ceiling. Either she has forgotten another Chinese saying or is trying to recall it.

All beings are on the same path, all victims of the same existence. No one is better than the next.

I raise my glass and propose a toast, to mothers, grateful that neither of ours can witness what we have become. And step-mothers, I add, to see what buttons that might push.

Missy exhales a thick plume of smoke.

Horoko had no pride and no honour. She had no respect for the family, for my father, or for herself. I tried to tell him but he wouldn't listen. He didn't want to hear how she would ruin our family and everything he'd worked so hard to build. I had to show him what she was, and all the things she wasn't.

What wasn't she?

She wasn't one of us. She wasn't worthy of my father. She wasn't like my mother. She wasn't like me.

She was a woman of shallow learning who swallowed the lessons of the past, without digesting them. I know. I get it. Maybe that's why he liked her.

Missy swills the last of her liquor. A damp leaf of mint masks a tooth and paints her a Wiccan's maw.

You think we weren't good enough for him? You think that's why he abandoned my mother?

I don't know. They say when women marry again it's because they detest their first husband, and a man remarries because he adored his first wife. Maybe Tolstoy was right and each unhappy family is just unhappy in its own way. It's foolish to look for logic in the chambers of the human heart, Missy. Men do things.

I can tell she has grown weary of literary digressions by the way she shrieks and smashes her Cohiba into the ashtray.

I have seen what men do! What he did to my mother! What Liu did to my mother! I watched my father with those women and I saw what he did with *her*. Never once did he look at me with the same adoration, or present me to his friends with such pride. I had to show him what she really was. She had no love for him. She loved only what he gave her, not what she could give. Not what I could give.

For the second time in twenty-four hours I'm amazed at her transformation. The impigrity of her escalation from Tokyo Rose to hysterical banshee.

A good person will be reborn, how much more so the evil person.

In addition to navigating The Eight Gates Of Deceit, I realize I've played a part in the grievous manifestation of an off-the-rails Elektra complex.

In my father's house there are many rooms, I recall aloud.

Are you quoting scripture now?

Oh, no. The Bible's got nothing on this. What about Liu? The photos? The video?

He would do anything we asked of him. Such is our position in society. People do not question motive or action, only what is in it for them. He was willing, even if he was not able. Would you like to see the pictures? The film?

We could be talking about holiday snaps from a family trip to Tokyo Disney, or renting the latest release from Blockbuster, so matter-of-fact is her tone.

I tell her I've seen enough.

IT'S OKAY.

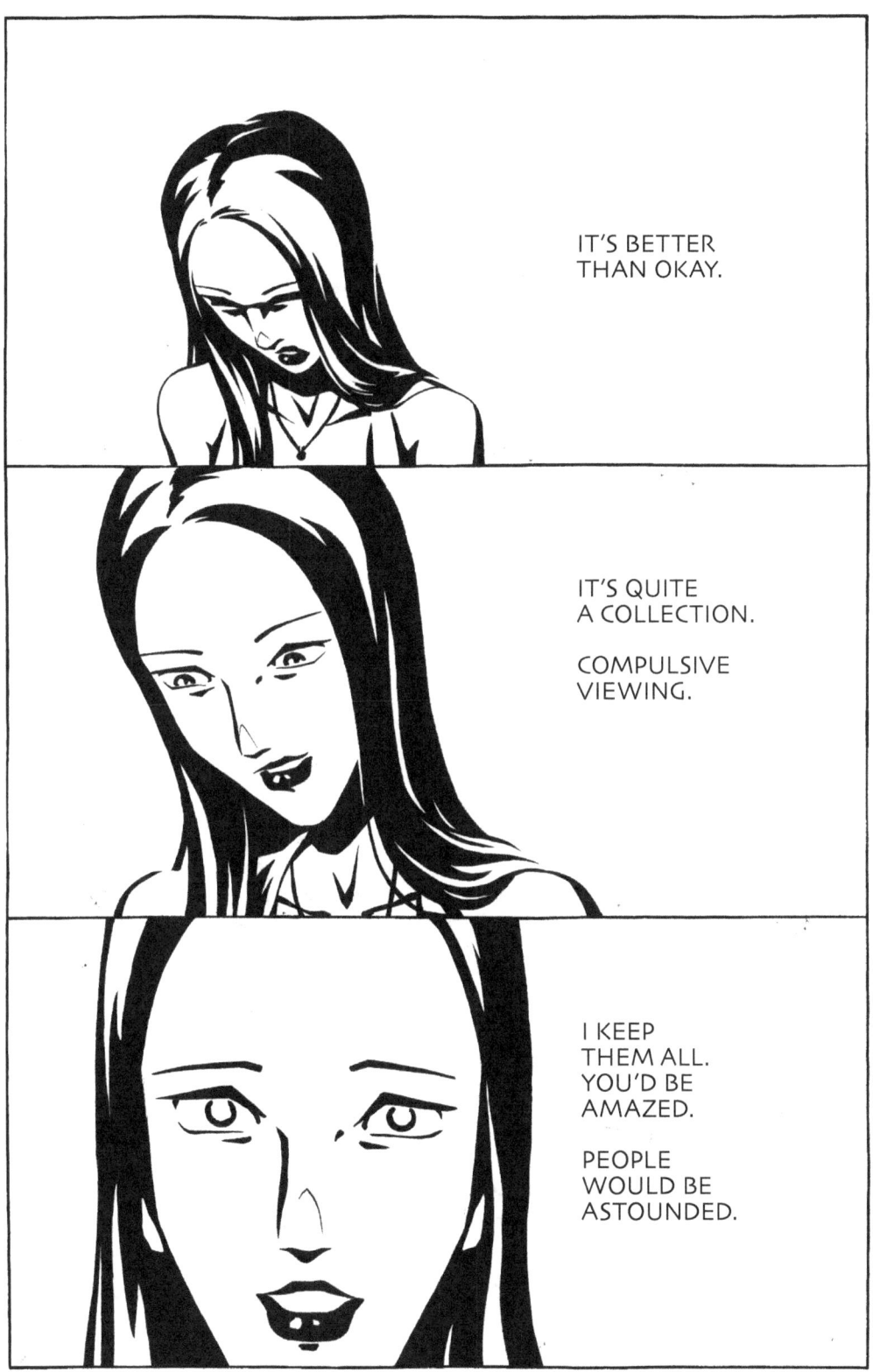

WHAT I'VE SEEN THESE WOMEN DO WITH MY FATHER.

WHAT HE MADE THEM DO. THE DEPTHS THESE WOMEN WOULD PLUMB. THE LENGTHS SHE WOULD GO, TO DEGRADE HERSELF.

TO SAVE HERSELF.

SO LITTLE DIGNITY.

NOT SO BEAUTIFUL OR PROUD.

I SAW HER WITH YOU TOO, JACK SO. HERE.

AMEN.

Now is probably not the time to tell her that, in her quest for redamancy, she did more than see off the main competitor for her father's affections. She was responsible for his demise and the ruin of his wife. She destroyed her step-mother and, in doing so, killed her step-sister too.

In revenge and in love a woman is more barbaric than man.

Kitty Ho may have screwed the pooch when it came to The Eight Virtues but Horoko Kitajima, in her own sweet way, nailed the feminine imperatives of The Three Obediences.

First to father, then to husband and finally to heir.

Had Kitty Ho subconsciously solicited her conceiver, or did familial fate find and fornicate with Horoko Kitajima in biblical style?

Vengeance is mine, I will repay.

Misuki Man walks to the window overlooking the South China Sargasso Sea and the cold, dark waters that wait for her. For us all. Her father had probably said that one day all this would be hers. And now it was. I hope it's everything she dreamed it would be.

Mei runs across the grass.

I contemplate the bond a father and child rely on, to do what they must to survive, as they walk through life, hand-in-hand.

What kind of world was I leading my daughter into?

All beings are on the same path, all victims of the same existence. Our enemies are not demons, but human beings like ourselves.

SHE'S A BEAUTIFUL GIRL, JACK.
SHE WILL DO ANYTHING FOR YOU. TRUST ME,
A GIRL WILL DO ANYTHING FOR HER FATHER.

A FATHER KNOWS
HIS CHILD'S HEART,
AS ONLAY A CHILD
CAN KNOW
HER FATHER'S.

NEVER
TAKE THAT
UNCONDITIONAL
LOVE FOR
GRANTED.

A SMALL
GIRL'S HEART
IS EASY
TO BREAK.

AND VERY
HARD
TO MEND.

The falling neon sky
renders Misuki Man
a vacivitous silhouette.

Like all of us,
she stands
in darkness,
surrounded
by light.

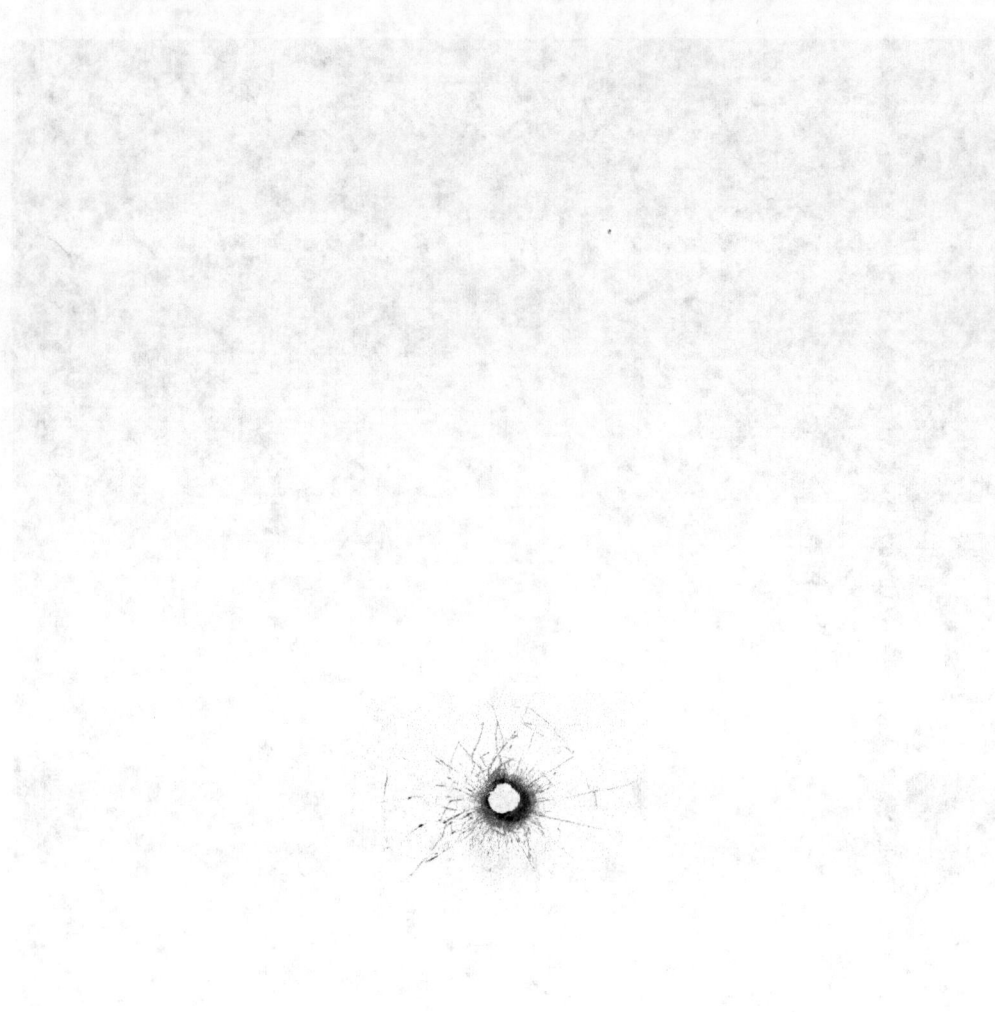

THE MISADVENTURES OF JACK SO CONTINUE IN

HAPPY
BIRTHDAY
B*tch

THE MISADVENTURES OF JACK SO CONTAGIOUS IN

DISCOVER THE ORIGINAL
JACK SO MISADVENTURE

"A viscerally enjoyable ride...
powerful narrational voice...
laugh-out-loud witty...

BITCH
ON HEAT

Intrigue, sex and violence...
a riotous rendering of noir
with Chinese characteristics."

 THE REVIEW, S(

"A revved-up
action packed tale...
a bitchin' read."

TIME OUT

BITCH ON HEAT

RICHARD TONG

1987. Jack So is a hard-boiled, not-so-good Samaritan and single father. When a bombshell drops into his lap, it sets off a journey through the simmering, Neon Noir™ shadows of Hong Kong.

I'M OFFERING YOU ALL I CAN, JACK.

THAT'S NOT WHAT I'M LOOKING FOR.

THEN LOOK A LITTLE LONGER. AND HARDER.

Navigating perilous curves in pursuit of an ancient artifact, he soon discovers the past is not finished with him, yet. History still has some harsh lessons for Jack So to learn. And history, when it comes unbidden, can be a bitch.

AVAILABLE IN HARD-BOILED, PULP & DIME-STORE EDITIONS

 FOLLOW JACK SO

 LIKE SO FUK YU

ALSO BY RICHARD TONG

SECOND **THE** EDITION

DURIAN

EFFECT

An oriental oddyssey
of epic distortion.

RICHARD TONG

In 1991, Richard Tong came home to a place he'd never been before. Hong Kong. With no money, no experience and absolutely no idea of what awaited, he embarked on a 10-year journey, exploring the alien corners of Asia and discovering the darkest regions of his soul.

"OH, EAST IS EAST AND WEST IS WEST, AND NEVER THE TWAIN SHALL MEET."

A BALLAD OF ONE MAN, TWO WORLDS AND THE SPINIOUS FRUIT THAT DIVIDES, CONQUERS AND BINDS.

Acerbic, poignant and witty. Raw like sushi, brutal like Bukowski and dry like the mouth of the Yangtze. The Durian Effect puts the odd in odyssey. It takes you swiftly to the edge of the great cultural divide... and throws you into the abyss.

ME&MY POTATO

One man, two worlds and a baby.

RICHARD TONG

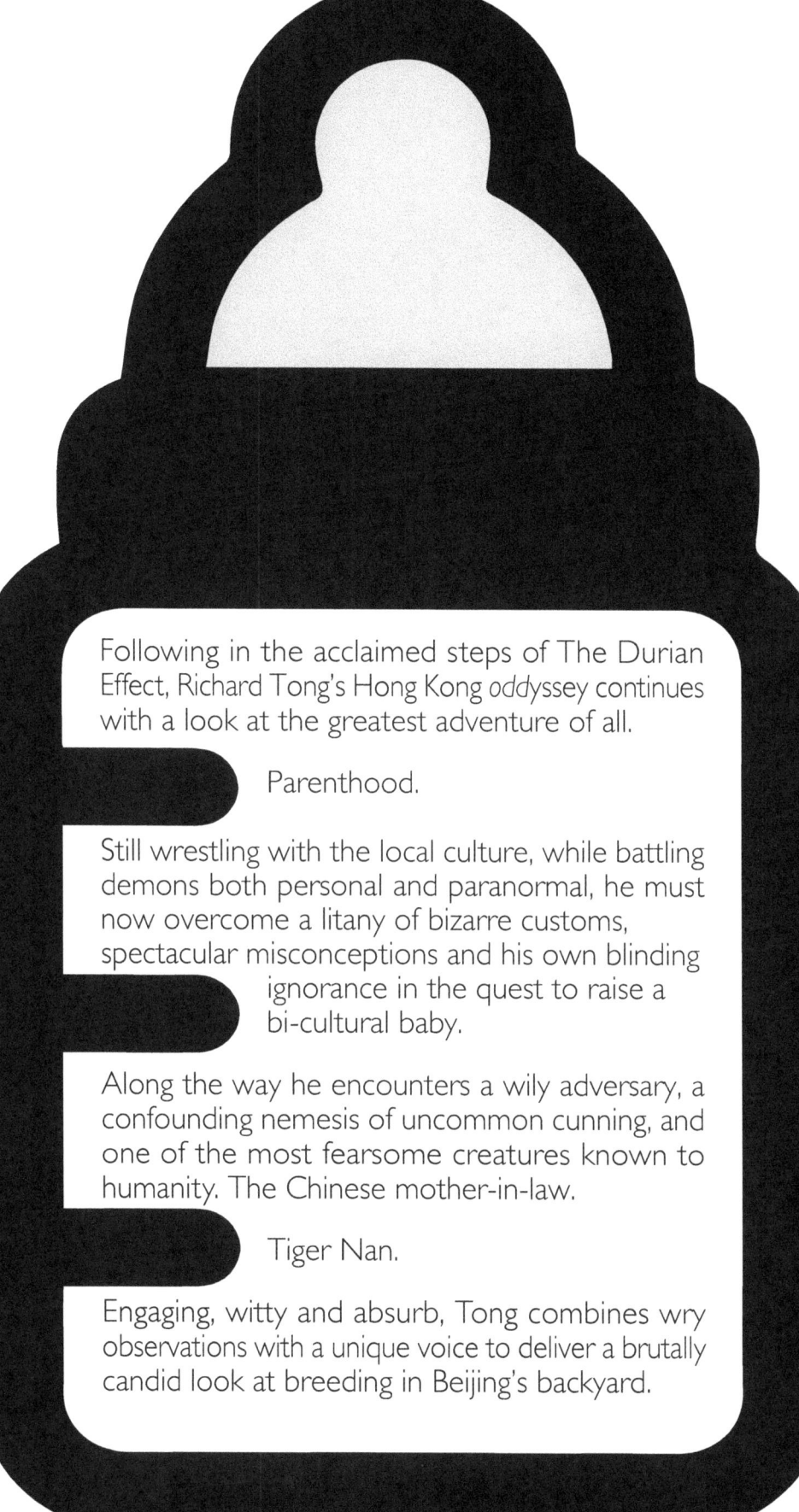

Following in the acclaimed steps of The Durian Effect, Richard Tong's Hong Kong *oddyssey* continues with a look at the greatest adventure of all.

Parenthood.

Still wrestling with the local culture, while battling demons both personal and paranormal, he must now overcome a litany of bizarre customs, spectacular misconceptions and his own blinding ignorance in the quest to raise a bi-cultural baby.

Along the way he encounters a wily adversary, a confounding nemesis of uncommon cunning, and one of the most fearsome creatures known to humanity. The Chinese mother-in-law.

Tiger Nan.

Engaging, witty and absurb, Tong combines wry observations with a unique voice to deliver a brutally candid look at breeding in Beijing's backyard.

www.ingramcontent.com/pod-product-compliance
Lightning Source LLC
Chambersburg PA
CBHW080716020726
47501CB00010B/2445